MW01106119

RAISING
SPIRITS

Outskirts Press, Inc.
Denver, Colorado

Outskirts Press
http://www.outskirtspress.com

ISBN-10: 1-4327-0153-3
ISBN-13: 978-1-4327-0153-6

Outskirts Press and the "OP" logo are trademarks belonging to
Outskirts Press, Inc.

Printed in the United States of America

There are many people who've passed through my life and to whom I owe a great deal. Friends who inspire, encourage, and motivate are rare commodities. Those who remain faithful in both good times and bad are even more precious. This book is for them, with profound gratitude.

May your spirits be raised as well.

Foreword

In the beginning, there was the book. I had hoped that A Wanderer's Wisdom would be declared at least a good first literary effort. To my absolute amazement, the publishers kept reporting an ever-increasing sales volume. So much so that my creation achieved a very lofty status on best-seller lists across the nation. Retailers had difficulty keeping copies on their shelves. Foreign translations appeared around the globe. Studio production bosses found themselves in competition for the movie rights. There seemed to be no shortage of people willing to shove money down into my pockets.

Fifteen minutes of fame? Hardly! I found myself giving interviews on television and radio for over a year! I did the morning tv shows in New York and Los Angeles. Afternoons were devoted to talk radio. Days sped by quickly as I was professionally shunted from one well-stocked limousine to another. Champagne flowed in continual rivulets at celebrity cocktail parties nearly every night. I attended more A-list fund raisers than I ever dreamed existed. Politicians brazenly sought to have their pictures taken by my side. Captains of industry suggested I might want to address their board of directors, or perhaps cut a deal to endorse their products. Women seemed unusually captivated by my charm and wit. I indulged shamelessly and denied myself nothing.

Of course it had to end.

Chapter 1

When the ancient prophet Moses ascended the mountain of Horeb, he had no clues about the mystery and wonder that awaited him at the summit. Mountain wilderness is funny that way. You go looking for one thing and end up being completely bowled over by something you never expected to find.

I was in need of a real break. Some serious downtime. My normal workaday world was now a thing of the past, hardly more than a washed-out memory. I had become a very wealthy and much sought after socialite. The problem is, I find the life shallow and lacking meaning. Being seen with all the right people at all the correct events, and always with the right 'game face' on no longer holds any allure. A small but persistent group of well-meaning brain cells kept sending out the same coded message: "get a grip on things you idiot, while you still can!"

I didn't much like being called an idiot by my own brain cells, but then I've noticed that brains often lack decorum. It's probably the result of their having been ignored so often in the past.

Seeking peace and isolation in the mountains seemed an inspired idea. A few days of quiet introspection would (I hoped) help me to sort out the ball of confusion my life had become.

There are a multitude of bold, grand mountain ranges in the wondrous state of Arizona. But I had chosen a smaller, less remarkable group called the Harquahalas. Those in the know will tell you that the Harquahala range isn't all that spectacular compared to its cousins elsewhere in the state. Its short, stubby peaks aren't especially awe inspiring, with the whole collection extending but a mere handful of miles.

Winters in the Harquahalas produce a raw biting cold, but seldom will any snow appear. In contrast, the long summer days invite sunstroke, heat exhaustion, and even death to anyone foolish enough to be caught unprepared during that inhospitable time. After the nearby copper and silver mines played out in the early part of the 20th century, most people wisely abandoned the area to the handful of hardy species that call the place home.

All of which suited me just fine. The chance encounter of an agent, producer, lawyer, or other human pariah in the Harquahala mountains seemed mighty unlikely.

I had abandoned my ancient Jeep earlier in the day, leaving it just off a trail head at the foot of the mountains. Part of my self-imposed penance for a great many sins included whipping what remained of my body back into something I could tolerate, if not gloat about.

The trek up the mountainside after months of shameless gorging on caviar, pate, and champagne was proving to be a bigger challenge than I'd reckoned. The big gray nylon backpack loaded with all the gear deemed essential to survival was feeling a lot heavier than it should've. Most of the trail, except for a few switchbacks, led unendingly uphill. It took only a handful of minutes tramping up the steep grade before I began gasping for air, my lungs protesting like an overworked bellows.

"What a useless fop you've become," I muttered to myself as I trudged along the little-used game trail. "It'd serve you right to fall down right where you are and STARVE. They'd never find you, you know..."

Okay, brain. Enough with the self-mortification. Let's keep it going here...left, right, left, right, left. That's it. Shades of Navy boot camp, with its precision marching on that blistering grinder in San Diego, huh? You can hack it, kiddo. You still got what it takes. Left, left, left, right, left...

By late afternoon, I decided to call it a day's work. I was hot, dirty, and unappealingly aromatic. Besides, there was a good reason to get camp set up before dusk. The radiant glowing sunsets in these parts are exquisite. I was planning to improve my photographic talents a little with the new digital camera I'd brought along for the occasion.

For anyone who hasn't yet experienced it, the peach-golden-orange Arizona sunset is a sight to behold.

I didn't plan to miss this one.

Chapter 2

Strictly speaking, I wasn't alone in my self-imposed wilderness exile. My little pal Zoom, a companion cat of the Scottish Fold variety, was along to take in the sights. Zoom is silver and black with the classic tabby markings and ears that fold forward in keeping with his curious breed. He has a round, almost owlish face, and is extremely smart for a feline We've been together for a long time now, having traveled far and shared in many adventures. Zoom is genuinely devoted to me and tolerates my follies with an easy going nature that makes him very special.

Prior to Zoom, I had always assumed I was pretty much a dog-type person. After all, dogs are utilitarian. They'll happily bring in the newspaper for you at the end of a long day. Home invasion thugs will generally avoid residences where a loyal hound is on duty. For the sight-impaired, a properly trained guide dog is a genuine blessing. The truth is, I enjoy almost any animal. But cats just never seemed that manly to me.

Preconceived notions are dangerous things, and all of mine

pertaining to cats came crashing down upon my head a few years back. A chance meeting with a generous couple in Mendocino (on the northern California coast) would forever change my silly notions about things feline.

Standing in line awaiting my turn at the local post office, I couldn't help noticing the elegantly dressed woman just ahead of me. And perched on her arm was a smallish, blazing orange cat with odd-looking ears. He was obviously content with his surroundings and purred gently while the line moved slowly ahead.

Being curious, I asked the lady about her unusual cat. She smiled graciously, having attracted such attention many times before. And after our business at the post office was completed, she invited me to lunch with her husband who awaited her at a nearby inn. I, being intrigued and having no other pressing business, happily agreed.

And so it was that Astrid Burns and her devoted husband Jake entered into my life. The three of us dined outside on the restaurant patio, so close to the blue-green Pacific waters as to hear the waves breaking gently upon the rocks below. Jake is a retired FedEx pilot who now runs a skydiving school at the local airport. Astrid has her own cottage business involving interior design and antique furnishings. And as luck would have it, both are devoted care givers (and breeders) of the exotic looking Scottish Fold cats.

A couple of months later I had occasion to visit Astrid and Jake at their private residence upon the bluffs just outside of Mendocino. Theirs was obviously a dream home - not so much large as it was welcoming. Nearly every window had a generous view of the azure Pacific waters below. In the late afternoons, herds of local seals would haul themselves out on the rocks to bask while squadrons of gulls on the wing soared, whirled, and dove for their supper. And it is in this house that Astrid's gift for interior design shines brilliantly. Rarely have I seen such genius in the display of fine antique treasures. And topping it all off were the dozen or so Scottish Fold cats that called the place home.

Each seemed to have an assigned role within the household. There was a greeter kitty, a lap kitty, a foot-warming kitty, a nurse kitty (for anyone not feeling well), at least three play kitties, a roving patrol sentinel kitty, and so on.

Of these, Zoom was the youngest. He had just abandoned the pleasures of nursing in favor of joining the others around the communal kibble bowl. A young and naive adolescent, the world was quite clearly his oyster. Sitting in an antique rocker enjoying the afternoon sun, I watched Zoom play with a wild reckless abandon that warmed my heart. He concentrated so fully on just having FUN, no matter what the undertaking. And I noted that his older siblings tolerated his antics with an understanding that his silliness was just a feline right of passage.

And yet, this tiny ball of fur had learned his lessons well for one in the world only a brief march of days. With a subtlety and stealth that only a cat is capable of, Zoom set about quickly capturing my heart. I thought it was cute the way he batted a toy mousie around on the hardwood floor, soccer style. And he would happily chase a toy bird attached to a string for as long as I would make it fly around the room. He also excelled at con artistry, his starving kitty routine easily overcoming my reluctance to feed him a last morsel of chicken off of my dinner plate.

I awoke much too early (about sunrise) in Astrid's elegantly attired guest room to the gentle sound of waves breaking on the beach below. It was predictably chilly, and I instinctively burrowed down under a hand made quilt that did an excellent job of warding off the damp sea air. It was then that I noticed Zoom, curled up nose-to-tail and appearing to be fast asleep at the foot of the bed. He'd apparently wandered in during the night and decided that this was where he wanted to be. I reasoned that it was (after all) his house and noted with appreciation that he made a darn fine foot warmer. Feeling luxuriously comfortable, I sank back into a serene slumber.

The unseen reality was that I was being sucked in, big time. And I was completely oblivious to this certainty. Didn't have the slightest clue that I was being set up. Nada.

My hosts (of course) knew full well what was going on. They'd seen it all many times before. Zoom came from prolific stock. His kin, being spread all across the continent, are highly prized and respected among the cat show types. His clan have had generations to perfect their craft when it comes to the precision-seduction of we poor humans.

"Amos," Jake and Astrid told me, shaking their heads in unison, "there really isn't anything you can do about it. He already OWNS you!"

Good grief! Ambushed! By a CAT? Not possible....or was it?

After promising to give Zoom a home he'd be proud of, I became a cat owner in this marvelous fait accompli. Little did I know just how different life would be for both of us from that day forward.

Zoom enjoyed seeking out new sights, sounds, and experiences, I joyfully discovered. And he would sulk mightily at being left behind for ANY reason. Thus the two of us became constant companions, road warriors with lives curiously entwined for the duration.

I love it. I'm pretty sure he feels the same.

Chapter 3

The hike up into the mountain wilderness shouldn't have been that big a deal, but I was so pathetically out of shape that it felt like I'd crossed the Alps by the time my sleeping bag was rolled out. Gradually the local cricket population began drumming out their steady metronomic beat. God's little lanterns twinkled on and off in the otherwise pitch black sky, their numbers beyond reckoning. Both Zoom and I enjoyed pleasantly full bellies, having devoured a couple of mesquite-broiled game hens. Zoom preferred to eat his plain, while I enjoyed my share topped by an excellent coconut-mango salsa. Our friendly little campfire crackled in the still night air, attracting a legion of small white moths.

Massaging my tired calf muscles, I had the satisfying feeling of accomplishment despite the aches and pain. Tomorrow would be tougher still, but for now I was content to sip hot coffee and savor a serenity that had been absent in my life for many months.

Zoom cocked his head, listening closely to the night

sounds. In the not-too-distant darkness, a family of coyotes had pulled down their nightly meal and were celebrating with unrestrained song. I listened to their yowls and shivered a bit at the thought of some poor woodland creature being viciously torn apart alive. Zoom seemed fascinated though, his predatory instincts being clearly aroused.

"Don't go getting any ideas," said I, basking in front of the fire. "Coyotes will often mate with stray dogs. Cats they just EAT."

Zoom glanced over at me, shuffling his feet beneath him. And then, sporting a tiny oh-so familiar grin, winked at me.

I couldn't do anything but laugh! Zoom's act is always calculated for maximum effect, and at night you couldn't possibly miss his round, luminescent eyes. He's a very special piece of work indeed.

I watched the fire slowly burned down, and, despite the early hour, decided to turn in. By now Zoom had already sought the shelter of his smallish nylon knapsack, a favorite sleeping spot of his since kitten hood. Inside I had stuffed a cat-sized bit of sheepskin for his comfort, and I knew he'd pretty much spend the night in there unless feeling the need to relieve himself in the early morning hours.

With the glowing embers of the fire now nearly spent and the gentle familiar night sounds in my ears, it didn't take long before I sensed myself dozing off into a comfortable sleep. It didn't feel like I'd been asleep long when the warning cries of a distressed cat, followed by unfamiliar hissing roused me from whatever dreams I might've enjoyed. I blinked twice, gathered my senses, and rolled over to see what was causing the ruckus.

Zoom was still inside his bag about ten feet away; I could discern his outline within. He continued to growl and hiss, standing up high on all fours with his back in full arch. I had to look closely or I'd have missed it, my night vision not being well-tuned. There coiled on the ground, directly in front of my anxious pal (still growling inside his knapsack) lurked a snake with bulbous, glowing red eyes.

Cold adrenaline stabbed my heart. I'd never heard of a snake coming this close into a camp. Usually they avoided men at all cost. Just our luck!

In the dim night light, I couldn't tell if this night stalker was a rattler or not. But in these parts it was very likely. A small nip to Zoom might be fatal. And if the snake happened to nail me instead, I was going to have a mighty hard time marching out of here. This was going to be tricky.

I didn't trust myself to go after the viper with a wooden stick; I just wasn't experienced enough to try that. If I got disoriented or lost my footing in the sand, the snake would have a better than fair chance at me. I carried no firearm. Zoom continued to sound warning growls, and I knew time wasn't on our side. I watched with horror as the snake slithered up even closer to the bag, raised its triangular head, and tested the air with a forked tongue.

I grabbed the closest thing to me (a chunk of rock) and prepared to launch it while at the same time praying for accuracy. If the rock hit the snake, or was a near-miss, I fervently hoped it would distract him and make him opt for the self-preservation route out of here. Missing the snake and accidentally hitting Zoom wasn't desirable, but it wouldn't be as bad as a set of hypodermic fangs in his neck.

It was then that the night sky exploded with a terrible fury.

Chapter 4

I was never quite sure which event came first; the brilliant lightning that temporarily blinded me, or the long blast of rolling thunder that rang in my ears. In this I had been taken completely by surprise because there was not a single cloud in the night sky.

My senses were assaulted violently, and I instinctively rolled up in the classic fetal position in a vain attempt to shield my eyes and ears. In a small (but still functioning) part of my brain was the notion that I didn't want to roll over on that snake if it could possibly be avoided. Even so, the bright light penetrated my closed eyes. I wondered about a nuclear explosion - they were supposed to be something like this, weren't they?

Slowly, the ringing in my ears began to subside and the spots in front of my eyes began to dissipate. Anxiously looking adjacent to the fire pit, I could see Zoom's bag. And (mercifully) no sign of the coiled snake.

"Zoom? You there?" came my voice, barely a croak.

"Maa-ow!" Everything ok.

Waves of relief swept over me as Zoom's small round head popped out of the bag. No signs of further trouble. I stomped on my boots, and after grabbing a small flashlight quickly surveyed our campsite as best I could with the narrow beam. I found no trace of the snake; not even a sign of his trail in the sand. Very strange indeed.

Collapsing in a near-dead heap atop my sleeping bag and with the adrenaline wearing off, I'd have given a lot just then for a shot or two of even mediocre brandy. Alas, to my great sorrow, there was none -probably for many miles. All the same, I was relieved the danger had passed with no ill coming to Zoom or I.

"Be not afraid," a soft voice said. "The Old Serpent is driven away."

Eeeeeeeeeeeeeyow!!! Caught totally off guard, I nearly suffered cardiac arrest for the second time that night.

"Be not afraid," repeated the voice of a soft white apparition, now coming into focus. I blinked again, and the soft white became more clear, turning to a radiant blue-white. But not so bright as to bring pain to my still-smarting eyes. A faint tinge of gold seemed to surround him. He looked like every picture I've ever seen of an angel, minus the wings.

Not able to respond, I sat there dumbly. I have never known such blind, all-encompassing terror. It was as if an ice pick had embedded itself in my spine. Paralyzed with fear, my only sensation was that of mild electric charges racing wild within me.

Muscles contracted involuntarily.

Knowing my fear, the night visitor softly repeated his words, "be not afraid....."

I was even less prepared for what happened next. Zoom exited his shelter, and after stretching himself out in the manner of cats everywhere, slowly walked towards us. As I sat there slack-jawed and completely dysfunctional, the angel stretched out a soft, glowing hand in his direction. Without hesitation, Zoom marched straight up to him and gently rubbed his nose and whiskers on the angelic fingertips. At this, the angel appeared pleased and smiled in appreciation. Zoom's back arched slightly and he began purring loudly.

"You are indeed fortunate," the angel said to me as he gently rubbed Zoom's folded ears. "Freely you have received. Now freely give. Your time here is not unlimited."

A pitiful babbling idiot might have at least responded with a grunt, or slobber. In my case though, even the smallest, most primitive response was beyond my ability.

With a final nod at Zoom and I, the angel spread himself thin on the night breeze and all trace of him disappeared. I remained sitting, still in a state of paralysis and shock.

Zoom, not at all bothered, gave me a head-butt in the chest and curled up to sleep in my lap.

Chapter 5

The night seemed to pass very slowly. I continued to sit in the same spot, frozen and unmoving, except to occasionally stroke Zoom's soft fur as he slept peacefully in my lap. Much later, all my emotions spent, sleep mercifully overwhelmed me.

Late the next morning with the sun high over the horizon, my abused senses began reporting for duty. Not quite asleep, but not awake either, I became aware of the sound of many, many voices. They were SINGING of all things! And this was clearly NOT your average bunch of well-tutored madrigals either. The music they made was so pure, so crisp, and so unlike anything I'd ever heard before. I was afraid to open my eyes; I wanted to drink in these sounds forever. It was a comforting, healing, and incredibly joyous sound that they produced.

Laying there in a half-daze, the thought came clearly to me that this was no dream-state that enraptured me now. This was the REAL DEAL. Mere mortals weren't (in my experience anyway) capable of producing any such music. This host was clearly of heavenly origins!

Now that was an extremely odd thought for me to have. But as quickly as I pondered the notion, I knew it was the absolute truth. A shot of frozen adrenaline pierced my spine and thus confirmed it.

I became aware of Zoom stirring on my lap as the singing slowly faded away. The sounds had been so special, so deliciously sweet. When they had gone, I felt saddened as if I had suffered a loss of great magnitude. None of this made any sense, but there you have it.

Eyes now open, I sat up with a groan and began to take stock of my situation. Coffee. I desperately needed coffee. Zoom, never one to waste time, was already poking around in my backpack in search of breakfast. It was already long past the normal breakfast hour, and I was hoping there might be some hot coals left in the fire pit for the coffee pot.

A little later, with our hunger pangs having been satisfied, I sat sipping coffee for a while and pondered exactly what had happened the night before. Part of my brain tried to examine the situation clinically, but kept coming up dry. Childhood memories of weekly Sunday school lessons offered no real understanding either.

Feeling quite unsettled and truthfully more than a little afraid, I decided to cut this trip short. Decision made, Zoom watched me curiously as I gathered up our gear from around our dry camp.

"Get ready to move out," I said. "We're heading back down the mountain early....."

No reply. Zoom didn't seem to care one way or the other. Blissful ignorance. Well, whatever our encounter with the angel may have signified, I was still worried about that horrid snake with the flashing red eyes that had paid us a visit. He might still be around. I couldn't seem to shake the feeling that

Zoom was in some kind of danger here.

Taking no chances, I had my little furry pal ride atop my backpack. Normally he'd walk alongside of me, or sometimes range out a little ahead.

But today he didn't seem to mind the free ride as I trudged slowly along the trail down into the desert valley below.

Chapter 6

My old Jeep was mercifully intact and right where I'd left it the day before. Its eight cylinders fired up without any protest and had us underway a couple of minutes later. I set a mostly southerly course back towards Highway 70. Zoom wasted no time finding a comfy spot in the back seat and promptly went to sleep.

There isn't any real road in that area, so I had to zig-zag , constantly keeping an eye on the ruts, rocks, and cactus. It wasn't a comfortable ride, but the old Jeep did the job it was designed for without complaining.

About an hour later we arrived at the paved highway. After stopping for a second to get my bearings, I turned onto it and headed west towards the little town of Negus. Twenty minutes later I could see a small group of buildings in the distance.

Actually, Negus isn't much of a town. A post office, a small grocery store with gas pumps out front, and a handful of other tiny businesses that manage to eke out a living for their owners was about it. A dusty rural town like so many others in

Arizona. But it had a rugged appeal and I have always found it charming in its own way.

I pulled the Jeep up in front of the gas pumps, filled the tank, and went inside the town's only grocery store. Deke Chavez, owner and proprietor, was busy stocking cans of vegetables on the long narrow shelves.

"Why, howdy Amos!" he said cheerily. "You know, I been tellin' folks you'd come back here. Every time we'd see you on the tv or read about you in the papers, folks here would say you made the big time; that we'd never see the likes o' you again. I kept tellin' them they was wrong."

"Well, Deke," I said, "it was quite a ride. Nothing like I ever imagined."

"Well, I'm glad to see you again," said Deke. "Say, where's that cat of yours? Loved the way he jumped up on Letterman's desk, right there on national TV!"

"He's outside, doing what cats do best. Taking his afternoon siesta."

"By the way, real sorry to hear about the fire."

"Huh? Say what?"

"Maybe I spoke out o' turn," said Deke, shuffling his feet nervously. "Fire up at your place last night. You probably ought to stop by the volunteer fire station and see the Chief. Sorry, Amos. I really am. Don't want to be the one bringing you bad news."

"Anybody hurt?" I asked.

"I don't think so, but I ought not be sayin' any more."

"It'll be okay, Deke. I know how you feel. I'll go see about it," I said, turning towards the door.

Some years back I had bought a little mobile home that had grown roots in a seasonal RV park out by the airstrip. Its previous owner, a widow, had decided to sell the place after her husband had unexpectedly passed away. I'd kept the place as a weekend retreat and had enjoyed many a fine sunset there whenever I could spare the time. My little getaway was only a two hour flight from home and was within walking distance of the airstrip. It wasn't elegant, but Zoom and I liked it just the same.

I drove right to the RV park, eschewing a visit with the fire chief. He was something of a blowhard and mostly to be avoided. To my regret, I found him standing at the charred ruins of what had once been my mobile home. I guess Deke had called him from the store and told him about my being in town. Whatever.

"Hey boy! There you are!" said volunteer fire chief Larry Crank.

"Yeah, hello there, Chief," I said without much enthusiasm. "What happened here?"

"Well, as you can see, not much left but a pile of ashes."

"You didn't answer my question."

"Well, hey, I don't know, really," he admitted. "We got a call late last night that your place was burning. When we got the engine here it was fully afire. Nothing to save by that time."

"So, like, you just let it burn?" I said with a touch of anger.

"Seemed like the best thing to do. We kept watch for a while, making sure the fire didn't spread. Where were you last night? I been trying to find you. Called that agent of yours, but couldn't get past the secretary."

"I've been up in the mountains," I said somewhat lamely.

"Really? I figured you gave up life around here, you bein' famous and all...."

"Anybody hurt?" I asked.

"Naw. Say, you insured?" he asked, a tone of suspicion creeping into his voice.

"Probably," I answered. "You know how it is with we rich and famous types. We tend to leave the details to the little people," I added, egging him on.

"Well, you can get a fire report from my office later," he said, giving me a hard look. "Let me know."

"I will."

With that, volunteer fire chief Larry turned his back on me and climbed into his beat up Bronco. I made a point of not waving as he drove away.

My nearest neighbor, Mortie Maguire walked up as I stood looking at the rubble.

"Hey there Amos!" he said, sporting a welcoming grin.

"Howdy, Mortie," I replied. "You know anything about this?

Mortie chuckled. "You mean our illustrious fire chief didn't tell you everything he knew?"

"Well, that took about five seconds. You know Larry. Spends most of his time trying to impress you with what a herd bull he is."

"Ain't that the truth! Well, it's good to see you, man!" exclaimed Mortie as he extended his hand. "Come on over to our place; you look real tired. Maude's got some elk stew on."

"Thanks partner. I could really use some. And a little coffee if you have any to spare," I said.

Zoom, never one to miss elk stew, quit nosing around the ashes of our former lodge and took off ahead of us.

By the time Mortie and I arrived at the door, Zoom was already having his ears scratched by Maude, who was clearly delighted at our arrival.

Chapter 7

Maude Maguire was one of those rare women who seem to get prettier as they age. I'd known her for about five years and had long since decided that her husband Mortie was one lucky guy. Maude sported long auburn hair, large doe-like eyes, and a mighty quick wit. It was hard to say how old they might be, but I figured them both to be well beyond what most of us consider normal retirement age.

Maude had been a school teacher back in Kentucky while Mortie ran his own truck repair facility. Never able to have children, they'd made the best of it by sponsoring a number of youth sports teams organized by their country recreation department. This was a couple totally joined at the hip. Mortie and Maude now spent the cooler months in Arizona. I knew that before the oppressive summer heat set in again, they'd pack up and hit the road in their big diesel motorhome.

"Amos, I declare you look like you been rode hard and

put away wet!" Maude exclaimed as Mortie and I walked up. "And poor Zoom here looks positively famished! Y'all get yourselves in here pronto!"

"Looks like you been given your orders," said Mortie, flashing me a quick grin.

"Wouldn't be polite to refuse," I said.

"Or wise."

We both made a point of stomping our shoes clean on the doormat (Maude is a fastidious housekeeper) and entered through the kitchen door. It was immediately apparent that today was Maude's baking day; the inviting aromas immediately stimulated my appetite.

Zoom was already half way through a kitty-sized bowl of elk stew. He carefully avoided the carrots and onions, but aggressively sought out the tender morsels of meat and potatoes. Pausing briefly to glance up at Maude, he rewarded her with a quick "m-rr-ow" which we took to be his approval of Maude's culinary abilities.

"Amos," said Maude as she set her big serving pot down on the table, "you look very tired. Tell Mortie and I what you've been up to. And then we'll tell you what we know about the fire at your place last night."

I looked at both of them closely, carefully weighing what I should (or should not) tell them. I was, I realized, becoming jaded from having dealt with so many agents, lawyers, and the like. But Mortie and Maude were my friends. I decided to hold nothing back from them.

"Maude," I replied slowly, "this is between the three of us here, you understand? You may think I'm losing my mind when I tell you my story. But all the same, I need to talk to someone about it and I respect your judgement."

Mortie and Maude, both sensing that something important was about to be revealed, just nodded and said nothing.

"It all started last night," I said, helping myself to a bowl of elk stew. "Zoom and I were tramping around in the Harquahalas...."

Between mouth fulls, I poured out the amazing tale of what had happened to Zoom and I the night before. I told them both about the snake, the deafening explosion in the night sky, and the appearance of the angel. Even about the singing I'd been treated to by the great heavenly choir. Incredibly, Mortie and Maude just sat there taking it all in until I'd finished my tale. Then they looked at each other curiously, and simultaneously nodded their heads in some kind of agreement.

"Amos," said Mortie as Maude began clearing away the dishes, "there's something we want to tell you before commenting on your little adventure.

It was me that called the fire department last night. Maude and I were sitting here on the porch swing looking at the night stars when the lightning struck your place. Craziest thing I ever saw. Not a cloud in the sky, and yet this bolt of electricity clobbers your little trailer. It began to burn fiercely, and immediately. Almost like it'd been soaked in gasoline. But that's not the strangest part. The flames were all light-blue colored. Not orange or yellow like you'd expect. Just blue...."

Maude sat down beside me, took my hand, and looked at me square in the eyes.

"Amos, you know that Mortie and I are only casual church people. But we are believers just the same. We think you and Zoom have lived through an amazing experience, and for that we're thankful. There's almost certainly some connection between what happened to you in the hills last night and the fire here. But exactly what it all means is a mystery to both of us. Anything else we say is just going to be so much speculation. And we believe that God has something special planned for you."

"It's all so confusing," I replied. "Why me? I'm no saint. Sure, I've tried to live a decent life, mostly. Always figured I was somewhere in the middle. Not as good as some, but better than others. Why would the God who created the universe single me out when he could easily have His pick of countless who are, well, more worthy?"

"Amos," said Mortie as he stuffed his after-dinner pipe, "our God is nothing if not awesome. His way, His thoughts, His plans, well, they're beyond the comprehension of we poor humans. Left to our own devices, I'm convinced we'd all surely perish from our own foolish excesses. Yet, He sustains us all out of pure love. You know I'm no preacher or learned scholar. But I've been allowed to live on planet Earth a long time, and like to think I've acquired a sort of rudimentary wisdom. A lot of that I owe to Maude," he said, winking at his wife.

"Think back to your early days, and what you read in the Bible," said Maude.

"Been an awful long time," I admitted sheepishly.

"Well, you'll remember that God's angels are sent as messengers. They didn't appear often in the Bible, but when they did show up it was always with a specific message from God. Here, it seems to me like you and Zoom have been given one such message. Seems to us there's only one sensible thing to do, " said Maude knowingly.

"What's that?" I asked.

"OBEY!"

Chapter 8

Leaving my trusty Jeep in Mortie's care, I walked down to the airstrip and prepared to get underway. It was late afternoon, but a call to the FAA weather briefer confirmed friendly winds and fair visibility all the way to the L.A. basin. Barring anything unforseen, Zoom and I would arrive at the John Wayne Airport in Orange County before sunset.

Mortie and Maude had asked us to stay the night at their place, but after everything that we'd been through over the last couple of days, I just wanted to go home.

Zoom seemed fine with the idea. He watched for a few minutes as I untied the Cessna Skyhawk and performed the usual pre-flight safety checks. Then he curled up in the back seat as was asleep before I taxied out for takeoff.

"Darn cat can sleep anywhere," I muttered to myself as I pushed the throttle wide open, pouring on the coals.

I've flown Skyhawks for a long time and have grown comfortable and confident in their high reliability. I'd purchased this particular one three summers back and had never regretted it. Cessna One Sierra Tango was over twenty years old, but had aged gracefully and always got us where we needed to go.

Piloting my own aircraft is sacred to me. I've owned a pilot's license almost twenty years, and yet I still feel like an exuberant child every time I take to the skies. From the time I took my first ride in my uncle's old Piper Cub as a small boy, I knew that somehow, in the fullness of time, I'd earn my wings. Many years would pass, and many dollars would be sacrificed. When the FAA decided in its wisdom I was at last worthy to be designated a pilot in command, it was a day to celebrate. I had joined what amounts to a unique club; there aren't that many of us. And we're blessed in being able to engage in one of the world's few remaining pristine endeavors.

Anxious to be in its element, Cessna One Sierra Tango quickly gathered speed down the runway and launched herself into the bright afternoon sunshine. I trimmed the nose up a bit, turned downwind, and headed for the Colorado River. Thirty uneventful minutes later, the Blythe airport came into view and I radioed for a landing advisory. Information received, we thumped down on the runway shortly thereafter behind a Piper Cherokee doing practice landings. I taxied us over to the fuel pumps and killed the engine. While the lineman filled our tanks, I headed over to the terminal for a men's room. Zoom, familiar with this particular airport routine and being uninterested, curled up and went back to sleep. We were on our way again about fifteen minutes later.

After departing the traffic pattern at Blythe, we continued our westerly course through the Coachella Valley, past Palm Springs and up into the Banning Pass. I monitored the Flight Watch frequency on the radio, listening for other pilot reports and occasionally getting updated weather information.

The closer we got to our destination, the visibility got predictably worse. Skies around Riverside and San Bernardino are often murky owing to air pollution, and any pilot worth his salt keeps a constant vigil for other aircraft. There are multiple airports in the area and it's not uncommon to find yourself sharing the airspace with several other planes.

Fortunately I had the benefit of years of experience operating around here, and knew to watch out for everything from a B-52 heavy bomber out of March AFB to a tiny Aeronca Champ from Chino. The air traffic controllers were helpful and issued traffic advisories, of course. But in the end, responsibility for safe aviating always rests upon the pilot.

Today we zipped through the area without any close encounters. Just after clearing the Santa Ana range, I radioed the approach controllers.

"Coast Approach, Cessna One Sierra Tango is over Lake Irvine at four thousand five hundred for a possible straight in approach to John Wayne...."

"Cessna One Sierra Tango, squawk 1415 and ident...." came the reply.

I dialed in the transponder code which allowed the approach radar to paint me on its screen, and waited.

"Cessna One Sierra Tango, radar contract. Straight in is possible. Descend to three thousand and remain on station at Lake Irvine."

"Roger, down to three thousand and orbit the lake," I replied.

"Cessna One Sierra Tango, expect a four minute delay due to jet traffic..."

"Cessna One Sierra Tango, roger, no problem, please keep me advised," I said.

It was close to sunset, and I knew from experience that everyone would be headed for the barn right about now. Even with the slight delay I'd still save time and fuel as opposed to making the longer standard approach from the south.

A few minutes later I heard, "Cessna One Sierra Tango, continue your straight in approach. Descent to two thousand at your discretion..."

"Cessna One Sierra Tango, roger..."

I turned us west, pushed the nose over, and sped on towards the parallel runways at John Wayne. A few minutes later, the approach controller handed us off to the airport tower. I switched frequencies, lowered the flaps to slow us down, and was cleared to land after being warned of wake turbulence caused by the heavy transport planes.

Cessna One Sierra Tango plunked down on runway 19L, rolled out, and cleared the active runway at the second intersection.

"Cessna One Sierra Tango, welcome to John Wayne. Contact ground control on one-three-two point five...."

"Roger, contacting ground...."

Once again the intrepid birdman has soared with the eagles and lived to tell about it.

Chapter 9

Mickey, the duty linesman at the FBO, was waiting for us in the parking area as I taxied to the tie down area and shut down the engine.

"Already called the fuel truck, Mister Westergaard. But it's their busy time and it'll be a while."

"That's okay Mickey," I said, tossing him the keys. "Ask them to top her off when they show up. And please schedule a wash and wax as soon as possible, would you?"

"You betcha!" said Mickey with a nod.

With that, I grabbed our gear out of the baggage compartment and started for the parking lot to retrieve my car. Zoom knew I always took our stuff to the car first, where I'd also roll down the windows and cool the interior. So he relaxed in the pilot's seat and allowed Mickey to scratch his ears while he watched the other aircraft coming and going.

We were home within the hour. My modest condo in Newport Beach was a welcome sight to both of us. Zoom made a bee line for his litter box while I opened all the windows and patio doors. The cool Pacific breeze began wafting in, quickly replacing the stuffy interior air.

There was a substantial pile of mail that had accumulated during our absence. I sat out on the patio sorting through the mess, most of which went unopened into the trash. Anything requiring further attention I tossed on my desk to be dealt with later.

Checking the contents of the refrigerator, I happily discovered there was enough food for the evening meal. I took out a couple of frozen chicken breasts and doused them with a sweet and sour marinade. There was also a package of baby peas that looked okay, and half a bag of Tater Tots. Haute cuisine. I opened a bottle of Rolling Rock Extra Pale, savoring it while I worked on mixing up batter for corn meal muffins and listened to a Dodger game on the radio.

The Dodgers beat the Padres while I ate, and three bottles of beer later, I went to bed and slept soundly.

Zoom woke me up at seven the next morning, reminding me that he needed to be fed. After refilling his kibble bowl, I put on a tank top and headed down to the beach.

Newport Beach is great for morning walks. The salt air is pungent and invigorating. I trudged along for a couple of miles, observing great multitudes of sea birds out foraging for their breakfast, while I worked on figuring out my 'To Do' list for the day.

An hour later I was back at home, having showered, dressed, eaten, and ready for anything. I made a few phone calls, arranged a couple of appointments, grabbed Zoom, and headed out the door.

First stop was Bernie the Attorney. Bernie and I had known each other for years, and I'd referred a lot of business to him back in my days as an investment advisor. His business had grown to the point where he did little except handle estate planning matters for wealthy individuals and lavish attention on his string of losing race horses at Los Alamitos.

Raising Spirits

Bernie's office suite was just up the coast in nearby Huntington Beach. Besides plush carpeting, impressionist paintings, and French Provencal furniture, these offices also housed Bernie's bevy of incredibly gorgeous private secretaries. A fringe benefit for all the rich old geezers who were Bernie's clients. Oh, it was all very honorable and above board, mind you. It's just Bernie's way of keeping you on the hook. Market appeal.

While the valet parked my car, I took the elevator up to the third floor with Zoom riding on my forearm.

Drop dead gorgeous Peaches Calderone was on duty at the reception station when I walked in. Peaches is a California blonde with eyes the color of cornflowers and legs that stretch all the way to heaven.

"Why, Mister Westergaard! How nice to see you again! And Zoom is with you!," she exclaimed in her delightful southern drawl.

"Of course, Peaches! You know I couldn't come in and not bring Zoom along to visit his number one fan," I said, flashing her a smile.

Peaches is in fact a big admirer of Zoom and always manages to have a packet of his favorite salmon flavored treats available whenever we come to visit. True to form, she produced a small cellophane bag from her desk drawer. Zoom meeow-ed in appreciation and jumped to the floor to receive his tribute.

I found myself admiring her shapely backside and world-class thighs as she happy fed my furry pal. I wondered if this was considered sexist, politically incorrect thinking and decided it probably was. Ah well... I'm probably too old to change now.

Bernie came in, shook my hand, and escorted me to his inner sanctum.

"Good to see you, Amos," he said, exhibiting his best poker face. "Did I just observe you leering like a gargoyle at my secretary's derriere?"

"You know I admire finery in any form, you old shyster," I said with a grin.

"And you know I wouldn't let just anybody talk to me that way. But since you're here on a mission and obviously just DYING to tell your favorite lawyer all about your debauchery with the rich and famous, I'll have to let it pass."

"Attorney-client privilege?" I asked, laughing.

"But of course!"

Chapter 10

"**B**ernard," I said, "prepare to be overwhelmed. But first let us take care of some of the boring, routine housekeeping."

"Yeah, sure." he said. "I figured that's what you really came in for. Got your file and all the most recent statements here. You know Amos, there's quite a LOT of money. I don't have to tell you that you're gonna take a huge tax hit this year."

"I know, I know......We'll get together and work on that issue before season's end," I promised.

"Don't put it off. You know most of the tax rules as well as I do. By the by, I know where there's this really great house in Newport for sale. Owned by a family trust - clients of mine. The original owners have died, and the surviving heirs want the place sold. Gorgeous home - you oughta see it. About three point two million, I'd say. You need to start living a little, Amos."

"Maybe I'll go see it," I allowed carefully. "I'd miss my

little condo; it suits me. And I can't see feeding the IRS needlessly either."

"Now you're talking!" said Bernie. "You and your cat will love it. Great house for parties, inside and out."

"Meanwhile," I said, "let's review a few things. My younger brother stays on as my successor trustee. He's recovered nicely from his hospital stay."

Bernie just nodded, his best poker face intact.

"He's smarter than I am anyway," I continued. "He'll make sure Mama is taken care of and help to carry out the other provisions of the trust if anything unexpected happens to me. I know you and he don't much like each other, Bernie. But I'm counting on the two of you to close ranks and get the job done if I'm not around to see to it."

"It'll be okay, Amos," said Bernie with a sigh. "I'm not worried about the legal aspects; you know I'm superb at what I do. All the bequests and transfers will be made on a timely basis. The money and other assets will get where they're supposed to go. As to your brother, he's just another in a long line of stuffed shirts I've had to work with over the years. Dandies like him grate on me, but you can count on me to suck it up and carry out your wishes."

"I know I can, Bernie. You and he seem to be on the very short list of people I can trust lately."

"I hear you," said Bernie with a knowing nod. "Celebrity isn't all it's cracked up to be, at least not in my observations. I've known you a long time, Amos. I'll bet hard cash you're feeling the same way after all your experiences in the past couple of years."

"The truth is what it is," I acknowledged. "It's been a wild ride. And don't get me wrong, I'm thrilled with all the loot that's come my way, but I just can't continue living on that kind of roller coaster. I'm determined to reclaim something of a normal life again."

"Well, it looks to me like that, in the life of a book, 'A Wanderer's Wisdom' has about run its course," said Bernie, glancing down at my file where it lay on his polished Brazilian cherry wood desk. "I talked with your publisher last week. She says the paperback issue should continue to sell quite well for a while. But that the major hurrahs are behind you."

"Yeah, that's kind of what I was hoping," I said.

"So what are you planning to do now?"

"Well, I've taken an advance on my next book. The problem is, I don't really have any brilliant ideas for a new novel. I'm hoping not to be a one-hit wonder in the literary world, but right now my normally fertile imagination seems to have taken a powder."

"Are you getting any pressure from your publishers?" asked Bernie.

"Not so far. They're still busy counting their take from the first book. But the honeymoon probably won't last long," I said.

"Well, you and Zoom take it easy for a few days. After the merry go round you've been on, you certainly deserve a break. Let the mental fog clear. Something will develop," said Bernie knowingly.

"Now TELL ME about all those New York actresses you were doing," ordered Bernie. "I can't stand it any longer!"

We talked on for a long while. I filled my old friend Bernie in on all the wild, unrestrained parties I'd been a willing participant in. Stories involving celebrity wives and their unusual appetites. My encounters with morally bankrupt politicians and their insatiable quest to widen their powers and prestige. And a near-unending river of tales featuring nymphomaniac starlets, wannabe's, and hanger's on. It was, I began realizing sheepishly, a sorry saga involving out of control debauchery. By the time I'd finished my salacious saga, I was feeling rather embarrassed.

"I don't know if I can go on," I said.

"Trust me, man, I CAN handle it," said Bernie, clearly arroused.

"Very well, then, " I said. "But remember, you asked for it!"

It was then I told Bernie about my overnight trip in the Harquahala mountains. I did the best I could to explain the terrifying encounter with the snake, the explosion in the night sky, and the appearance of the angel who'd probably saved Zoom and I.

For the first time since I'd known him, Bernie the Attorney just sat there in his large overstuffed leather chair and said nothing. I could hear a clock ticking somewhere, and that was all.

"Amos," he said, finally speaking, "you know I'm a cynical old SOB. In my line of work you have to be. I've known too many certifiable fruitcakes in my life - most of 'em rich - to allow me to be any other way. If it was anybody but you and that blasted cat, I wouldn't believe a word of this. Never! But you're too much of a straight shooter, aren't you?"

"Bernie, as surely as I draw breath that's exactly what happened to us. I've rolled it over in my mind countless times since that night, and there's nothing that explains it. There was no booze to be had, and you know I don't touch drugs. Zoom stretched out and touched that Angel as easily as I could stretch out and shake your hand. The whole episode terrified me so much I couldn't move or speak to save my own life."

"Great grinning geckos!" exclaimed Bernie. "I simply don't know what to say!"

"Kinda unusual for you, isn't it old man?" I asked, sporting a tiny grin. "And just to add a little more intrigue, many miles away, my little home down there burned to the ground that same night. My neighbors said it was like no fire they'd ever seen. Eerie blue flames that quickly incinerated the whole structure."

"Damn!" said Bernie, all but overwhelmed. "I presume it was empty? Nobody hurt? You were insured, you know. I'll get claim underway."

"No physical injuries. The place was empty at the time.

Raising Spirits

Just very weird is all," I said.

"Amos," said Bernie in a serious tone, "you know I am your lawyer and your friend. I'll help anyway I can. But your tale just stuns me; I'm really rattled. I know I won't sleep well tonight."

"Aw heck, Bernie," I said, "it'll be okay."

"Will it? Look at yourself, Amos. You're a changed man. Your life will never, ever be the same! A nocturnal visit from an angel sent by the living God! You know, I"ve never been very religious. Spent my life chasing the big bucks. Determined to 'be someone,' whatever that means. But there's always been a belief of sorts buried deep within me. I always knew that the faith of my fathers was true. And yet I've managed to ignore it all my adult life. Then you come walking in here and announce a close encounter with God's own angel!"

Bernie was clearly agitated. I knew the feeling only too well.

"Listen my friend," I said, trying to exert a calming effect on my old friend. "I didn't ask for any of this, and I don't know what it might mean. But I do know that God loves us all, great and small. In the centuries since the Bible was written, despite never ending analysis and commentary, that's the one underlying, undeniable, unending truth. He loves us. It's so simple that it eludes people."

"What're your plans?" asked Bernie in a low voice.

"To try and find some answers," I replied.

Bernie nodded and rose from his chair. Our time together was up. I shook his hand, promised to keep in touch, and went out to retrieve Zoom. Bernie looked so sad when I left, and I wondered if I should've kept my mouth shut. But by then it was too late, and destiny would unfold as it would.

I found Zoom on the galley/lunchroom area used by the staff. He was hunkered down on the big dining table, surrounded by a collection of the most gorgeous T&A ever assembled. Bernie's Brigade continue to fuss over him until they saw me standing there watching.

"Oh Mister Westergaard, he's just SO precious!" gushed one - a shapely red haired dream girl whose name I couldn't seem to recall.

An old friend in my stomach began to uncurl. The thought crossed my mind that I too would have trouble sleeping that night.

Chapter 11

Following that unsettling meeting with Bernie the attorney, I drove out the old Harbor Freeway to the fishing port of San Pedro. Traffic was heavier than expected for the time of day; Zoom and I shared the highway with legions of fuming, ill-tempered motorists. The congestion didn't bother me very much. I'd been traveling these roads long enough to know that it was just part of life in southern California. But some people just never seemed to get it and various displays of road rage were common.

San Pedro is unique in that many of the residents are second or third generation, born and raised there. The area doesn't suffer as much from constant transient turnover as do other nearby beach communities. Thus the atmosphere tends to be more hometown, and I like it a lot.

Pastor Miguel Papadoukis ministers to the faithful at the Safe Harbor Church of Jesus Christ on the south edge of town. A small white traditional chapel with attendant steeple beckons to worshipers twice each Sunday. During the rest of the week a large volunteer organization tends to the needs of the elderly, single moms, lonely sailors from distant lands, local school children, and a host of others needing help.

Miguel himself is a fascinating story. The union of a Hispanic mother and a Greek father, he cuts a dashing figure even in his fifties. Tall, wolfishly lean, sporting jet black hair and his ear pierced with a tiny gold loop, Miguel appears every inch the modern day pirate. Which is very close to what he once was.

His father disappeared when he was six, and young Miguel took to running the streets. Later, flush with cash from a successful drug running operation, Miguel reclaimed his Greek roots and bought an old sixty foot fishing trawler. With the courts handing out ever-stiffer sentences to drug traffickers, Miguel rightly figured he could make nearly the same money smuggling illegal aliens into the U.S. with much less risk in terms of jail time.

For years he plied his illicit trade and was never caught. The only time he was ever boarded by the Coast Guard was off the coast of Monterey. Even then his luck held. Miguel was dead-heading south that afternoon and the only thing onboard besides himself was a lot of well-worn fishing gear.

Miguel's secret was in working mostly alone, keeping a low profile, and trusting precious few. The illegals never knew where they'd be landed along the coast. No one ever complained; his charges were taking big risks and they knew it. And Miguel made a point of waving around his big .44 magnum (and who knew what else?) from the time his passengers came shuffling nervously aboard.

The big change in his life came during a savage February storm. Despite his years of experience at sea, things went horribly wrong. Miguel's boat sank with a full cargo. In this case it meant that thirty-six men, women, and small children seeking the good life in L.A. would never find it. An angry gray Pacific ocean would be their grave.

Miguel found himself alone in the water, without a life

jacket and fighting hypothermia. Cursing God for his foul luck, he somehow hung on through the darkest of nights. The dawn finally came, and with it a calming of the angry waters. But by now the unlucky smuggler was nearly spent. Through salt-abused, blood red eyes, he spied what appeared to be a bit of flotsam nearby. Summoning the last of his reserves, Miguel paddled over to the debris, hoping to find something to help him stay afloat a little longer.

His heart shattered when he discovered that his find was nothing more than the corpse of a drowned two year old girl. Miguel recalled with horror that this tiny China doll had been aboard before his ship went down. Alone, exhausted, and figuring to die, Miguel begged God not for mercy, but forgiveness. He cried alone for what seemed to him an eternity.

The vagaries of the ocean current floated the tiny corpse away, never to be seen again by a human eye. When Miguel saw a pair of fins cutting the gray water nearby, he resolved to dive down as deep as he could and drown himself. Even in his emaciated condition, he still had enough presence of mind to reason it was better to drown than be torn apart while living by hungry sharks.

But he was mistaken; these were not sharks out on the prowl. The fins belonged instead to a pair of dolphins. Sailors have a long-cherished belief that dolphins bring good luck, and so it was with these two. No sooner had the finny mammals passed Miguel by than out of the morning gloom appeared a commercial fishing boat.

Miguel Papadoukis would live, the only survivor of a crime to which no physical evidence would ever appear.

Chapter 12

Zoom and I sauntered casually past the little chapel and down the cobblestone driveway towards the rectory. We were a few steps shy of our destination when a door flew open and out rushed Maria, Pastor Miguel's long-suffering housekeeper.

"Senor Amos! Welcome! And you have brought also Senor Zoom to visit!" she exclaimed with delight.

"Hola, Maria! You know I couldn't come here without bringing my fuzzy companion. What would the children think of me?" I asked, laughing.

"Well, you are just in time. You may share a late lunch with HIS HIGHNESS in the study. Senor Zoom, please to come with me...."

Zoom needed no coaching. He'd been here before to the delight of the pre-schoolers at the day care room. Being something of a ham, Zoom loved being shown off to the toddlers under the watchful gaze of Maria. And he knew that before leaving, there was almost always a dish of cold milk to be had.

Raising Spirits

I threaded my way down a narrow hall to the study, knocking softly on a well-worn and familiar door.

"Enter," commanded a strong baritone voice.

I stepped into the study and confronted Pastor Miguel Papadoukis, his mouth around a giant submarine sandwich.

"Forgive me, padre, for I have sinned," I said, not being able to resist a small giggle.

"Well I'll be hung," exclaimed Miguel, his eyes widening. "The prodigal son returns at last! And I'll wager you've sinned more than a little!" he added thoughtfully. "Come in my old friend; come in and be welcome!"

No handshakes here; Miguel's customary greeting involves a great bear hug which I dutifully reciprocated.

"I can't tell you how good it is to see you again, Amos. Maria was just saying the other day that she hoped you'd not forgotten your friends and moved to New York."

"No chance of that," I said, shaking my head. "New York, the book tour, doing all the tv shows - they were an enlightening experience."

"Indeed! Do you know how many people lust their entire lives hoping for just a little of that kind of fame?" Miguel asked. "Do you know what they'd GIVE?"

"Sadly, they'd likely give much more than it's worth. At least to me."

"So you didn't find all that fast luxurious living to your tastes, eh?" asked Miguel.

"Oh, in the beginning I went willingly enough," I said. "The cars, the women, the booze, the nightlife - it can all be pretty seductive. I understand now why so many of the rich and famous in our society tend to crash and burn."

"Well, fortunately you discovered this for yourself, before being completely consumed," observed Miguel.

"The Lord looks out for fools and sailors, remember?"

"So it is, amigo. Who knows this better than I? Tell me, is Senor Zoom well?

"Down in the nursery, being adored as we speak," I said with a grin.

"Bravo!" said Miguel, obviously happy. "We have some special ones there today. Poor little waifs not quite right in the head. He'll brighten their day as surely as you have mine."

"Cocaine babies?" I asked.

"I'm afraid so," answered Miguel with a sad little nod.

"Listen, Miguel," I said, changing the subject. "I need to talk; I need your observation and counsel. Zoom and I have recently had an, uh, encounter that's really rattled me."

"Amos, my friend, you may speak freely as always."

I told Miguel about my retreat into the mountains, and about the intruding snake with the oversize bulbous eyes that had stalked Zoom. And especially about the visit from the angel of the Lord, noting that his appearance may well have saved Zoom from death. Miguel listened patiently, only interrupting me a few times to ask for clarification. He then pondered what I had told him for a few moments. I could hear the wall clock gently ticking behind me.

"Amos," he said. "You are one of the few living people that know the details of my former life. You know that after my ship sank, I gave up my wicked life and committed myself to God's work and this ministry. Oh, I jumped through the requisite hoops. Went through the seminary and was legally ordained. But in fact, great and perceptive wisdom eludes me."

"But still, you must have SOME thoughts on this," I said, feeling a little panicky.

"I have learned in the past that, when confronted with a situation that seems to have no ready answer, one does well to consult the owner's handbook," said Miguel, leaning forward.

"Owner's handbook?" I asked.

"Some call it the Holy Bible."

"Oh."

"In the bible, angels appear several times. Most often they bear an important message from God. In your case, the message 'freely you have received, now freely give,' is a quotation from the book of Matthew," said Miguel.

"Explain."

"Okay, this part of the book of Matthew tells of the time when Jesus sent the apostles out to preach the word to the lost sheep of Israel. As my biblical translation reads, they were to 'heal the sick, cleanse lepers, raise the dead, and cast out demons.' The last part of verse eight reads 'freely ye have received, now freely give.' What I find curious is that the second part of the message you received is NOT in the bible. When your visiting angel said that your time here was not unlimited."

"Bingo," I said, becoming suddenly uncomfortable in my chair.

"Don't let it trouble you, my friend. For reasons not yet understood, God in His infinite wisdom has taken notice of you. You should take what the angel said seriously and NOT be afraid. Go forth, live your life, and be secure in the knowing that God is with you.

"That strange, awful snake still worries me," I said. "Something about it was just all wrong."

"In the bible, the snake's presence usually represented the evil one, Satan. Or perhaps a demon. But did not your angel also say that he had been driven away? I would take comfort in this. I believe you are under a protective guard."

"A guardian angel?" I asked, feeling a little skeptical.

"Perhaps several. Apparently we're not to know. But I believe you and Senor Zoom have become an integral part of a great and holy drama, being played out in the heavens and upon the earth even as we speak."

"I just can't get my head around that," I said. "Until recently I was just an ordinary guy, struggling to make his way in the world like countless others. On something of a lark, I write a book that propels me into the limelight. And suddenly the creator of the universe, the Big Guy Himself sits up and notices me?"

"I think it is unwise to associate your newly won fame with

the visit by one of God's angels, Amos. God doesn't care bit about such things as celebrity status. He'll use you wherever you are. My advice to you is that you accept what has happened and carry on," said Miguel sternly.

"And do WHAT?" I asked, my voice tinged with anger. "Heal the sick? Raise the dead? Do you know how crazy that sounds?"

"Amos," said Pastor Miguel, his jet black eyes piercing me, "have faith. God will help you find your way down whatever path he has chosen for you. The burden will not be more than you can bear."

"How long do you think I have?" I asked, feeling somewhat resigned.

"I don't know," answered Miguel. "Many learned scholars seem to be in agreement that we're in the last days as have been described in the bible. That we are indeed witnessing signs of the end of this age as spoken of by Jesus. It could be so, but I just don't know. And anyone who tells you they DO know with certainty is a liar."

"I feel unequal to it," I lamented. "And I don't even know what IT is!

"Come with me, my old friend. We will go down to the chapel and pray together.

Prayer calms a troubled spirit and helps us see more clearly. Prayer works."

I nodded and the two of us got up and walked over to the chapel. The sun was shining and the air fairly hummed with the sounds of many birds and tiny insects. I still felt very unsure of myself.

Miguel detoured slightly and pulled me into the tiny library alcove.

"I have two copies of your book in here," he said. "Would you do me the honor of signing them for me? We're having a fund raiser next week, and I believe your books will bring more at the auction if they've been personally autographed."

"Of course," I said as I whipped out my checkbook. "But

just in case folks don't think as highly of me as we might hope, this will make up any difference." I wrote out a check for $50,000.00 and handed it over, along with the two books that I'd signed my name to. For the first time since I'd known him, I saw tears begin to well up in Miguel's eyes.

"Amos," he said, his voice cracking, "this is so generous. It will help many more than you can know. May God bless you....."

"Pleeeze Miguel! I'm having enough trouble with all this NOW," I pleaded. "Just take care of the little ones, okay?" I added softly.

Miguel only nodded, and then led us both into the sanctuary where we prayed together. Afterwards, I felt as if a burden had been lifted. I was really no closer to understanding the visit from the angel, but all the same I was less fearful.

I found Zoom asleep in the day care room, curled up and napping between two toddlers. I tiptoed in quietly.

"Zoom?" I whispered.

"Mrr-r-r-?" he trilled softly.

"Time to go, pal..."

Zoom got to his feet slowly, stretching carefully as cats will do. Very gently he rubbed his whiskers on the cheek of the napping children who continued to sleep undisturbed. We crept silently out of the room and into the hall where Maria and I exchanged our goodbys. She escorted us down the driveway to our car, waving as we drove away.

"Padre Celestino," Maria prayed, "please to watch over Senor Amos and Senor Zoom. Keep them safe that they might one day return here to those who love them...."

Chapter 13

The following day was Saturday and I decided to lay low and do nothing. I was finding that the idea of days without meetings, interviews, and fund raisers was growing on me. The day dawned typical California sunny. Standing on my balcony I could see lots of leggy, well-endowed beauties making their way down to the sea. The afternoon exodus would show which sun worshipers had tanned well and which ones had been neglectful of tanning oils and sun screen.

I spent most of the morning catching up on mail and doing some light reading. The afternoon cable lineup included a Dodger game, which suited me just fine. I watched the lads at Chavez Ravine pull out a close one in the 9th, after which I drove out to the grocery store for essential supplies.

Standing in line with a half-full cart of goodies, I couldn't help but glance at the rows of tabloid newspapers beckoning to the unwary shoppers. They didn't seem to change much over the years, I noticed. Mostly the same stuff about alien visitations, salacious innuendo about current celebrities, and absurd predictions of future events. I decided (as I always do) that none of these issues were worth the asking price and moved along with the line in front of me.

Safely back at home and with groceries stowed, I put a couple of sole filets in marinade and listened to a local FM jazz station while I mixed up a green salad. The ocean breeze picked up as the sun began to set, and I was struck yet again by how much I enjoy my little home near the beach.

Come Sunday morning, Zoom and I slept late. Finally rising about eleven, I fixed us a large breakfast of fresh fruit, toasted bagels, and Canadian bacon. After cleaning up the kitchen and finishing the last of the coffee, the rest of the afternoon was spent browsing the immense Sunday newspaper and enjoying a nap. Zoom didn't much care for reading, so he mostly spent his day curled up on the big leather reclining chair, snoring only occasionally.

By Monday both of us were well rested and (I fervently hoped) ready for whatever lay ahead. I dialed the offices of Delores Dithering (my booking agent), identified myself, and asked for an appointment.

"I'm sorry, sir. Ms Dithering isn't presently taking appointments," came a rather haughty reply.

"And why would that be?" I asked. "She run off with to Barcelona with that bull fighter again?"

"REALLY, sir, I can't say....."

"Listen, get a hold of her - wherever she is - and tell her I'm only in L.A. briefly and need to speak with her. Call me back at this number, got it? I'll be waiting for a call."

"I can't promise you anything, sir," came the reply, thinly veiled with contempt.

"Yes you WILL promise! If nothing else, you'll promise to call me back. Failure to do so isn't an option and only guarantees unpleasant repercussions! Do you understand?" I asked, my voice betraying anger at being treated so poorly.

I hung up the phone, my mood having darkened already and it was still early yet. Amazing enough though, my cell phone rang about ten minutes later.

"Amos, darling, how ARE you?" came the screechy voice of Deloris Dithering. "I've been worried to death about you and Zoom for just AGES! When did you get back in town?"

Believe it or not, booking agents really do talk this way. I suspect it might have something to do with their fetish for designer clothes and all that bottled water they drink.

"I'm fine, Deloris. Zoom's fine too," I replied. "Listen, I'm only in town briefly and I need to see you. Where are you?"

"If it was anyone but you sweetie, I'd beg off. We're frightfully busy here."

"So your wonderful secretary informed me. Where'd you dig her up anyway?"

"Oh Amos, don't be angry with me. It's hard to find good help you know. Besides, she came highly recommended. Her last job was at the National Organization for Women."

"Somehow that doesn't surprise me," I said, laughing.

"Listen, I can work you in this afternoon at two, but you'll have to meet me here. Do you know where CID Studios are in Burbank?"

"Sure do," I said. Near the Burbank airport."

"That's the one. Ask for me at the security desk. I'll tell them you're expected."

"What the heck are you doing at CID?" I asked, curious.

"Well, I sort of fell into this deal. Friend of a friend of a friend. You know how it goes in Hollywood. I'm writing and co-producing a new prime time sitcom. We're calling it "Heavy Load," she said with excitement.

"Heavy Load?"

"Yeah! It's about a bunch of not-so-bright high school cheerleaders."

"Just what the world needs," I muttered.

"Now just you be NICE, Amos!" warned Deloris sweetly. "See you at two, darling, and don't you DARE forget to bring Zoom!"

Chapter 14

At two that afternoon, Zoom and I arrived at the visitor parking lot of CID Studios. Actually, the studio provided valet parking for the heavies and their limos, but I wasn't quite sure we qualified, so I didn't bother.

After tucking Zoom inside my windbreaker, I headed over to the main entrance and approached the security desk.

"Pearock Productions?" I asked.

The guard on duty was all of four feet, ten inches in height. She sported a baton, handcuffs, and sidearm. More captivating was her glittering smile, perfect teeth, and blonde hair cut short. She was cute as a bug, and her name tag identified her as Mindy.

"Yes sir, " the mini-cop answered sweetly. "Do you have an appointment?"

"At two with Deloris Dithering," I answered, returning her smile.

"Your name please, sir?"

"Amos Westergaard,"

"Yes sir, I have you scheduled. Pearock Productions is on the second floor, past studio three, and on your right. Will you be needing an escort, sir?"

"No, thank you, Mindy. I'll risk it alone. I navigate fairly well," I said.

"Well, just the same, if you need any help at all, please ask," said Mindy, favoring me with yet another glittering smile.

As I walked away from her desk, I found myself liking her a lot. I stepped aboard the escalator moving relentlessly upwards and ascended slowly to the second floor of the CID building.

After the ride was over, I unzipped my windbreaker and allowed Zoom to peer out. He squirmed a bit, wanting to be let down.

"Not just yet, pard," I said. "Wait 'til we get down the hall a little further."

Zoom let out a big sigh, but stopped wiggling.

I came to studio number three. So far, so good. A big sign out in front announced that Danny Buonaguidi (child star of the 1960's) was hosting the pilot for a new program called "Refuse Heap." Apparently yet another in the endless parade of daytime talk show experiments.

The door was slightly ajar, so I peeked inside. It looked like ole Danny was no longer the darling little blonde haired elf that had once dazzled households and commanded stratospheric ratings. Danny was now mostly bald, sporting a walrus mustache, and carried the better part of three hundred pounds on his frame..

It appeared that the studio was producing an episode that revolved around canine stars of yesteryear. On stage there were several bored looking hounds sitting on stools and looking out at the assembled audience. Danny waddled around, pointing out this or that, gamely trying to look cool and inject some life into the show. I thought the whole idea was silly, but what do I know?

Zoom pawed my arm, reminding me of our business, and I continued walking down the hall until we found Pearock Productions. I pushed the door open and found no one in the outer office. Either they'd forgotten about us, or that charming secretary was out powdering her nose. (Do they still DO that?)

There was a door leading to another office, so I knocked and entered without being told. Inside was Deloris on the telephone. She motioned for us to sit.

I pulled up a comfy chair and gave Zoom his freedom. He immediately hopped up on Deloris' desk and allowed her to stroke his fur while she talked. The thought came to me that it'd been a while since anyone stroked MY fur.

Trying to look nonchalant while sitting in the tiny office, I glanced around while Deloris continued yakking on the phone. There were three computers, a half dozen monitors, four printers, and a long ugly green leather sofa. No windows. I figured I'd last maybe a half hour in this cubby hole before I ran amok. Deloris is extremely fond of tobacco, and the smoke residue didn't add anything to the ambience of the place. Oh well. I supposed it might be worse in a Calcutta prison. Maybe.

"Well let me LOOK at the two of you!" exclaimed Deloris as she hung up her phone. "Zoom baby, you look just STRIKING! And YOU Amos," she added gleefully, "some of the gossip about you in New York would make a sailor blush! Naughty, naughty...."

"Don't believe everything you hear," I said lamely.

"Uh huh!" said Deloris, shaking her head and continuing to smile. "Listen sweetie, I don't have a lot of time. I'd LOVE to take you both for dinner but that's not in the cards. This new sitcom....."

"It's okay," I said, interrupting her. ""I just wanted to see you before I leave town again. To confirm a few things between us."

"Sure, baby, sure. What do you need?"

"First, no more gigs for me right now. My book seems to have about finished its run.

There's only that one show up in Reno I'm supposed to do next week. I'll make good on the appearance unless they decide they no longer want me," I said.

"Fat chance of that, Amos. Reno's a small market relatively speaking. They're not going to let a national celebrity like you off the hook."

"I sorta figured that. But no more after that, right?"

"So what are you up to, lover? Care to share?" she asked, flashing a tiny, wicked grin.

"I'm just going to kick back for a while. Do some research. I took the advance on the next book. But I don't figure to complete anything until sometime next year," I said.

"No problem. With me spending so much time in television production, I don't have the time to work bookings like I used to. But the MONEY - lordy Amos - the MONEY here is unbelievable! Promise me you'll do a guest appearance sometime?" she asked. "The fees we pay even the no-names are stupendous. For a real SOMEBODY like you...well...you get the idea."

"If it'll help you, I'll bite my lip and do it. You know I never have gotten really comfortable in front of the camera," I said sadly.

"Give it time, Amos. You really do have a certain, well, PRESENCE in front of the lens. It's a gift, and it shows."

"And you could charm a rabbit out of a carrot patch," I said, smiling.

Deloris got up to see us out, and it was then I realized that Zoom didn't seem to be anywhere around. In fact, he'd disappeared.

Chapter 15

Eventually the insurance investigators working on behalf of CID Studios would piece together the cause of the afternoon riot. Zoom's role in the donnybrook would become the stuff of legend. I was sort of hoping that the CID executives would exhibit a sense of humor about the whole thing, but as it stands now, both Zoom and I remain sort of unwelcome.

At the beginning, all I knew was that Zoom had crept out of the Pearock Production offices while Deloris and I were talking. I knew he wouldn't go far; it's not his nature. All the same, I didn't want my little pal wandering around the studio unescorted.

Deloris and I moved slowly down the hall, peering into offices and inquiring of the various personages if they'd seen a silver and black cat. Mostly we were answered by blank stares.

This was getting us nowhere. I rode the escalator downstairs thinking to enlist the help of Mindy the mini-cop who was still on duty at the security desk. No sooner had I poured out my tale of woe than Mindy's radio crackled to life. Someone was reporting a disturbance at studio three. This was followed by an immediate alert, directing all security personnel to the second floor studio NOW.

There were screams, barking dogs, equipment crashing, with lots of angry shouts emanating from the floor above us. It seems that my furry pal Zoom paid a visit to the set of Refuse Heap. Zoom, ever a ham for the cameras, couldn't resist the temptation to do a couple of circuits around the stage in front of the audience and all the bored looking hounds that were on display.

The results were predictable. Those tired, arthritic canines took one look at Zoom and the game was on. Sort of. Most of the pack were well past their prime it wasn't much of a contest for an agile cat like Zoom who can leap and soar like an NBA superstar. Even so, except for an ancient bulldog that stopped to pee every three steps, the rest of the aging hounds were determined to give chase as best they could.

Zoom scooted up the main aisle of studio three, dashed laterally across a row of spectators, past a startled camera operator, and out the side door into the main hallway. The baying hounds were not far behind, with a few of the smaller breeds trying to jump over the seats and scaring the daylights out of several people in the audience.

Everyone scattered, trying to avoid getting stampeded in the rush. Some people panicked, tripping over dogs and each other. There was much cursing and a couple of fistfights broke out with the contestants having to be subdued by the studio security teams.

As the down-escalator delivered the first of this tumbling mass of humanity to the main floor, I couldn't help but notice Zoom was at the head of it all being aggressively pursued by two bloodhounds and a three-legged terrier.

My little pal was either too busy evading the dogs, or perhaps having too much fun to notice me standing there next to Mindy with my mouth agape. I watched in amazement as

Zoom did an end-run that would've done the NFL proud and expertly mounted the up-escalator heading back up to the second floor. The surviving members of the pack followed almost immediately, still intent upon capturing their quarry.

Fortunately and despite all the hysteria, no one was seriously hurt. A couple of older ladies had fainted but were quickly revived, no worse for the experience. Others required modest first aid for bumps and bruises, but that was about the extent of it. A member of the camera crew had the presence of mind to keep the cameras rolling, and the results were later edited to make for some fun fodder on the five o'clock news.

Zoom made his second circuit upstairs and again evaded capture by the struggling security team and the now-tiring hounds. This time around he opted to avoid the escalator and instead scooted skillfully down the stairs just a few steps ahead of the red-faced, panting, and totally enraged Danny Buonaguidi.

Scooping up my companion, I hurried out the front doors of CID Studios, being VERY anxious to leave the commotion behind. In an act of incredible heroism, Mindy the mini-cop stepped in front of the doors and prevented anyone else from following directly behind me.

I took off across the parking lot at a fast trot with Zoom secure on my forearm. I knew full well that Mindy the mini-cop couldn't hold off the angry mob for long. Jumping in the car and dumping Zoom carelessly in the back seat, I fired up engine and got us moving as fast as I could. By now lots of people were streaming out of the studio building.

Danny Buonaguidi angrily waved a clenched fist and screamed a familiar, time-honored Hollywood oath at me as I drove past.

"You'll nevah woik in dis bidness again!"

I waved as we sped by, and sent Mindy a dozen red roses the next day.

Chapter 16

"Mammoth radio, this is Cessna One Sierra Tango on a one mile final, runway 27...."

Zoom and I were underway again, having departed the John Wayne airport earlier in the day. After threading the tight airspace around L.A., we'd cut across the Antelope Valley and then headed north, following Highway 395 that runs sort of parallel to the eastern Sierra Nevada mountain range. It was a clear and spectacularly gorgeous day to be high in the sky. Below I had seen huge stands of timber and many, many alpine blue lakes where I knew the fishing would be fabulous. Some of those locations are so isolated that even today they are rarely visited by man. America the Beautiful on display.

We were about at the halfway point in today's journey. Prudence dictated we stop for fuel and lunch. The Mammoth Lakes Airport is a fine facility, having everything the wandering airman might need. Cessna One Sierra Tango plopped down at the edge of the long runway (owing to the expertise of her pilot, of course) and exited at the first intersection convenient to the terminal building and restaurant.

There were picnic tables thoughtfully placed outside, so Zoom and I opted to dine al fresco while we waited for the fuel truck to come and service our plane. The lunch special was smoked trout salad and served with sourdough bread. The waitress didn't even bat an eye when I ordered two. I guess they get all kinds passing through there. And some dude flying with a cat probably doesn't rate highly on their "you ain't gonna believe this" scale.

The trout salad was delightful and had obviously been prepared by someone very talented in the kitchen. I finished mine off quickly and sipped iced tea while I watched the lineman refuel our winged chariot. Zoom took his time, carefully picking out the succulent bits of smoked trout and avoiding the vegetables. I asked our waitress for a small bowl of water for him.

I paid our waitress for the fine meal and then walked inside the terminal to use the men's room and settle our fuel bill While I did this, Zoom trotted across the tarmac and hopped into the back seat of the Cessna to await my return.

After draining a little water out of the fuel sumps and doing a careful pre flight inspection, I fired up the engine and taxied out for takeoff. There being no other traffic in pattern, I poured on the power and we slowly accelerated down the runway. With the air being so thin at Mammoth Lakes, it takes a while longer than normal to build speed and generate enough lift to get airborne. Being full of fuel and close to our maximum takeoff weight, we used most of the 7000 foot runway to make good our escape.

I flew along happy and satisfied. Zoom slept in the back seat. Life was good. We passed over Bridgeport, Walker, and Topaz Lake, all tiny mountain communities mostly dedicated to the outdoor life. Fishing, hunting, and tourism keep them economically afloat most of the year. Pretty soon Carson City began to appear on my horizon. An interesting collection of period architecture, gambling halls, saloons, and state buildings dot the main highway. Halfway through town I added a little power and put us into a gentle thirty degree bank to port. Sure enough, just over the ridge Lake Tahoe came into view, right where I knew it'd be.

Zoom, now awake after a suitable cat-nap, hopped into the co-pilot's seat and stared out the window at the magnificent lakeshore below. He's been to Tahoe a time or two and seems to appreciate the area as much as I do, but probably for different reasons.

I flew along, passing by the big casinos at Stateline, crossed over Emerald Bay, and then radioed the tower at the South Lake Tahoe airport for a landing advisory. Information received, I dropped a few rpm's, lowered the flaps a notch, and began a slow descent.

The tower cleared us on to final approach, and Cessna One Sierra Tango touched down right on the numbers as if her pilot had been making mountain top landings all his life. The ground controller directed me to proceed north on the taxiway where I'd find the FBO and transient parking areas.

There seemed to be plenty of vacant tie-downs, including one that faced the FBO office. I carefully guided us between the tie-downs, killed the engine, and switched off the main electrical circuit. The linesman heard me coming in over the radio and the fuel truck came to a stop in front of us before I'd gotten my seat belt unhooked.

"Good afternoon, Sir! And welcome to South Lake Tahoe," he said.

"A good day indeed, amigo! Listen, top off my tanks with 100LL, will you? And maybe clean the windshield for me?" I asked. "I'll be here a couple of days, so I'll leave the keys in the dispatch office," I added.

"No problem, Sir! Just leave her as she is. I'll tie her down for you after I'm finished. Will you be needing a cart for baggage?"

"I don't think so, but thanks for asking," I replied. "My cat's in the back. I'll just leave him there for a few minutes while I take care of some business inside. He won't bother you," I said, turning and walking towards the office.

Inside the FBO building I found the dispatch desk manned by a young woman wearing a scarlet red polo shirt and tanned shorts. She smiled, welcomed me, and asked how she could be of service.

I gave her my name, the tail numbers of the Cessna, a VISA card,, and told her we'd likely be here a couple of days. While she was busy processing me, I also asked her to call the transportation captain at Caesars and request they to send a limo down to pick me up. And, if there was no limo available, to call me a taxi. She nodded, and I walked off towards the men's room.

Actually, I wasn't quite sure I still rated limo service, but I figured it didn't hurt to ask. My luck held, and Caesars dutifully dispatched a white limo to pick Zoom and I up in front of the main terminal building. The driver, a tall black man whose name tag read "Curly Mike" gently put my one bag in the truck, looked at Zoom, and then looked at me inquiringly.

"That's okay," I said. "My furry pal will ride in back with me."

"Yessir," said Curly Mike. "There's a full mini-bar and snacks in back. Sorry we didn't know you were travelin' with your cat, or we'da stocked some special treats for him too!"

"My fault, Curly Mike. I didn't allow enough lead time for that kind of special service. But I thank you just the same," I said cordially.

"Are you familiar with Lake Tahoe?" inquired Curly Mike. "I'm authorized to take you on a sight-seeing tour, if you like."

"Thanks, but no thanks," I replied. "I've been fortunate enough to visit Lake Tahoe many times. I think today we'll be happy enough just to drive directly through town and to the hotel."

"As you wish, sir."

It only takes about fifteen minutes to drive from the airport to Caesars. Zoom and I rode along in silence as the huge limo took us through town past dozens of small motels, restaurants, and shops all dedicated to the tourist trade. By now it was late in the afternoon, and the sidewalks were full of all kinds of people. Women, children, teens, men, and no small amount of elders all out enjoying a fine time.

We crossed the border into Nevada, and a couple of blocks thereafter pulled into the VIP parking area in front of the huge Caesars resort.

The huge marquee above the entrance proudly proclaimed that Miss Cyndi Cheyenne was the headline act in the main showroom, performing two shows each evening.

"Zoom," I said, "it would appear that we've arrived."

Chapter 17

Standing in front of a beveled full length mirror, I admired myself attired in a chestnut grey three-piece suit. A medium width plum-red tie over a white-on-white shirt completed the stylish look. Hair combed, shoes resplendent, eyes clear, I was indeed the fine figure of a man.

Zoom was ready too. He'd taken his version of a shower, I'd clipped his claws and he now sported a kitty sized, red bow tie around his neck instead of the usual collar and ID tag.

I picked him up so's he could ride on my arm, walked out the door of our hotel suite and headed down the hall towards the elevators. As we stood waiting for the elevator car, a young couple with their daughter joined us.

"Look at the kitty, mama! He's pretty! What's his name, mister?" the little girl asked me.

"His name is Zoom," I said. "And he likes to have his ears rubbed by pretty girls."

The little girl glanced hopefully at her mother, who nodded her head. I lowered my arm a bit so she could pet him. Right on cue, Zoom began to purr.

Our elevator arrived, and we all entered the car. It was a short ride to the main floor, and I motioned to the others to exit ahead of us.

"Bye, Zoom!" the little girl said, waving over her shoulder.

"Good job Zoom," I said to my furry pal.

The two of us walked around the perimeter of the main casino floor. Most of the people were busy gambling, but a few took a time-out to notice the guy with the cat on his arm and either smiled, pointed, or waved at us as we made our way over to the main showroom.

The head maitre d' smiled at our arrival.

"Good evening, Monsieur Westergaard; it is a great pleasure to have you with us again," he said. "It has been too long. We have your places prepared. Come and I will seat you myself. Will you be needing anything special for yourself or Monsieur Zoom?"

"Merci, Pierre. I apologize for being away so long. Nothing special this evening. Perhaps some champagne, well chilled, is all. I'm looking forward to the show," I said.

"Tres bien," said Pierre, bowing. "Please follow me."

I trailed the head maitre d' into the main showroom and down a wide aisle. The huge amphitheater appeared full, with the other revelers already having been seated and awaiting the opening act. The VIP tables were long, narrow affairs laid out at 90 degree angles to the stage. Zoom and I found ourselves seated at an elegantly adorned table about eight seats from the front of the stage.

The staff at Caesars, never missing a chance to perform small extras for their guests, had placed a fluffy satin pillow on Zoom's chair for his added comfort. We were the last ones to be seated, and a few of our table mates smiled and nodded knowingly at Zoom and I. A silver-haired lady dressed in white silk and emeralds reached over and petted Zoom, who dutifully purred for her.

A waiter appeared with a chilled bottle of champagne, and

held it up for my approval. I nodded, and asked him if he could provide the entire table with the same.

"Certainment, monsieur. Right away," he answered, hurrying away.

While the opening act (a comedian) did his thing, I reviewed what I knew about Cyndi Cheyenne.

She and I had met at a series of New York fund raisers for a cause I couldn't quite remember. We'd become fast friends, mostly because neither of us took ourselves too seriously. She was about five foot six inches tall, with coppery-blonde hair that fell to her shoulders. She'd been further blessed with large brown doe-like eyes and long lashes. A stunning figure, especially when dressed in black and adorned with gold, Cyndi was every bit the contemporary country-western diva. The music she wrote and sang was top drawer. She also would occasionally do a crossover, changing from country-western themes to more steamy torch music. Her records sold millions, and she had at least a couple of Grammy awards that I knew of. Off stage, Cyndi had a reputation of being an incredibly sweet person. I liked her. A lot.

With a drum roll, the master of ceremonies introduced the star attraction, Miss Cyndi Cheyenne. The crowd went wild as Cyndi strutted confidently out on stage for her opening number. I sat mesmerized while she sang, conscious only of a small electric current zinging continually up and down my spine. Zoom was hunkered down on his pillow, tail flicking to the beat, eyes with a radar lock on the beautiful Cyndi Cheyenne.

Chapter 18

Cyndi Cheyenne certainly knew how to work her audience that night. Looking drop-dead gorgeous in a black pantsuit trimmed with gold sequins and a come-hither smile, she continued to perform old favorites and new material aided by a superb band and an expert stage crew.

About an hour into the show, Cyndi got her first standing ovation as the final notes to her Grammy winning song "Lonely Lessons" faded away.

"Thank you folks! Thank y'all kindly! Now how about a hand for the band?" Cindy asked as her musicians all stood and took a well-deserved bow.

As the applause died down, Cyndi turned and slowly walked across the stage.

"I'd like everyone to bear with me for just a moment, please," she said. "Down in the audience I see a very special friend. Some of you probably know him from his writing and television appearances. Let me tell you he's so much more than that. Ladies and gentlemen, I'd like you to give it up for Mr

Amos Westergaard, visiting us here this evening with that coolest of cats, Zoom!"

I was stunned and amazed at roar of the crowd.

"C'mon, Amos! Stand up and give us a wave," shouted Cyndi from stage.

Pasting on my best smile, I stood up and waved to the crowd, who continued their applause. I reached down and picked up Zoom, holding him high for everyone to see. I think he got even LOUDER cheers than I did, truth be told.

"Thank you, Amos! And Zoom!" said Cyndi. "We're mighty proud to have y'all here with us tonight!"

I nodded her way, picking up my champagne flute and toasting her. This brought another standing ovation from the crowd. Cyndi Cheyenne just beamed. The glow around her was infectious.

Zoom was up on the table being petted and adored by those nearby.

"Thank you again, folks. I mean that sincerely," said Cyndi. "Now I'd like to do a favorite song of mine for you. My great grandpa, the old Scottish highlander taught it to me shortly before he passed on at the age of a hundred and three. He was very special to me, and I miss him very much."

The band began to play some light, haunting chords with a Gaelic flavor. And it was then that Zoom saw an opportunity.

After giving me a sly look and a quick wink, Zoom took everyone by surprise as he quickly accelerated down the length of the VIP table and launched his nine pound frame across the chasm onto the stage and made a perfect landing next to Cyndi Cheyenne.

The crowd went wild and whooped with delight when they saw this. Zoom, ever the ham, just stood there at Cyndi's feet, rubbing her pretty ankle with his whiskers and looking up adoringly at her.

Cyndi, being the professional that she is, just smiled and motioned for the band to extend the opening bars, which they did without missing a beat.

"Goodness, Zoom! Are you planning a duet?" asked Cyndi.

An alert stage hand brought out two stools; one for Cyndi and one for my furry pal, who was obviously quite pleased with himself. The audience loved it, loved Cyndi, and I knew the experience would create memories they'd talk about years later.

I sat quietly, sipping my champagne and watching Cyndi Cheyenne perform as only she could. Zoom stayed right were he was, perched on a stool and obviously content to bask in the adoration of the audience for the duration of the show.

At the end, there were two more standing ovations for Cyndi. Finally the performance was over and people began slowly filtering out of the ampitheater. A courageous few battled the human wave of traffic. Some wanted to shake my hand, others to have their picture taken with me. One lady actually had my book with her, which I happily autographed for her.

A very large, fit man appeared at my side.

"Sir, my name is Graham. I'm hotel security. If you'll follow me backstage, we'll see about reclaiming your cat," he said with a smile.

"Lead on, good sir," I said. I wasn't worried about Zoom, but I knew these people had a job to do.

So I followed Graham backstage, passing by musicians, sound and lighting crews, and a few more security officers. A few smiled and waved. There were also some high-five's exchanged. I've always liked stage people. They seem to be mostly hard working, cheeky buggars who don't get overly awed at the celebrities that are always passing through their world.

We came to a door that led into the Star's Dressing Room.

"Here, sir," said Graham. He knocked, and then inserted a coded card key into the reader. The door lock would then retract electronically and admit me.

"Thank you, Graham," I said.

Raising Spirits

Graham opened the door, peeked in, nodded at Cyndi Cheyenne who then nodded in return. I walked in and Graham closed the door behind me. I could hear the electric locking mechanism re-engage.

Cyndi Cheyenne was seated at a large vanity cleaning the makeup off her face. Zoom had assumed the napping position nearby on an overstuffed sofa.

"Oh Amos!" she said, "I'm so glad you and Zoom could come tonight! I've been feeling so lonely."

She stood up and I swept her into my arms, drinking in the scent of her perfume.

"Woman," I said, my voice quivering, "I love you. I think I have always loved you."

I kissed her deeply, feeling her body shudder next to mine.

"I love you too, Amos," she gasped. " Isn't it about time we did something about this?"

Chapter 19

Rays of early morning sunshine streaming in through the balcony glass woke me. Zoom was beside me on the bed, still snoring gently. I noted that his fur smelled faintly of tobacco smoke, no doubt the result of last night's activity in the ampitheater.

Feeling absolutely fabulous, I hopped out of bed, dialed room service to place a breakfast order, and skipped off to the shower.

I had just finished shaving when I heard a discrete knock at the door. The room service steward had arrived, pushing in a silver cart laden with fresh squeezed orange juice, hot coffee, and a toasted bagel with Marionberry preserves. I signed the check, adding a generous tip, and bade the man a good day.

By now, Zoom was up and pecking in his kibble bowl. He wandered over to see if I had anything suitable for a kitty appetite, and I offered him a little of the Marionberry preserves. He licked the sweet goo from my plate and then began to wash his paws. Morning's work accomplished, my furry pal then returned to bed and the first of several scheduled morning naps.

I sipped coffee and thumbed through USA Today. Didn't seem to be much out of the ordinary going on in the world. Reports from the usual trouble spots. Economic indicators were either good or bad, depending on where money was invested. The Dodgers were making a serious run for the pennant once again.

Picking up the phone, I dialed the concierge desk.

"Good morning, Mr Westergaard," came a cheery voice. "What can we do for you and Zoom today?"

I would soon begin to understand that the Adventures of Zoom the Wonder Cat were making the rounds among the resort staff.

"Good morning to you, too," I said. "I need your help with a few things."

"Your wish is our command, sir," replied the concierge.

And so it went. I learned that, yes, the hotel could arrange to deliver Zoom to the Sierra Pet Salon to be fumigated and groomed. And that they'd return him to my suite later that afternoon. Yes, a rental car could be arranged and delivered. A convertible? Yes, certainly. It would be there for me at the valet entrance at noon. Unless I'd prefer the use of a hotel limo and driver instead? No? Very well, then. And yes, hotel security would be tipped off that Miss Cheyenne would require an escort out of the building at noon. And, be advised that hotel protocols suggested that VIPs be picked up in front of the north entrance, not the main driveway that faced west.

It's always a pleasure dealing with people that know their business. True to their word, a cherry red Mustang convertible was waiting for me downstairs at noon. I signed the rental agreement, hopped in, and drove it around to the north entrance as the concierge had advised. No more than two minutes later, Cyndi Cheyenne appeared, being escorted out of the building by Graham the security officer. I do SO love it when a plan comes together!

I got out of the car, went around and opened the car door for her, and thanked Graham. He just nodded and walked back into the building, his task properly completed.

Cyndi gave me a peck on the cheek and asked where we were going. I needed a moment to take her all in. Tousled coppery blonde hair, white silk blouse open at the neck, tailored jeans. My heart began doing flippity-flops all over again.

"We're going to play tourist," I said. "We're going to visit a couple of my favorite places along the Lake," I said.

"Lead on, good sir!" Cyndi said with a grin. "Nobody takes me anywhere!"

I put the car in gear, drove out of the parking lot, and headed to South Lake Tahoe.

"Isn't this the way to the airport?" asked Cyndi.

"Same road, but we'll turn off before we get there. Ever been out to Camp Richardson or Emerald Bay?"

"No. Seen some pictures of Emerald Bay is all."

"You'll like it," I said.

"Long as I'm with you, it's good," Cyndi declared.

My heart did a few more flippity-flops and I did well to keep the car under control. We cruised through Camp Richardson and I pointed out some of the historic sights. About a mile beyond, I turned the car off onto the road leading to the visitor center.

"Cyndi, this is a favorite place of mine along the lake. There's a nature trail that winds around a feeder creek. Lots of native plants and wild flowers. Squirrels, lizards, all kinds of birds. Small bridges that span trickling waters. And benches for resting along the way," I said.

Cyndi removed her large sunglasses and looked me square in the eye.

"Amos," she said, "this is beautiful! A perfect sunny day. A walk in the woods. A handsome gentleman....."

I smiled, taking her hand in mine and we began walking

together, side by side, along the dirt trail. Every so often a squirrel or tiny lizard would dart across our path. The bird life seemed to be especially industrious today, with most of them busy snagging small insects off trees or from the forest floor. I sent up a quick prayer of thanks, knowing that (for me) days don't get much better than this.

Cyndi laughed at the antics of the tree squirrels and pointed out different bird species to me. Across the creek, a deer and her fawn trotted purposefully downstream towards Tahoe. Neither of us thought to bring a camera. I told myself it didn't matter; that the visions of Cyndi and I here in this place would remain bright and clear in my mind forever.

We stopped to talk for a while, seated comfortably on a bench, our legs dangling over a slow running creek.

"Amos," Cyndi asked in a tiny voice, "did you mean what you said last night?"

I looked at her face, my eyes betraying me completely.

"I have always loved you," I said, my voice almost a croak. "Ever since we met at those fund raisers in New York. It's more than just your incredible musical gifts, or your outward beauty. You're beautiful inside, with a wit and wisdom that makes my knees buckle, Cyndi. You walk in the room and I get this little jolt of electricity running up and down my spine. Nobody's ever done that to me. Ever."

Cyndi looked over at me, her hand still in mine, and said nothing for a moment. It was so quiet I thought I could hear both our hearts beating.

"Being a recording artist, I have men sniffing around me most of the time," she said. "But they all seem to need something from me in an exploitive sense. Money, contracts, promotional deals, endorsements, sex, and the list goes on. I've never been married, so it seems I'm fair game. I've had a couple of proposals of marriage, and while the guys were okay, I honestly didn't love them. Not knowing any better, I just keep on doing what I do best - make good music."

Not knowing what else to do, I just nodded and continued to listen.

"I've had some luck, some good people around me in key positions. I don't take drugs and I drink sparingly. I've made a few mistakes, but in the process I've learned which deals are good for Cyndi and which ones to steer clear of."

I took a deep breath. "I come at this from a different direction," I said. "Sure, I understand that to some extent Cyndi Cheyenne is a business and that a lot of people depend on her. But my focus is different. When it comes to a man and a woman, I have a thing about loyalty. Loyalty breeds respect, integrity, and eventually a deep abiding intimacy. Without loyalty, most couples fail."

Cyndi seemed to think about that for a moment before she answered.

"What you say makes sense, Amos. And when you think about it, the lack of loyalty is probably why so many celebrity couples fail. Their loyalty is more often given over to things other than their mates."

"You also need to know that I don't really care much for the limelight," I said. I've had my fill of it, and found it lacking. I figure to continue writing as long as people like my books. I'll deal with the cameras and the microphones as best I can, but I won't be seeking them out, either. Seems to me that I won't be stepping on your action any more than you would on mine. And with each of us utilizing our own gifts to help the other, we'll become better than we are separately. Cyndi Cheyenne, if you'll have me, I'll love you the rest of our lives," I said gently.

"Zoom's part of the deal, right?" asked Cyndi, smiling.

"Are you KIDDING? Zoom adores you! You think he'd have put on that show last night for anyone else?" I said, laughing at the memory.

Just then my stomach let out a powerful rumble, reminding me of the need for feed.

"Come, my love," I said. "time we moved along."

"It's practically perfect here. I hate to leave."

"The good news is, there's more of the practically perfect just up the road."

Cyndi Cheyenne stood up, gave me a squeeze, and kissed me sweetly. I felt my knees begin to melt, and the thought came to me that just MAYBE I'd get to live the rest of my life insanely happy with this beautiful woman.

I managed to get us back into the car and pointed it in the direction of I wanted to go. But the truth is it was mostly instinct. My senses were overwhelmed by Cyndi Cheyenne.

We drove through the tall pines to Emerald Bay, and I stopped the car on the shoulder of the narrow road. We both got out and walked over by the small ledge that protrudes off the ridge. From there is a stunning view of the bay and the tiny offshore island. One of the paddlewheel steamers that ply the route between Zephyr Cove and Emerald Bay was slowly circling in the clear blue-green water below us.

"Oh, Amos! The pictures I've seen can't compare! It's breathtaking!" exclaimed Cyndi.

"I think the same can be said of you, beloved," I answered.

"You just keep that up and you'll NEVER be rid of me," she said with a grin.

"That's the plan, baby. Now if you look below, and to your left, you'll see a real Viking castle through the trees. It was build decades ago by a wealthy dowager, and it's been maintained by the parks department in recent times."

"Can you get us inside?"

"Of course. But it's a long hike. About three miles down, and three miles back up."

"We can't do that today, can we? Promise me we'll come back though, Amos."

"It shall be as you say, my love."

I was rewarded with a brilliant smile, and with that we returned to the car.

"I know a good restaurant ahead near Meeks Bay," I said.

"You seem to know a lot about this area, Amos."

"Been coming here since I was a boy," I said. "The thing is, there's always something new, something more I discover each trip."

There is a restaurant in Meeks Bay that tends toward French/Swiss cuisine. I'd eaten there before and always found it excellent. It being a practically perfect day, I asked the hostess to seat us outside on the patio. Cyndi Cheyenne and I shared a tureen of vegetable soup and some brie cheese spread on crusty bread. For desert there were luscious, ripe strawberries hand-dipped in dark chocolate. We both said little while we ate, our eyes communicating a joy at just being with each other.

There was a small green meadow in back of the restaurant, and after our meal we walked there, her arm around my waist. I picked a wildflower, and she wore it in her hair. I stopped at the foot of a majestic Ponderosa pine, sat down and leaned my back against it. Cyndi sat down too, resting her head in my lap.

"Amos," she said. "I want to stay here and listen to the wind for a while," she said.

I nodded, and once again nearly passed out from an overload of happiness.

Chapter 20

"**A**mos," asked Cyndi Cheyenne, her head still resting on my lap, "do you believe there's a God? This isn't just a philosophical question. It's important to me."

"That's a complicated question just now," I said, taking a deep breath. "Here's what I want you to know. First, the answer is yes. I went to Sunday school as a kid and was taught about God and his son Jesus. I would later go through a rebellious period and turn my back on Him. But as in the tale of the prodigal son, I returned later. I've screwed up more than once since then, but He knows I'm not perfect. I depend a lot upon forgiveness. My days start with Him and end with Him. How about you?"

"Something like you, but not exactly the same," replied Cyndi. "My great grandpa lived a long life, and I remember him teaching me about God when I was just a young girl. And something else. He was from Scotland, and in that time and place they believed in "demons and haunts" as he called them. I know he believed in them. And that he'd never lie to me, either. When he died, my grandma (who was his daughter) took over, reading lots of bible stories. I remember being especially fond of Old Testament heros. And yes, I believe in God. Made my peace with Jesus a long time ago. Oh, I've had to compromise a lot since then. Had to deal with some thoroughly rotten people to advance my career. But He's always been there with me, even though I suspect He didn't always approve of my behavior."

It was then that I told Cyndi Cheyenne about the encounter Zoom and I had in the Harquahala Mountains. How the snake with the large red bulbous eyes had so terrified us. And about the appearance of the angel that intervened just in the nick of time. I told her about the message he delivered to me.

I waited nervously for Cyndi's reaction, hoping she wouldn't think I was nuts.

"Amos, that's incredible! I don't think you'd make something like that up. Have you seen the snake, the angel, or had any other unusual things happen since then?" she asked.

"Mercifully, no. " I replied. "I consulted an old friend about it, though. He's the minister of a church down in San Pedro. He says he believes that not only has God taken special notice of me, but that Zoom and I might be under continual angelic protection from some kind of satanic or demonic threat. I felt a little better about it after that, but honestly I'm still pretty much in the dark."

"Well, it scares me," said Cyndi. "But you're a strong man, Amos. My great grandpa, may he rest in peace, would tell you to always put your hopes in God, especially when things got dicey."

"Your great grandpa sounds like a wise man, Cyndi. I'm sorry I never knew him."

"You'd have loved him too, Amos. He understood the world better than I do, I think. And he played the flute so beautifully. Haunting, Gaelic tunes long forgotten. It might be from him that I inherited my musical ability."

And then she began to hum. I didn't recognize the song, but it sounded Gaelic. And her humming expanded into a beautiful trilling. Gentle, though. So very restful. I could feel my spirit relax inside.

"What family do you have, Amos?" asked Cyndi.

"Just my mother and a younger brother," I answered. "Mom lives and teaches at an assisted living facility in San Diego. My brother's a corporate tycoon down in Las Vegas. My dad died when I was in my teens."

"Ever married?"

"Once, a long time ago. It didn't last. No children. Your turn," I said.

"I'm an only child. Grew up around New Orleans. My daddy moved us to Montana when I was 14. He's gone now, died four years ago. Mama runs the ranch herself now, along with a foreman. And of course the cowboys."

"I'm impressed," I said. "Takes guts to run cattle these days."

"Mama's a very capable woman. And the ranch is her life since daddy died. All the same, I see her getting on in years and I feel like I need to be there more for her. She's determined to pass the property on to me when her time comes. She knows I don't need it, or the money, but it's the clan tradition she's obliged to uphold."

"What about you, Cyndi? Where does life take you after your tour at Caesars ends?"

"I'm off to Marin County for a couple of weeks. There's a production company there that I've hooked up with. We're going to do a new kind of movie, completely digital and no actors. The cool thing is, there's a digital ME in the film. I get to play myself, and do a couple of my songs. It's a big gamble, but I've cut myself in for a piece of the pie when the movie gets released for distribution. If the concept works, I'll do more of these projects and spend less time touring. I always want to tour some, though. A long as people like to hear me sing. I just can't continue doing it ten months a year. You?"

"Zoom and I are headed east. I have a radio interview to do in Reno tomorrow. After that there's some small business matters and visiting a few long-neglected friends around the country. Should be back home in California in a couple of weeks, more or less."

"And you fly your little plane to all these places?"

"Mostly. She gets Zoom and I where we need to go. Beats driving. And I can come and go pretty much whenever I want to, as long as the weather cooperates."

"You're an amazing man, Amos Westergaard," said Cyndi, shaking her head.

"Stick with me baby and you'll go places," I said, doing a bad impersonation of a long-dead movie actor.

"I'm findin' myself loving you more and more, you know?" said Cindy, her face turning serious.

I didn't know what to say, so I didn't say anything at all.

"I have an idea, Amos. Tell me what you think. I'll be finished in Marin County by the middle of the month, and after that I'm scheduled to take four weeks off. Mama's expecting me at the ranch, and I don't plan to disappoint her. How about you and Zoom coming there instead of heading back to California when your own business is finished back east?" she asked, a touch of anxiety in her voice. "The ranch is huge, and the two of us can walk and talk unmolested. Mama will like you too, once she figures out you're not after my money or chasing the cameras yourself."

"Did you know one of my very first jobs as a teen was teaching younger children how to ride horses?" I asked

"Oh Amos! Does that mean you'll come?"

"Well, only if your invitation includes Zoom too," I said with a grin.

We sealed the deal with a kiss.

"We have to go," announced Cyndi. "Don't forget I have two shows again tonight."

"Will you be able to see us off at the airport tomorrow?" I asked.

"Just you try to keep me away."

Chapter 21

Neither of us wanted our afternoon together to end. I drove slowly in the far right hand lane of the highway and allowed faster cars to pass by as they wished. Cyndi Cheyenne laughed and joked, regaling me with tales of her youth on a Montana cattle ranch. I mostly just listened, and she occasionally favored me with a meaningful smile. With the convertible top down, we soaked up the warm afternoon sun, breathed pure alpine air, and delighted in each other's company. There were many, many boats out that afternoon and in my mind's eye I envisioned the two of us sailing around the lake during a future visit to the Tahoe Valley. I know that life offers few guarantees, but I was feeling some guarded optimism that in the end, Amos Westergaard would win the hand of the fair Cyndi Cheyenne.

I pulled off the road onto a small spur that I discovered years back.

"This'll only take a minute," I said. "Come with me."

Her hand in mine, I led us down a tiny, narrow trail that

wound around an immense pine tree and into the brush. The wind blew gently, and if you listened closely you could hear the trickle of water.

"Ooooh Amos it's INCREDIBLE!" exclaimed the love of my life the first time she saw Pilgrim's Pond.

"It's a sight, isn't it?" I said. "Not many people even know it's here, right off the highway. Watch right above that big tree by the ridge."

As if on cue, a splendid golden eagle appeared and circled the pond, giving us the eye as he passed.

"If that's not the livin' end," said Cyndi, clearly in awe of the magnificent predator.

"Come," I said. "We're intruding on his territory. Golden eagles are solitary birds, and he'll be happier when we've gone."

"Thank you for showing me this place, Amos. I know it's special to you."

I nodded guided us back to the car. Cyndi seemed a bit more quiet, introspective and lost in her own thoughts. I smiled, put our chariot in gear, and got us rolling again. The road at this point became one of many curves and the occasional switchback as we headed down the mountain. A dark sedan hurried by, its driver obviously not enjoying the splendid views.

It was only a couple of minutes later that Cyndi and I both heard the scream of tires and the sound of a collision. Rounding the next curve we saw that same dark sedan smashed, crumpled, and merged into a giant boulder on the side of the road. The driver was motionless and slumped over the steering wheel.

I'd seen enough accidents to know this was a bad one.

"C'mon," I said to Cyndi as I stopped our car in front of the mangled wreck. "Somebody needs help."

"Right behind you."

Inside, the passenger still wasn't stirring.

"Can you hear me?" I asked in a loud voice.

Nothing, no response.

I opened the door and peeked in. The driver was a young black woman, very pregnant, and bleeding from several places including her head.

"Got to get her out," I said. "I'll start her, and you help with her feet, okay?"

Cyndi just nodded, grimly determined.

Between the two of us we managed to extricate her from the car. There were so many things to be fearful of in moving a victim like this. But there didn't seem to be any other options at the moment.

"Okay listen, you're going to have to sit on the ground. We need to elevate her head a little, " I instructed Cyndi.

I grabbed my cell phone and dialed 911, hoping we'd get a signal out here. Mercifully, there was an answer.

"Nine-one-one emergency," came the voice at the other end.

"Listen up," I said. "Injury accident on Highway 38, maybe a mile west of Emerald Bay. Victim is a young female, very pregnant. We need the paramedics and an ambulance immediately!"

"And your name, sir?"

"Don't have time for that stuff now. If I don't get the bleeding stopped, she's not gonna make it!" I yelled. "Do your job!"

Looking down, I realized the woman had a compound leg fracture. The bone must've nicked a vein, because there was blood spurting on the pavement. Luckily I was wearing a web belt, which made a passable tourniquet.

"Baby," I said, "keep some pressure on that head wound. Use whatever you can."

Cyndi Cheyenne nodded and began tearing strips from around the lower part of her blouse. A few cars drove by, slowed, and quickly moved on. None stopped to help.

My makeshift tourniquet stopped the flow of blood, but her breathing seemed very shallow. And I could just barely detect a pulse. As for the baby, there was no telling.

The woman began to moan and stir.

"Shhh! Shh! Y'all just lay quietly," said Cyndi. "Help's coming."

With that, Cyndi Cheyenne began singing gently, her silky voice calming the gravely injured woman.

I began looking for other injuries. I was worried about broken ribs and perhaps a punctured lung.

Cyndi abruptly stopped singing.

"Amos," she said, her voice trembling, "behind you!"

Now what? I twisted myself around best I could while at the same time hanging on to the tourniquet. I was completely unprepared for what I saw.

Slithering up the slight grade of the roadway was a fair sized snake with large bulbous red eyes. He stopped, raising his head to peer inside our car with its driver side door still open.

I knew this snake. And while I couldn't tell you why, I knew it was responsible for this accident. And I was really, really ticked off.

"You there!" I yelled at the serpent. "Forget it! The cat's not there! You set up this accident to get us, but you screwed up! You failed! Now get out of here! Come any closer to this woman and I'll surely crush your head under the heel of my boot!"

The snake continued to slowly slither towards me. Its eyes flashed a red warning, I was beginning to fear my gamble hadn't worked.

And then to our horror, Cyndi and I watched as the snake wriggled with glee in a small pool of blood that had collected on the asphalt. Raising its triangular head in my direction, the snake hissed at me before shooting across the highway into the brush. Sadly, it managed to avoid being run over by an approaching car that passed us by without so much as slowing down.

"Amos," asked Cyndi, her voice quivering, "was that....."

I nodded. "I can't tell you how, or why."

Just then a thundering herd of bikers approached us from the rear. Probably a dozen of them out for a joy ride around the lake. The guy in the lead slowed as he passed by Cyndi and I. Relief washed over me as I saw them come to a stop and dismount.

A very large bald man walked up to us, surveyed the situation and asked, "how can we help, man? Aw, she's really pregnant, isn't she?"

"Listen," I said. "Take the cell phone out of my shirt pocket and call 911. See if they'll tell you how far out the paramedics are. If anyone of you has a first aid kit with some bandages, or even a clean t-shirt, we need a better bandage for her head. And then we need to get her head elevated a little higher."

The biker nodded and stripped off his leather jacket, which he placed on Cyndi Cheyenne's lap as she raised the poor woman's head a bit.

"Yo Bozz! Need a clean tee up here, fast! In my bag!"

Snatching my cell phone and dialing 911, the dispatcher confirmed to my biker pal that the ambulance was on its way, probably about three minutes out.

Bozz brought up a white t-shirt, and I watched while he turned it into a respectable pressure bandage.

It was getting later in the afternoon, and traffic seemed to be picking up.

"Listen," I yelled. "Some of you guys that can, direct the traffic, okay? Keep it moving. We don't want a jam when the ambulance tries to get through here."

"You got it, bro!"

The rag-tag bikers responded like they'd been doing this all their lives. Sitting there with this poor injured woman, I was really thankful they'd stopped to help.

"Is she going to make it, Amos?" asked Cyndi.

"I wish I knew," I said, shaking my head.

Chapter 22

The ambulance showed up a couple of minutes later, escorted by two of the bikers on their fully dressed rides. A few car lengths behind it were two police cruisers. It began to look like our immediate problems might be over. The paramedics scrambled out of their emergency vehicle and hustled over to where Cyndi and I were tending the accident victim. Seeing the arrival of the cops, the rest of the bikers quickly bugged out.

"Okay, sir. Ma'am. We'll take over from you," one of the paramedics said.

"Cyndi," I said, "looks like the cavalry has arrived."

Cyndi Cheyenne just nodded, looking a little pale.

I left the medicos to do what they do best, arising to meet an El Dorado County sheriff's deputy that was walking in our direction.

"Tell me what happened," he said.

"Can't say," I replied. "Didn't see the collision. Came upon it after the damage was done and stopped to help."

"Did you see any other cars?" asked the deputy.

"No. Just the crumpled one you see there," I said, pointing to the wrecked vehicle.

The other cop was examining our rental car and the demolished sedan.

"Do you know the injured woman?"

"Nope. Never saw her before this afternoon. All I can tell you is she's badly injured and pregnant. I hope she makes it."

The other cop took a few pictures, and then walked over to us.

"Rental car's clean, Stan, not a mark on it," he said. "The wrecked car has some scrapes on the right rear quarter. Too soon to say if this might be a hit and run, but it's a possibility."

"I recognize Miss Cheyenne," said the cop who was interviewing me. "But who are you?" he asked.

I gave him my name, and told him how he could contact me.

"Deputy," I said, "I can't speak for Miss Cheyenne, but I'd consider it a kindness if you'd keep my name out of the news. I'm not looking for any publicity or camera time."

The other cop went over and had a few words with Cyndi, both watching as the paramedics loaded the young woman into the waiting ambulance. He nodded at her, and walked back to where I stood with his colleague.

"The smart money says the local tv crew's on the way. I'd just as soon you and Miss Cheyenne be gone before they arrive. It'll make my job easier."

I nodded at the deputy and shook his hand. We had an understanding of sorts, it seemed.

I joined Cyndi, put my arm around her, and led her over to our convertible. She looked at me, but said nothing. In fact, she didn't say anything until we'd put some miles between us and the wreckage. Finally she took my hand, gave it a little squeeze, and rested her head on my shoulder.

"Rough afternoon," I said.

"Amos, I've never been part of anything like that. Not ever."

"You did just fine, baby. Rose to the occasion."

"You did most of the work. I couldn't have done what you did."

"It's mostly a matter of putting the fear behind you and letting your training take over. I haven't taken a first aid course since I was a kid, but in times of crisis, it's surprising how it all comes back to you."

"That woman was still alive when the ambulance took her away. I hope her baby makes it. And what about that awful SNAKE? Good grief!"

"Dunno what the deal is with that snake. But I know deep down he had something to do with that accident. Sounds crazy, I know. But I'd bet hard cash on it. You saw the way he went over to OUR car first? He was looking for Zoom. Same as he did that night we were camping in the mountains."

"Creepy."

"You got that right. But he failed again. And I'm taking comfort in that."

"I've seen plenty of snakes on the ranch, but nothing like this one. There was a, a wickedness about it," said Cyndi, shuddering.

"My friend the padre says the snake usually represents the Evil One, Satan."

"Well, he can't HAVE you! Or Zoom!" cried Cyndi Cheyenne.

"Well, baby, neither of us figures to go gently," I said, looking at her seriously.

I pulled into a drive-thru and ordered us both a peach smoothie. The cashier looked at us funny, and it took a moment for me to figure out why.

Cyndi got it the same time I did.

"Amos," she said, giggling, "you should see us! We're a fright! My top is ripped to shreds and has dried blood all over it. Your sleeves are bloody, and your jeans are stained!"

"Egads, you're right! We look like a couple of refugees from a B-grade zombie movie!"

We both laughed hysterically, and the tension was broken. We'd done a tough job, faced down an unknown danger, and walked away from it unharmed. We were both feeling a little better.

Cyndi flipped open her cell phone and dialed for some help.

"Nicki? It's Cyndi. Yes, I know I'm late. Listen, there was an accident and we stopped to help. No, we're fine. The show goes on. But my friend and I are a mess. We can't go traipsing through the hotel looking like we do. Find us a couple of those gray dressing smocks and meet us at the VIP entrance. We're about ten minutes away. We're in a red convertible. Thanks."

"Okay," said Cyndi, "I think we're covered. The troops will meet us when we arrive. With any luck, we'll avoid scaring anyone."

"Woman," I said, "you're a marvel. One in a million. One in a BILLION!"

Chapter 23

We were met at the hotel entrance by Cyndi's makeup artist Nicki Jerome. Not knowing entirely what to expect, she'd brought us each a long silver-gray smock, some large sunglasses, and a couple of floppy black hats. Accompanying Nicki were two hotel security guys and the concierge assistant.

"Cyndi darling, are you okay?" asked Nicki, her voice betraying excitement. "You're all over the news! They're carrying on about how you stopped at the scene of a horrible accident and bravely helped the victim! They're showing pictures of the wrecked car, and old file photos of you!"

Cyndi Cheyenne gave me a puzzled look. I just smiled and shook my head.

"Folks, we need to get you inside," said one of the security guys.

I nodded, tossed the car keys to the concierge assistant and asked him to check the car back in. I struggled into the too-small smock, donned one of the floppy hats. I thought it looked ridiculous, and Cyndi couldn't help giggling at me.

The security team did their best to remain poker faced as they ushered us through the hotel and into a waiting elevator. It was a strange procession, but nobody seemed to notice.

With Cyndi's hotel accommodations being the top floor penthouse, I got off first.

"See you in the morning?" I asked.

Cyndi Cheyenne nodded, her moist eyes betraying more than she was comfortable saying in front of the others.

"Give Zoom some ear rubbies from me," she said, her voice a little wobbly.

I stepped out of the elevator car and heard the door close behind me.

Walking along the hallway towards my suite, I was vaguely aware that there was no one else about. It seemed unnaturally quiet, especially after all the day's excitement.

I inserted the card-key into the locking mechanism and entered my room. Zoom the Wonder Cat came prancing over to greet me, all clean and sweet-smelling. He wore a white bow around his neck, and was obviously quite pleased with himself. I sat down on one of the casual chairs next to the oval coffee table. Zoom jumped up onto my lap, hunkered down, and proceeded to purr happily while I rubbed his ears.

"Little buddy," I said in a low voice, "you don't know how happy I am to see you."

We sat there for a while, each of us content with the other's company. I finally got up and walked to the bedroom, carrying Zoom with me. Stripping off my blood-stained clothes, I realized I never wanted to see that outfit again. I rolled the ill-fated shirt and jeans into a ball and dropped them into a waste bin. Walking into the spacious bathroom, I washed my face and hands and imagined the tension of the accident experience disappearing down the drain. Joining Zoom on the bed, I slipped off into a comfortable, dreamless nap.

By the time I woke up it was well after sundown and the glittering neon lights outside were making their presence known.

I closed the window drapery and donned my back-up attire.

"I'll be back in a few," I said to Zoom, who was still half-napping on the bed.

As one would expect, there is a fine gentlemen's clothing store located inside Caesars. I strolled down the arcade, paused to admire a couple of sport shirts on display in the window, and then entered.

"Good evening, sir," said the salesman, wearing a splendidly tailored blue pinstriped suit. "How may I help you?"

"And a good evening to you. Listen, I had a bit of an accident earlier and ruined one of my casual walk-about outfits. I'm traveling on tomorrow and need a replacement. Something comfortable, a bit understated. All natural fibers, if you please. No synthetics."

"Certainly, sir."

The salesman then measured me for size and asked me to follow him.

I ended up buying a superbly tailored pair of black straight-legged jeans. Its partner would be a gold button-down shirt of highly polished cotton. These would do nicely.

Thanking the salesman, I reversed course and rode the elevator back up to my suite. Not feeling much like being around people, I dialed room service for dinner. A couple of toasted club sandwiches, piled high and accompanied by cole slaw and chilled beers would be just the ticket.

A little later our meal arrived. Zoom and I watched the Redskins battle the Broncos on the television while we munched our dinner. The late local news featured a story about the "heroic efforts of country western singer Cyndi Cheyenne battling to save the life of a pregnant accident victim near Emerald Bay." I smiled, flipped off the tv, and tuned the radio to the local jazz station.

Setting the alarm clock for the desired wake-up time, I fell into bed and slept soundly.

Chapter 24

The next morning I busied myself with packing and engaging in the usual pre-flight activities. I called an FAA weather briefer and after listening to his spiel gave him our aircraft particulars. He filed my flight plan and provided me with the proper radio frequency on which to activate it later. Zoom and I were just finishing breakfast when a discrete knock came at the door.

I opened up, admitting Cyndi Cheyenne and Graham the hotel security officer.

"I'm not quite ready to go," I said. "Need another ten minutes."

Graham nodded. "I'll just wait outside and advise the rest of the team," he said as he walked out the door.

I pulled Cyndi close and once again my senses were overwhelmed by the experience. I kissed her gently on the lips, and she responded with a fervor that I'd never known from her before.

"Amos," she said, finally coming up for air, "I lay awake

half the night thinking about the two of us, and how it might be. I'm lettin' myself fall in love with you, and I'm a little scared."

"I'm a little scared, too," I said. "But after yesterday's experience and watching you rise to the occasion, I'm more in love with you than ever, my little songbird. If the two of us can peer over the horizon, hand in hand, I think we can deal with just about anything that comes our way. And be better at it together than we ever could apart."

"Mrrrrr-ow?"

"Zoom's just puttin' in his two cents worth," laughed Cyndi. "How are YOU this morning, old fellow?" she asked, rubbing his ears.

"Come on," I said. "The staff's waiting on us. Let's get out of here and head over to the airport."

Cyndi picked up Zoom and I grabbed my modest suitcase. Graham the security officer escorted us down to the VIP entrance where we were met by Curly Mike tending a sparkling white hotel limo.

"Good morning to all of you," he said, tipping his hat. "Airport, Mr Westergaard?"

"Yes," I said. "General aviation terminal, right?"

"I remember, sir," said Curly Mike.

Cyndi and I rode in silence, her hand in mine all the way to the airport. Zoom just stared out of the window, watching the world go by.

All too soon, Curly Mike turned off the main road onto the airport loop. Stopping in front of the GA terminal, we all exited the limo and Curley Mike went around to retrieve my suitcase from where it had ridden in the trunk.

"Curly Mike," I said, "it's always a pleasure to ride with you."

"Thank you, sir. Um, I'd like to know if you and Miss Cyndi can spare me a moment?"

"Certainly," I said, wondering what was up.

"Heard about what the two of you did yesterday, helping that accident victim. Means a lot to me. What you don't know is, that young woman is my niece Shannon. My brother's eldest daughter."

"Oh MY!" exclaimed Cyndi Cheyenne, not knowing what else to say.

"How's she doing?" I asked.

"When she got to the hospital, the docs said it was touch and go. My family got together and prayed over her all night. Early this morning the decision was made to induce labor. The doctors said it would ease the stress on her mangled body."

"How'd it go?" I asked, almost afraid of the answer.

"She made it," said Curly Mike, beaming. "Came through and surprised us all. Twins. A boy and a girl."

"Well I'll be skinned," I said. "Congratulations!"

"Thank you, sir. But the truth is, none of us did anything. If you and Miss Cyndi hadn't stopped when you did, three people would've died at the side of the road yesterday."

"Mister Mike," said Cyndi, "I can't tell you how happy I am for you and your family!"

"It's Curly Mike, if you please, Miss Cyndi. And, there's something else. My brother asked me to ask you. He'd like your permission to name the babies after the two of you. When they're old enough to understand, we'll tell them the story, and all about you."

I stood there stunned, not knowing what to say. I looked at Cyndi, who smiled and nodded.

"Curly Mike," I said, "Cyndi and I would both be honored. And, in the fullness of time, I hope we're able to visit your niece and the two little ones."

"My family would be thrilled, Mr Westergaard. You tell us when, and I'll organize the best outdoor BBQ party you can imagine!" said Curly Mike with enthusiasm.

"You got a deal," I said, shaking his hand.

Our day brightened by that bit of good news, Cyndi and I walked into the GA terminal while Curly Mike stood attending to his car. I settled my fuel bill, made a last-minute trip to the men's room, and escorted Cyndi out to see my airplane. The lineman had already released the tie downs, removed the wheel chocks, and towed it out onto the taxi way.

"Oh, Amos, it's sooo cute!" exclaimed Cyndi Cheyenne. "I like your little red and white airplane!"

"She's a beauty, isn't she?" I said.

Zoom hopped into the back seat where he immediately assumed his customary take-off position. I put my small suitcase into the rear storage area and locked the access door.

Cyndi Cheyenne watched as I dutifully made all the essential pre-flight checks.

"You're really careful, aren't you Amos?"

"When you fly, being careful is what keeps you alive," I said. "We pilots really HATE unexpected surprises."

I pulled the love of my life close, openly kissing her deeply right there in front of God and country.

"You'll meet me on the ranch in a couple of weeks, then?" asked Cyndi.

"You probably ought to tell me where the nearest airport is," I said. "It would help."

"Missoula," she giggled. "The Missoula airport is about a half hour drive from the ranch."

"I'll be there," I said. "I promise."

"I love you, Mr Westergaard. It's gonna be hard for me to get any work done between now and then."

"Me too," I said, kissing her one last time before I entered the cockpit.

"Now listen, I need for you to move away. At least as far as the front of the terminal building there."

I watched as Cyndi Cheyenne walked slowly away. It hurt. I wanted this woman beside me.

"Clear!" I yelled out the window, just before I hit the starter.

The engine coughed a couple of times, the prop began to spin, and I started the sequence of checks and events to get Zoom and I underway. The ground controller cleared me to taxi down to the active runway. I waved at Cyndi as the plane began to roll, and she waved back.

A couple of minutes later we arrived at the departure intersection. I pulled over and did the requisite magneto checks, waggled the control surfaces, and set the radios to the frequencies I wanted.

"Tower, Cessna One Sierra Tango is ready for takeoff. If it's not too busy, we'd like a straight out departure," I added.

"Cessna One Sierra Tango, cleared for takeoff. Straight out's approved," came the reply.

I carefully guided us into position on the center of the runway and poured on the power. Gathering speed down the runway, I rotated the nose and we were flying once again. I waggled my wings just a tad as we flashed past the terminal.

Cyndi Cheyenne was standing up on top of Curly Mike's limo, waving her hat as we flashed by.

Chapter 25

Reno is only a short hop from South Lake Tahoe, as the Cessna flies. Its airport is a joint-use facility accommodating commercial jetliners, an assortment of warbirds belonging to the Nevada Air National Guard, and transient pilots like myself. It is always busy. The good news is, Reno air traffic controllers are some of the most efficient there are. I was cleared onto final approach and made a passable landing with almost no delay.

By the time I taxied over to the Alpine Aviation building, a lineman was waiting to direct me to a vacant tie-down space and refuel my tanks. Suitcase in one hand, Zoom riding on the other, I went inside the dispatch office, gave the attendant the requisite information, and asked him to call me a cab.

"Where to, sir?" asked the cab driver, a pretty Japanese woman with piercing black eyes.

"Do you know where WNWD radio is? On Virginia Street near Clover?" I asked.

"No problem," she said. "Pretty cat. Does he like to fly?"

"Mostly he objects to being left behind," I said.

"Well, I don't blame him, " said my cabby, laughing.

Zoom and I were left standing in front of the radio station a few minutes later. I glanced at my watch, noting with pleasure that I was a little early.

Inside a perky blonde receptionist greeted me, adored Zoom, and then zipped off to announce our arrival to the station manager.

"Mister Westergaard, I'm Ted Webster, station manager here at WNWD. We're very pleased you were able to make it. You'll be going on the air live with Barry Maivia in about twenty minutes. I'll escort you up to the booth shortly; right now our news guys are in there. Can I get you some fresh coffee?" he asked.

"No thanks," I said. "But I would like a large glass of chilled water, and something smaller for my little pal here," I said.

"Certainly," said Webster. "Um, would you like me to have our receptionist Sally tend to your cat while you're on the air?"

"Again, thanks. But no thanks. Zoom here is a pro, and has done these kind of live programs many times with me. He'll be fine."

Webster nodded but didn't look convinced. Not knowing what else to do, he scurried off to rustle up the water I'd requested.

Barry Maivia is a large Samoan fellow with a deep melodious radio voice. And as it turned out, also a consummate pro when interviewing writers plugging their books. Zoom took to him right away and began purring contentedly while we got ourselves organized in the cramped broadcast booth.

"Mr Westergaard, it's a pleasure to meet you," said Maivia. "I rarely read the books written by the people I interview. I simply don't have time. But I want you to know I did read yours and found it compelling. Now I want you to relax. We're going to have some fun here this afternoon."

"What's the drill?" I asked.

"Pretty much standard stuff. I'll introduce you and we'll do a little chit-chat small talk. Then we'll take some calls from listeners. Watch me for the cues taking us to commercial breaks."

I nodded and shook his hand.

"Does your cat always purr like that?" he asked.

"Only when he's going on the air live," I said, deadpan.

Barry Maivia roared with laughter and scratched Zoom's chin. Ice broken, we each settled in to do the job we'd signed on for.

The last promo faded away and I watched as my interviewer opened a live mic.

"This is WNWD radio, the voice of the eastern Sierra. I am Barry Maivia and I'll be your host this afternoon until three. Ladies and gentlemen in our listening audience, I'm very honored to be talking with Mr Amos Westergaard, author of the international best selling book, A Wanderer's Wisdom. Mr. Westergaard, welcome to Reno, sir..."

"Thank you, Barry. It's always a pleasure anytime I'm able to visit this area. The people in Reno have always made me feel welcome and I don't think I'll ever get tired of the stunning mountain views. Truly God's country."

"I should tell our listeners that in addition to yourself being here in our studio, there's also your cat Zoom."

"Zoom is something of a ham," I said. "He loves attention and pretty much goes where I do."

"So, your cat flies around the country with you when you do these interviews?"

"That seems to be the case," I said. "I pilot my own Cessna, and Zoom has staked out the back seat in my airplane as his own personal space."

"That's an interesting life you have going there. I wonder if Zoom has anything to add?" asked Barry as he lowered the open mic down in front of my furry pal.

Zoom took his cue expertly, increasing the volume and vibrato of his purrs.

"Well, thank you Zoom!" said Barry. "He's really something!"

"He'll take over the interview if you'll let him," I said, laughing.

"Sorry little guy. No can do."

His job done, Zoom curled up on the desk and took a nap while Barry and I continued talking on the air.

"Mr Westergaard, your book, A Wanderer's Wisdom, has sold something in the area of thirty five million copies worldwide in just over a year. Those numbers are staggering."

"Let me assure you and your listeners that no one has been more surprised or delighted than I have been," I said. "A Wanderer's Wisdom is my first book and, happily, it seems to have touched a lot of people."

"And you attribute that to what, exactly?" asked Barry.

"I think it's a combination of things involving some universal truths. A Wanderer's Wisdom is NOT is the latest new age thinking. And I'm definitely NOT some enlightened visionary or guru. I'm a very ordinary guy really, and I think my writing reflects that."

"You talk about universal truths. Can you expand on that a little for us?"

"Certainly," I replied. "Let me give you just one example. Almost all of us have experienced the morning alarm going off and dragging ourselves out of bed. We shuffle into the bathroom, stare at ourselves in the mirror, and think, man, I'm meant for something better than this. The truth is, most of us ARE meant for something better. But we don't focus on it and instead continue to live lives of quiet desperation. And what's universal about this scenario is that it applies neatly to people all around the world, regardless of race, gender, or social standing."

"And your writing helps people zero in on viable solutions?"

"It seems so, Barry. At least, I get a lot of unsolicited letters telling me that."

"Man, with thirty five million copies in print, I bet you DO get the mail. Let's take some calls now. Let's see......first up we have Ellen, from just south of here in Carson City. Ellen, you're on live."

"Thank you Barry. I love your show!"

"Praise is what keeps me goin' here, Ellen. Do you have a question for our guest Mr Westergaard?"

"Well, not so much a question as a comment. Mr Westergaard, I've read your book and think it's wonderful. You talk about focus. I just want you to know that, thanks to your book, I've been able to focus a little differently than I had been. I found solutions that helped me get my kid off drugs and back into college. I'm guardedly optimistic that instead of becoming a drugged out loser, my son's going to amount to something worthwhile."

"Wow! That's incredible, Ellen! Congratulations to both of you! Wish we had more time to talk, but we have to move on. Let's talk to Gary here in Reno. Gary, talk to us, brother."

"My story is a little like the last one, Barry. A friend gave me A Wanderer's Wisdom as a gift. Nobody's more surprised than me at how it's changed my life. Mr Westergaard, I focused in big-time on those chapters dealing with simplicity. It was like you were talking specifically to me. I simplified my life. I sold my boat, my truck, the snowmobiles, the jet skis, and my wife's car. I got the STUFF out of my life and it changed the focus for my whole family. My wife quit her job, tends the house, and grows hydroponic fruits and vegetables in the green house I built. My kid dumped his skanky friends and now hangs out with me. I bought him a new digital camera and he's becoming quite an accomplished photographer instead of wasting his time at the mall with the other losers."

"Incredible!" exclaimed Barry Maivia.

"It gets better," said caller Gary. "I'm sleeping better, eating better, and have lost forty pounds. My wife's lost two dress sizes. And we're lookin' at each other like we did when we first got married."

"Woo hooo!" exclaimed Barry. "You go, dude!"

"Yeah! And I want to tell the other listeners that we're experiencing a domino affect because of this. I bought the book for my business partner, and now HE'S doing better in his life. He and I decided to give A Wanderer's Wisdom to our twelve employees to see what would happen. Mostly we're seeing operations go more smoothly, and we're also witnessing our business become a team effort for the first time. Our financial bottom line is looking a LOT better."

"Amos?" said Barry, prompting me.

"Gary, I'm really happy for all of you. Now if you want to have some fun, pass A Wanderer's Wisdom around to your neighbors. Watch what happens when these things take hold on the street where you live!"

"Aw, man, I'd never thought about that!" said caller Gary. "That might be something to see! You oughta know some of my neighbors..."

"Gary, thanks for calling in."

"You bet, Barry. And thanks again, Mr Westergaard, for all you do!"

"Whoa! You know it sounds like you've got some real fans out there today, Amos!" said

Barry Maivia. " Folks, we'll be right back after the news break. This is WNWD radio, the Voice of the Sierra."

Barry closed the mic, an automated news program kicked in, and we both took a breather.

"Man, we're smokin' today, Amos. You can't BUY the kind of calls we've gotten so far."

I just smiled, by now an old hand at this.

"Before I forget, would you autograph my copy of your book?" asked Barry.

I inked his book and asked for another glass of chilled water. For some reason radio booths always seem too warm for me.

We started up again a few minutes later. Time went by very quickly as it always seems to whenever I do these kind of interviews. Zoom continued to nap.

One caller wanted to know how to get a better job. Another wanted to know if I was concerned about global warming. A couple of more calls showering me with praise and telling listeners how their lives were better because they'd taken the things in my book to heart. One woman caller wanted to know where I was staying and what my room number was. No, she hadn't read my book, but she thought I sounded hot.

Barry Maivia wound up the interview exhorting people to buy my book, available at the usual booksellers.

"Mr Westergaard, I just want you to know that I don't get many book interviews to go as well as this one did. Thanks for makin' my day easy."

"Barry, I recognize talent when I see it. You're a credit to your profession," I said, shaking his hand. "Be well."

I asked Sally, the cute blonde receptionist, to call me a taxi.

"Won't hear of it," she said. "I have my car outside. Just tell me where you and your precious kitty need to go."

"El Dorado Towers," I said.

"Let's do it, then."

I didn't say much during the short ride over to the hotel. I was feeling a little tired. It'd been a long day already.

"Thanks again," I said to Sally the radio station receptionist as I got out of her car. She looked a little disappointed that I didn't invite her in for a drink at the hotel bar, but them's the breaks.

The staff on duty at the front desk greeted me like any preferred guest.

Shortly thereafter, Zoom and I found ourselves standing in a room on the 17th floor with a good view of the airport runways in the distance. I grabbed a cold beer out of the mini bar and flopped down on a comfortable recliner.

Zoom hopped up on my lap, settled in, and was snoring gently by the time I'd finished my beer. I dozed off too. By the time I woke up, the sun was setting.

Raising Spirits

My stomach let me know that I'd skipped lunch. I went into the bathroom to wash up, broke open a new bag of kibble for Zoom, and took the elevator down to the hotel dining room.

The food at the El Dorado Towers has always been superb. I ordered a salad made with baby greens, a baked potato, and a small filet mignon cooked rare. Okay, so it's not very imaginative, but to me it's comfort food.

Afterwards I wandered aimlessly around the casino floor for a while. Checked out the posted spreads on upcoming NFL games in the cavernous sports book. Window shopped in the arcade. Nobody paid any attention to me. Just another nomad passing through Reno.

I rode the elevator back upstairs to my room. Zoom was asleep again. There was nothing on the television I wanted to watch. Opening another beer from the mini bar, I sat and watched the night landings going on over at the Reno airport from my window.

The truth is, I was missing Cyndi Cheyenne.

Chapter 26

The next day dawned clear and I woke up feeling rested. Zoom was busy worrying a tiny spider that was attempting to take up residence inside a lampshade. I showered, ordered a light breakfast from the room service operator, and began packing my suitcase.

Less than an hour later the two of us rode the elevator downstairs to the lobby. After checking out with the desk clerk, Zoom and I boarded the hotel shuttle just as it was leaving for the airport.

I logged on at one of the computer terminals thoughtfully provided by Alpine Aviation. Having checked the aviation weather and after filing a flight plan, I headed outside to start the pre-flight routine on our winged chariot. Zoom assumed the take off position (which mostly involves curling up for a nap inside his backseat basket) and we were taxiing out towards the active runway a few minutes later.

"Cessna One Sierra Tango, follow the Bonanza in front of you, number seven for takeoff," directed the ground controller.

"One Sierra Tango, roger," I said.

Busy morning there at the Reno airport. While we sat waiting our turn, I amused myself as best I could. The surrounding mountains were gorgeous as always. I wondered if Cyndi Cheyenne was awake yet. Probably not, I decided. Her nightly shows seldom allowed her to retire before three in the morning. I made a mental note to call Bernie the Attorney and find out if there was any news from the fire insurance company about my former weekend retreat down in Arizona.

"Cessna One Sierra Tango, taxi into position and hold," came a voice over my headphones.

"One Sierra Tango, into position and hold," I acknowledged, guiding us on to the center of the runway.

"Cessna One Sierra Tango, cleared for takeoff."

"One Sierra Tango is rolling," I said, shoving the throttle home.

My little airplane quickly gathered speed down the runway, anxious to be in her own element. I rotated the nose, adjusted the trim, and we were on our way.

"Cessna One Sierra Tango, maintain runway heading to Pyramid Lake. Make a right turn out at the lake, and contact Departure on one-two-seven-point seven five."

"Cessna One Sierra Tango, roger Pyramid Lake and Departure control," I said.

I navigated as directed, and kept a close eye out for other aircraft. The departure control guys were decent and allowed me to continue east out of their airspace without delay.

After requesting a frequency change, I got my flight plan activated in the ATC computers by yet another operative. Then I switched the other radio over to the Flight Watch frequency, allowing me to monitor any pilot reports that might be of interest. Just another day at the office, really.

Winging along through northern Nevada on a sunny fall day is good for the spirits. I mostly followed the meandering Humboldt River eastward, occasionally getting a hard navigation fix off a dam, reservoir, or mountain peak. We passed over Winnemucca where hardy farmers grow some of the region's finest potatoes. A little later I landed in the mining community of Battle Mountain to top off our fuel tanks and check the oil.

Thanks to a twelve knot tailwind we moved along smartly throughout the rest of the morning. It was shortly after overflying the city of Elko that I began thinking about lunch. Actually, I probably should've landed at Elko. Zoom and I had dined well there on an earlier trip. But since we'd already passed by that option, I grabbed my flight directory to see what other eateries lay ahead.

I found a small notation for the Pirate Cove Hotel and Casino, with a private landing strip adjacent to the property. Okay, there were some of these small time operations springing up along the eastern part of the state. They were usually in relative wilderness and the landing strips were most often built for the convenience of the casino management, but transient aircraft were welcomed too.

Checking my navigational chart, it looked like the Pirate Cove was about ten to twelve minutes northeast. I altered course slightly and began my routines for setting up a landing approach.

A few minutes later I spotted the Pirate Cove Hotel with its runway alongside. There were only a couple of other planes tied down and no other discernable aviation activity. I reduced power, dropped the flaps a notch, and circled to land. The narrow runway was uncomfortably short, but I managed to get us down safely with the help of gusting headwind.

"Lunchtime, Zoom!" I yelled over my shoulder. "What'll it be? Tuna or chicken?"

I got no audible response, but then that's not unusual.

Chapter 27

The Pirate Cove Hotel and Casino is similar to many other such places I've seen along the eastern and less populated corridors of Nevada. A modest two story hotel adjoined the smallish casino with its buccaneer theme. Inside it seemed moderately busy, with the majority of the patrons paying homage to row after row of clinking, clanking, flashing slot machines. Down in the pit I could see a few die hards playing cards and shooting dice.

Just inside the door and to the right I found the restaurant. A placard in front advertised the daily special, corned beef on rye. A cute twenty-something young woman with auburn hair and a prominent chest was at the cash register.

"Hi," I said. "We just flew in hoping to grab some lunch. Could you fix us a couple of tuna sandwiches on toasted wheat and an iced tea with lemon to go, please?"

"Well hi there, cute fellow!" she said, pointing to Zoom. "I'll get you fixed right up."

I gave her a twenty, and she gave me some change.

"We'll just wait right outside," I said.

"I'll bring your food out to you in a few minutes," she said.

Just then a thin, dark haired waitress with bags under her eyes came rushing over towards us.

"You can't bring that animal in here!" she screeched.

"Yes ma'am. I understand," I said, beginning to retreat. "Don't want to make any trouble."

The young auburn haired waitress winked, letting me know she'd bring our food out to us.

With Zoom still riding my forearm, I walked around the area in front of the restaurant. Every now and then someone would stop to admire Zoom, but mostly people just kept feeding money into the slot machines.

In a fit of boredom, I fed a twenty into one of the blinking progressive machines that promised a huge payout. Mostly I'm not attracted to slot machines, but every now and then when there's nothing else to do I'll play a little. This particular one didn't seem to be very enthusiastic, but neither was it greedy. It seemed to want to take a little of my money, and then every so often it would line up and spit it all back. It looked to me like I was just about breaking even. I was scooping out the coins and putting them into a big plastic cup when our waitress appeared with our to-go lunch in a large white paper bag.

"Here you go, sir," she said, smiling. "Hope you enjoy your lunch."

"Thank you, young lady," I said. "Good of you to bring it out here to us."

I handed her the cup full of coins.

"A little extra tip for extra gracious service," I said. "And there's a few coins still in the machine. Go ahead and try your luck."

"Oh, I never play these things," she said. "But maybe just this once...."

"Go for it, " I said.

She stepped in front of me and pulled the lever. I was really

hoping she'd win something, and held my breath while the wheels began to line up.

Nobody was more surprised than I to see the machine line up four sevens. Alarms began to blare and strobes flashed.

"Young lady, it looks to me like you've just won the big $136,897.00 progressive jackpot," I said over the noise.

She stood there stunned. "No, no," she said. "That was your money."

"Nope. I gave it to you, remember?"

The slot machine manager came running over, followed by a uniformed security guy.

"Congratulations, sir!" he said excitedly.

"I'm not the winner," I replied. "The winner is this young lady here," I said, pointing to our waitress.

"Oh, but employees on duty aren't allowed to play," he said.

"Well, she's the winner, just the same," I insisted.

The slot manager looked at the security guy, who just shrugged.

We were joined then by another very large man, about the size of your average wildebeest but probably not quite as smart.

"What's goin' on here?" he demanded.

"Well, we have a progressive winner on this slot," said the manager, pointing to the winking machine. "But this man insists the winner is Dolly here, works at the coffee shop."

"That's right," I said. "You'll make the payout to her, not to me."

The big guy's cell phone rang, and he stood there deadpan, nodding.

"You stay with the security captain," he said to Dolly the waitress.

Dolly just nodded, not saying anything.

"You come with me; the boss wants you upstairs," he ordered.

"And, what if I don't want to go?" I asked, not responding

well to shabby treatment.

"C'mon!" he snarled, grabbing my right arm.

Faster than your heart can beat, Zoom reached over, dug his claws into the back of the man's hand, and raked deep.

"Owoowow!" he howled.

"Not nice to lay hands on the customers, " I said.

"Don't make this any worse than it already is," he said, wincing in pain and beginning to bleed. "Follow me."

With a sigh, I fell in behind the big man and followed him through the casino. A lot of people stopped playing the machines long enough to watch as we moved past them. Every now and then the big guy would glance over his shoulder to make sure I was still following, and to glare at Zoom.

For some reason the phrase "dead man walking" flashed through my mind.

Chapter 28

After allowing the wounded wildebeest to escort Zoom and I upstairs, we were ushered into the executive office suite of one Stewart Thistlebane. Or at least that was the name elegantly inscribed on his desk placard.

Thistlebane was a small, severe looking fellow with dark receding hair. When we walked in, he was busy scribbling something on a yellow legal pad. Thistlebane looked up at me, scowled at Zoom, and continued writing. I sat down on one of two visitor chairs and placed Zoom on the other one beside me. Since it appeared like we were being ignored for the moment, I opened up our bagged lunch. Unwrapping a tuna sandwich, I began to eat. Every now and then I'd give Zoom a piece, which he seemed to enjoy.

"I don't allow no pets in here," said Thistlebane, finally looking up.

"Then put up some signs," I said, continuing to chew on my sandwich.

Thistlebane gave me a hard stare.

"You probably ought to dismiss your bouncer," I said, glancing over at the big guy. "He seems to be bleeding all over your carpet."

Thistlebane nodded. The wounded wildebeest turned and clomped out the door. Thistlebane glared at me again.

"That your tough guy look, Stewie?" I asked. "Needs work."

Just then, Thistlebane's eyes flashed red and gave himself away. I caught it, and instinctively knew what I was dealing with. It wasn't much of an edge, but it would have to do.

"Who are you?" demanded Thistlebane. "And what's your connection to that girl downstairs?"

"My name is Amos Westergaard. As for the young woman downstairs, I only just met her in the coffee shop. You could use a few more like her."

"Never heard of you," said Thistlebane.

"No reason you should have," I said. "I doubt we travel in the same circles."

"Anyway, it don't matter who you are. And the girl's fired. We're not payin' off that slot jackpot. We think you mighta cheated. Gonna do our own little investigation," announced Thistlebane, giving me a wolfish grin. "Probably take several weeks."

"Doesn't sound like the smart play to me, Stewie, " I said, shaking my head. "It'll bring trouble."

Thistlebane's eyes went red again, and I knew I'd scored.

"You're going to leave here," he said. "In exactly what condition remains to be determined."

"Oh come now, Stewie. I'm many things, but naive isn't one of them," I said, calmly feeding Zoom another piece of tuna. "We both know you answer to somebody else. He's not going to like it when your stupidity generates lots of negative attention to this little operation."

Thistlebane glared in my direction again.

"Tell you what," I said. "Here stored in my cell phone is

the number to the Nevada State Gaming Commissioner. And I'm sure he knows the Attorney General. And I bet they BOTH know scores of lawyers at the EEOC. Maybe, just to add my own brand of humor to your troubles, I'll arrange to have an investigative journalist and camera crew start digging around this place. Who knows what they'll turn up?" I said with a crooked smile.

"You're bluffing," said Thistlebane.

"I never bluff," I said. "Tell you what, Stewie. You dial the number on your desk phone. Better your dime than mine."

I read off the phone number. Thistlebane scribbled it down on his yellow pad. And stared at me again for a moment. Then shaking his head in disbelief, he dialed the number.

"Gaming Commissioner's office," said a voice.

"Uh, never mind. Wrong number," said Thistlebane, quickly hanging up.

"Stewie," I said, "I'm through screwing around here. Your butt's in a crack, and you're going to deal. Pay off the slot jackpot to that woman downstairs. You owe it, and the video surveillance will prove it. She and I are going to walk out the front door together and not look back. You'll be rid of us. And you'll avoid risking your own hide anymore than you already have. It's the smart play. And it's your only play."

Thistlebane just stared at me blankly, and nodded. He still didn't know who I was. He was used to cheating naive tourists from Nebraska and getting away with it. Resigned, he picked up his phone.

"Maxie? Thistlebane. Listen, pay off on that jackpot win to the coffee shop girl Burke's holding in security. Yeah, by the numbers. Withholding taxes, the whole bit. Cut her a check for rest."

"CASH!" I said loudly. "No check."

"Uh, never mind the check," said Thistlebane, scowling. "Pay her off in cash."

Chapter 29

Burke the security captain met Zoom and I outside Thistlebane's office and cautiously escorted us back downstairs to the cashier's cage. Dolly the coffee shop waitress was there looking confused and scared.

"You got the money?" I asked.

"Y-y-y-yes," she stammered. "In my shoulder bag. A little over ninety seven thousand dollars."

"Fine," I said. "You, me, and my furry pal are going to walk safely out of here together. The security captain is going to see to that."

Dolly just nodded and said nothing. We walked across the casino floor to the main entrance and out on to the street.

"Do you have a car?" I said.

"No," answered Dolly. I ride a bike to work. Car blew up last month. Had it towed away.

"Then we're going to need a taxi," I said, eyeing an elderly couple exiting a brownish cab. "C'mon!"

We quickly claimed the empty back seat. The driver looked

the two of us over and asked "where to, folks?"

Thinking on the fly, I asked our driver if there was a used car dealership nearby that might specialize in clean, late model vehicles.

"That'd be Kingsley's," he answered. "Bout ten miles from here."

"Tally ho!" I said.

The driver put the car in gear, and we rolled away from the Pirate Cove.

Dolly started to speak, but I put my hand in front of her lips.

"Young lady," I said in a low voice, "there's a time to talk and a time to be silent and listen. Right now it's your time to be quiet. You've just been fired, and you're in trouble. First order of business is to get you safely away. For that you need a car. You can now afford one, and I'm going to help you. Now, tell me your name."

"It's Dolly. Dolly Barton. And I can't believe they FIRED me," she said in a sour tone.

"My name is Amos," I said. "Amos Westergaard, to be exact. My little buddy sitting next to you is my cat Zoom."

Right on cue, Zoom began to purr. Which seemed to have an immediate calming effect on young Miss Barton.

We rode along in silence for a few minutes, until the driver announced "Kingsley's car lot just ahead, folks."

Kingsley's seemed to have more trucks than passenger sedans. But as we cruised past the front row of vehicles for sale, I saw what I was looking for.

"Just drop us off in front, please," I directed the driver.

We got out and Dolly paid the driver. A heavy-set gray haired fellow came out to greet us.

"I'm Tom Kingsley, folks," he announced as he offered his hand. "Can I be of help?"

"Good afternoon, Tom," I said. "My name is Amos, and this is my friend Dolly. We're both pressed for time, so you'll excuse me for wanting to dispense with the usual protocols."

"Certainly," said Tom, his face turning serious.

"Dolly here needs a good transportation car, and I saw one on your front row that we might be interested in...."

Thirty minutes later, Dolly Barton was the proud owner of a three year old Subaru Forester for which she'd paid cash. Tom Kingsley waved goodby as we pulled out of his parking lot.

"Okay," I said, "next order of business is the quick-lube down the street. Passed it coming in. We can talk while they're changing the oil."

Dolly just nodded, clearly delighted with her new car.

The quick-lube place wasn't busy. I told the service manager what we needed and Dolly handed him the keys. He motioned us towards the customer waiting area.

"Coffee inside, folks," was all he said.

There was no one else in the small lounge, and I figured we had about a half hour wait for the car.

"Now you can talk," I said to Dolly Barton.

"Who ARE you?" were the first words out of her mouth. "I mean, NOBODY does what you just did! Here, some of this money belongs to you...."

"I already told you. My name's Amos. Today I'm a pilot who just happened into the Pirates Cove looking for lunch. As for the money, it's yours. I already told you that, so forget about it."

Dolly gave me a disbelieving look. "Has to be some strings attached," she said.

"Not on my part," I replied. "You've got a decent car, and you've got money to go where you will. In a little while you're going to drop me off at the airstrip. Zoom and I are going to fly out of this place and not look back."

"Something's still not right," she said.

"Yeah, there IS a sticky part to this. And here's where you need to focus. The people running that casino are downright wicked. I had to push hard, very hard, to get them to pay you that money. Right now they're mad. Pretty soon they'll be thinking about getting even. You're in real danger, so you can't go back there. Not to say goodby to former co-workers, nothing. Do you understand? Zoom and I are at risk too, but you're the soft target."

"I have to get my baby," announced Dolly.

"You have a baby?" I asked, surprised.

"Four months old, a little girl. I named her Holly."

"Dolly and Holly Barton. I like it," I said, smiling. "Where's her father?"

Dolly looked at me sadly.

"He left us. About three months ago. Left us in this crumby motel with no money, nothing. It's why I've been waiting tables. Trying to save enough money to get out of this place, but I've barely managed to break even."

"Where's your baby?" I asked.

"At that same crumby motel," answered Dolly. "I rent a room by the week, and I pay the motel manager's wife to watch my baby girl while I work."

"Where's your family?"

"In Portland, Oregon. My parents were really upset when I told them I was pregnant. When they found out Bobby was the father, things only got worse. He had a bad reputation around town, and they said he was no good. But he told me he loved me, and conned me into going away with him. I had a few thousand dollars saved, but when it ran out, so did he. I hurt beyond imagination when I figured out he wasn't coming back. And I feel stupid telling you this."

"Well, Dolly, the thing is, you don't have a monopoly on stupidity. What counts is where you go from here," I said, gently.

"I want to go back to Portland. To be in familiar surroundings again. These past months have been harder than anything I could imagine," she said.

"Sounds to me like you've grown up some," I said. "Okay, Portland it is. But no matter what, you've got to leave town this afternoon. Your safety, and that of your baby depends on your getting away from here."

"Amos," she said, "I need disposable diapers, and I need a map. And then my baby and I are out of here. The sooner the better."

"Good girl," I said. "Let's go and get your baby; you can drop Zoom and I off on your way out of town."

On the road to her motel, Dolly stopped at a Walgreen's for diapers, bottled water, and a road atlas.

"Dolly, the smart move is to say nothing to ANYONE about the money you're carrying," I said. Play things close to the vest. Always keep your purse with you; never leave it on the car seat or anything like that. Carrying a lot of cash is dangerous. In three days you can be back in Portland. When you get there you can open up an insured money market account. Don't let any of the bank operators talk you into "investing" your money. Keep it in insured accounts. You've got a golden opportunity to start over and make a decent life for you and your baby. Keep it simple, and be wise about it."

"I have a friend who works for a credit union," said Dolly. "She'll help me."

"That sounds really good," I said.

We drove into the parking lot of a small, rundown looking motel.

"Let's go down to the front and I'll introduce you to my baby," said Dolly.

We walked down to the motel office where an overweight woman with a bad perm was at the desk.

"Hi, Shelly! How's my little bundle doing today?" asked Dolly.

"Been quiet since the noon feeding," said Shelly, walking to the back of the aisle and picking up a baby basket.

"I have some good news," announced Dolly. "We had some high rollers in today who tipped really well. I can pay you everything I owe."

Shelly took the money from Dolly, counted it, and then looked over at Zoom and I warily.

"Don't allow no pets in the motel," she said.

"Shelly, this is my friend Mr Westergaard," said Dolly. "He's a pilot! And, Mr Westergaard, this is my daughter Holly."

"Pleased to meet you, Shelly, I said. "No need for concern, though. I'm just passing through and won't be staying overnight. My furry pal here can stay in the car until I'm ready to leave."

Shelly just nodded and turned away to answer a ringing phone.

I peeked into the baby basket and was rewarded with the sight of a tiny blonde haired muffin, sleeping the sleep of the innocent.

Dolly carried her child and led us out of the small office and down the way towards her rented room. I stopped to tuck Zoom in the Subaru and locked the door.

"Won't be long," I promised him.

Dolly let me in her room, and I gave her some more advice while she busily packed her meager belongings into soft carryall bags.

"I don't mean to tell you what to do, Dolly. But I've traveled a great deal and have learned some hard lessons of my own. Remember the things I've told you, and you'll have a good chance of succeeding," I said.

"Amos," said Dolly, "I've never met a man like you. You've risked your safety, given me a lot of money, a new start for me and my baby, and asked for nothing but a ride out of town. Anyone else would've wanted the money. Or something," she added with a knowing look.

"Miss Barton, you're pretty as a summer day at the beach," I said. "And can turn any male head you've a mind to. But the truth is, I'm in love with another," I confessed.

"But, like, she wouldn't know if we, ah..."

"Yeah. But it wouldn't make it right," I said.

Dolly Barton thought about that for a minute.

"I think you just raised the bar for me, Amos."

"Dolly, you're pretty, single, and have a gorgeous baby girl. There's plenty of good guys out there who'd be thrilled to be your life partner. Just remember that you mostly won't find them in pool halls and beer joints. Make it a point to associate yourself with quality people. They'll value you in return, and you'll find you and your baby being nurtured by people you can count on instead of life's losers."

"I need to mend some fences with my parents," said Dolly.

"Take it slowly, and they'll come around. They won't be able to resist their granddaughter. Just let them see you're getting your life together and living responsibly. You'll do fine," I said.

"Time to go," said Dolly.

Chapter 30

"Don't drive into the Pirates Cove entrance, Dolly. Stop and let us out a block or so past it. I don't want anyone seeing this car on the hotel security cameras," I said.

"Always looking ahead, aren't you Amos?"

"I'm a pilot, and we pilots HATE surprises."

"You're also a kind man, Amos Westergaard. I won't forget you. And when Holly's old enough to understand, I'll tell her about the traveler who wandered into our lives and gave us a hand when everything seemed lost."

"You just get yourselves safely to Portland. And leave me a voice mail message letting me know you've arrived okay," I said, handing Dolly my business card.

"Will do."

Dolly pulled over to the side of the road to let us off. I retrieved Zoom and waved goodby. A farewell beep of the horn, and they were gone.

"Well little buddy, let's get ourselves out of this place,"

I said to Zoom.

I skirted the perimeter of the hotel parking lot and walked with purpose over to the airstrip. It was late in the afternoon, and I was anxious to make good our getaway.

Cessna One Sierra Tango was tied down right where I'd left her earlier. My spirits sank when I saw her nosewheel was flat as a pancake.

The thought came to me that this might've been deliberate. Petty revenge courtesy of Stewart Thistlebane? Perhaps.

I unlocked the cockpit and deposited Zoom in his customary place. Then I went around to the small cargo hold and retrieved a plastic emergency tool box.

There was, I reasoned, a chance that someone had simply let the air out of the tire, rather than having punctured it. I had a small hand pump that would allow me to test that theory. Pumping up the nosewheel wouldn't take long, and I had a pressure gauge that would tell me pretty quick what the story was.

Vigorously working the hand pump, I glanced around and noted that the sun was starting to set. We really needed to leave. It's not that I can't fly at night, it's just that I don't care to if I can avoid it.

I disconnected the hand pump from the tire valve and then began my walk around and standard pre-flight routines. I was particularly worried about the fuel, because if it'd been contaminated that changed everything. But after rocking the wings and draining a little from the sumps, the gas at least appeared normal. Noting no other discrepancies, I went back to check the air pressure in the nose wheel. I noted with relief that, according to the pressure gauge, the tire seemed to be holding up just fine. I stowed my little toolbox back in the hold, locked the hatch and then climbed into the cockpit.

Flipping on the master switch, I was just about to twist the ignition key when I had a premonition that something wasn't right. I couldn't explain it. I shut off the electrical current and climbed out again.

Raising Spirits

On the second walk around I did a really careful check of the control surfaces. The ailerons, flaps, and rudder all appeared to move freely. When I checked the elevator, I found a nasty little surprise waiting for me that I'd missed the first time around. Someone had removed the retaining nut and cotter pin from the pushrod assembly. And had then reconnected the elevator with what appeared to be a couple of winds of ordinary sewing thread. A shiver went down my spine. Somebody had been too smart by half. Ninety nine times out of a hundred I'd have missed this. I usually just moved the rudder up and down, and reached under to check the pushrod without actually seeing it. When that thread broke away, either on takeoff or during flight, the results would be catastrophic and lethal.

I was really angry but told myself to focus. I needed to find a way to get Zoom and I out of there, and quickly.

Retrieving the plastic tool box again, I took stock of what I had in the way of stray nuts, bolts, and fasteners. About twenty minutes later I'd fashioned a connection link of sorts that I felt might hold. It wasn't much to stake one's life on, but remaining where we were wasn't an option either.

After checking the nose wheel pressure one last time, I hauled myself back into the cockpit, connecting my seatbelt and shoulder harness.

Yelling "clear!" out the window, I fired up the engine and began to taxi. Stopping at the turnout area off the end of the runway, I did an engine run up and carefully scanned all the dials. Everything in the green, and the engine ran smoothly giving me no hint of fuel contamination.

"Lord, watch over us," I said, sending up a quick one just before I sent us blasting down the runway.

I rotated the nose quickly off the short strip and we were once again back in the air where we belonged. The elevator seemed to be working and the emergency fix holding. I turned us downwind and eased us into a more gentle climb just as the sun was disappearing beneath the horizon.

The next order of business was figuring out where we were going. I got on the radio and after a few fits and starts managed to raise the flight service people in Salt Lake City. The reports weren't good. A low pressure system was moving down from the north. Twin Falls was already reporting rain and lightning activity. Elko (behind us) was 'not recommended' citing high winds and blowing debris. Scanning my navigation chart, an idea began to form.

"Salt Lake, One Sierra Tango requesting most current weather in Ely," I said.

"One Sierra Tango, Ely AWOS reports clear, winds light and variable out of the northwest."

"Roger, Salt Lake. Looks like that's our destination. I need to make a precautionary landing as soon as possible," I said.

I filed us direct to Ely, arranging for flight following along the way just in case we had any further difficulties. About an hour later and with fuel running low, the little desert community of Ely came into view on the horizon. By now it was well after dark, but I could easily see the rotating airport beacon flashing south of town.

"Salt Lake, Cessna One Sierra Tango, over...."

"Cessna One Sierra Tango, Salt Lake, go ahead..."

"Cessna One Sierra Tango has the Ely airport in sight. Request any available weather or landing advisory, over..."

"Cessna One Sierra Tango, the Ely AWOS still reporting clear, winds light and variable. Notam indicates right traffic for runway two-seven."

"Roger that, Salt Lake. Looks like we're going to be okay. Thanks for keeping an eye on us," I said. "We're going to descend for landing shortly and I'll lose radio contact with you," I said.

"Cessna One Sierra Tango, roger that. Remember to call us and close your flight plan on arrival..."

"Cessna One Sierra Tango, roger, thank you, out...." I said.

Glancing over my shoulder at Zoom in the backseat, I noted he was fast asleep and obviously unconcerned.

I reduced power to the engine and began a gradual descent to pattern altitude. Switching the radio over to Ely's unicom frequency, I listened and heard nothing.

Ely radio, this is Cessna One Sierra Tango, inbound for landing Ely. If anyone's down there, request landing advisory, over...."

A few seconds later, I heard a female voice.

"Cessna calling Ely, this is Dutchess two niner seven. The airport is closed. We just landed on two-seven, right traffic. Winds calm."

"Dutchess two niner seven, thank you very much," I said. "Ely radio, Cessna One Sierra Tango entering a right downwind for landing runway two-seven."

I reduced the engine RPM's little more, lowered the flaps a notch, turned on my landing lights, and began a careful descent. Night flights always increase what pilots call the 'pucker factor,' and this one was no exception. A nice, well coordinated approach is the trick to night landings.

I radioed my position again as I turned onto the base leg, and lowered the flaps another notch.

"Ely radio, Cessna One Sierra Tango is on a one mile final, landing runway two seven, Ely."

By now I was fairly confident the elevator connection would hold, but just the same I flared gently as the runway numbers flashed beneath me.

My trusty airplane kissed the runway and rolled out, giving me every indication the nose wheel was still inflated. Life was good.

"Ely radio, Cessna One Sierra Tango is clear of runway two-seven, Ely," I said.

Breathing a huge sigh of relief, I taxied off in search of the transient aircraft tie downs. Finding an open spot not far from the FBO office, I pulled in slowly and cut power to the electrical panel and then the engine. The Dutchess pilot was right. There wasn't anyone around; the airport was deserted this time of night.

Opening the pilot's side window, I just sat there quietly for a couple of minutes. It had been a very long day, and our departure from Reno that morning felt like something long in the past. By now Dolly Barton and her girl child would be far away from danger, or so I fervently hoped. Next order of business was food, a shower, and bed for the night.

I flipped open my cell phone and scanned the numbers stored on it. Finding the one I wanted, I punched the buttons and got a satisfying ring tone.

"Ely Sunrise Bed and Breakfast."

"Elizabeth, it's Amos Westergaard," I said.

"Amos! You RODENT! It's been over a year since you've been to see us!"

"Well, I'm trying to make amends," I said, laughing. "Listen, I know it's late, but Zoom and I just flew in on a wing and a prayer. Would you have a room for us tonite?"

"Is the Pope a Catholic? We ALWAYS have room for you Amos! How soon can you get here?" asked Elizabeth excitedly.

"Ah, that's something of a problem," I said. "We just landed at the Ely airport, and there's nobody around."

"Never you mind," said Elizabeth. "I'll send Terry to fetch you. He'll meet you in front of the terminal building in about fifteen minutes."

"Liz, you're a gem," I said, meaning it.

"Just you remember that," she said, hanging up.

Next I dialed the FAA to report a safe arrival and close out our flight plan. Zoom was wanting out, and it occurred to me that he probably needed to relieve himself.

"Little buddy, we made it again," I said, letting him hop down onto the tarmac.

The Ely airport was serenely quiet. I paused briefly to admire the stars twinkling in the heavens. A gentle desert breeze caressed my cheek. Scooping up Zoom with my left hand and grabbing my overnight bag with the right, I began a slow trek toward the street.

Chapter 31

Some kind soul had thoughtfully placed a park bench in front of the airport terminal building. Zoom and I were sitting there quietly when a roving police cruiser appeared and stopped in front of us.

"Everything okay here?" asked the cop inside.

"Just fine," I said. "Waiting for a ride. They're on their way."

The cop nodded and drove on.

A few minutes later a gray Ford Explorer showed up. I waved, and the driver flashed his lights.

"Well, look what the cat drug in!" yelled the driver.

"Hey! Better watch that, mister!" I yelled back.

"Amos, it's good to see you," said Terry Portola, laughing. "And Zoom too!"

"Good to see you too, Terry," I said, sticking out my hand.

With Zoom and my bag safely riding in back, I hopped into the front seat.

"Um, Terry, we haven't eaten. Know anyplace still open

where I can at least get a sandwich?"

"No worries, old friend. I smoked a turkey yesterday. Plenty of leftovers at the house."

A long day full of uncertainties and danger was coming to an end, I thought to myself. And here we were in a safe haven, among friends. I looked out at the night sky and sent up another short prayer of thanks.

Elizabeth and Terry Portola own and operate the Ely Sunrise B & B. It's a good partnership they have. Elizabeth's a fastidious housekeeper and world class baker. Terry keeps track of reservations, welcomes guests, and performs whatever building maintenance the large two story refuge requires. And if that isn't enough, they raise Alpacas for the wonderful cashmere-like fleece the curious critters provide.

"Thanks for coming to get us," I said. "I'd have called sooner, but until a couple of hours ago I had no plans to be here."

"Somebody else's loss is our gain, then," said Terry. "Elizabeth's all excited you're staying. I'm really glad you made it in to see us again."

Elizabeth Portola was waiting on the porch when we drove up. Eschewing her husband and I, she opened the rear passenger door and extracted Zoom.

I looked over at Terry.

"Well, she always did like Zoom best, you know," he said, deadpan.

"Amos Westergaard, shame on you! I'll bet poor Zoom hasn't been fed, has he?" demanded Elizabeth.

"Truth be known, neither one of us has eaten," I said.

"Shame on you," she repeated.

Terry laughed and we all went into the house.

"Come on back to the kitchen RIGHT NOW," ordered Elizabeth.

Ten minutes later Zoom and I were dining like royalty on

delicately smoked turkey slices. And for me, Elizabeth also produced some freshly baked dinner rolls and a green salad with an herb seasoned dressing. I swear the woman's a magician in the kitchen.

"Beginning to feel some life comin' back into me," I said, now fully fueled and spirits rising.

Zoom was looking better too, I noticed. He'd knocked off an unusually large amount of smoked turkey, and was busy washing his face as cats do.

"Coffee?" asked Elizabeth.

"No thanks," I said. "But if you have any green tea, that'd be nice."

"Coming right up."

"Place is looking right smart," I said to Terry.

"Thanks. We've changed several things since you were here last. I just finished the big deck out back this past spring. Visitors enjoy sitting there and watching our Alpacas with the gorgeous mountain view in the background."

"How's your boy?" I asked.

"Jake graduated from college this year. Working at one of the mining operations up in Battle Mountain. Operates that giant machinery they use nowadays. I think he's found himself a woman, but he's being kind of quiet about that."

"Doing a man's job, sounds to me like," I said quietly.

"Wish he wasn't so far away," said Elizabeth sadly.

We talked late into the night, just old friends getting caught up on events. Terry eventually escorted Zoom and I up to our room. I took a quick shower and collapsed on the antique featherbed, totally spent.

Chapter 32

The local bird population began chirping earlier that next morning than I would've preferred. I rolled over and tried to go back to sleep, but the aroma of freshly baked pastries kept tickling my nostrils. Elizabeth was obviously busy downstairs in the kitchen. Zoom was no where to be seen; the odds favored him being down there supervising. Surrendering to the inevitable, I got up and trudged off to the bathroom.

Showered, shaved, and now wearing clean attire, things were looking up. Before heading downstairs for coffee I made a few phone calls. First in line was the Ely FBO, in order to plead the case for my airplane. The dispatch lady said she'd put us on her list for refueling as soon as the crew came back. Then she transferred my call to the local airframe mechanic (who just happened to be her son). I told him about the emergency patchwork job I'd done and the need for a proper repair with authorized parts. He said it probably wouldn't be any big deal, but he couldn't get to it before this afternoon. Two other planes waiting ahead of me. I gave him the number of the B & B, asking that he call me when he was finished or to let me know if there was any unexpected difficulty.

Next I called Bernie the Attorney. No, the insurance company hadn't settled my claim yet. They were still investigating, whatever THAT meant. And Zoom and I were still not welcome at CID Studios. The good news was, they hadn't sued. So far.

Saving the best for last, I dialed the private number of Cyndi Cheyenne. I got her voice mailbox, as I expected I would.

"Good morning gorgeous," I said after the beep. "I'm in Ely, staying at a fine old country inn. Missing you very much and wish you were here to share breakfast. Zoom's fine too. He's downstairs being pampered and adored by the proprietors. My airplane's being serviced, so I'll probably be here all day. Call me if you have time. Love you....."

After that I opened the drapes and was rewarded with a magnificent view of the mountains to the west. A few clouds hung around here and there, but it looked like it was going to be a pleasant and sunny fall day.

Following my nose down to the kitchen, I found Elizabeth Portola busy making her special cinnamon and almond bear claw rolls.

"Morning, Amos!" she said cheerily. "Coffee's ready; grab a mug there off the rack."

I poured myself a steaming cup, added a little creme, and sucked it down greedily.

"Seen Zoom?" I asked, the caffeine beginning to do its job.

"In the drawing room. Being fawned over by a couple of the guests. He's famous, you know!" said Elizabeth, giggling.

"Zoom the Wonder Cat never misses an opportunity to perform for an audience," I said merrily. "Look up 'ham' in the dictionary and you'll find a picture of Zoom."

"Well, we're happy to have him here," proclaimed Elizabeth.

"Going to be a pretty day," I said.

"This is my favorite time of year," said Elizabeth. "The weather's fine; we're not quite so busy and I can take a little more time to enjoy things."

"Where's Terry?" I asked.

"Out back in the garage. Working on my car."

"Wonder if he needs any help?" I asked. "Feels like forever since I did any honest work."

"Not until after you've eaten," said Elizabeth. "Peek in the oven. I saved breakfast for you. Everyone else ate long ago."

I peeked, and found a plate of heuvos rancheros waiting for me. Accompanying them were refried beans topped with jack cheese along with a generous dollop of steamed brown rice.

Elizabeth dropped a fresh bear claw on my plate and pointed me towards the kitchen table.

"Oh, yummm!" I said. "How'd you know this is one of my favorite breakfasts?"

"Zoom told me."

I laughed, and began happily wolfing down a VERY fine breakfast.

"You're looking better this morning, Amos," said Elizabeth. "I swear you looked about done in last night."

"Yesterday was one of those days that really tests a person," I said. "But it all worked out okay. And having you and Terry waiting at the end of it all helped more than you can know," I added.

"Just see that you don't stay away so long next time."

"I'll take that to heart, Elizabeth. By the way, it looks like Zoom and I are temporarily grounded. Plane won't be ready until later today. Can we stay over again tonight?"

"That would make me very happy, Mr Westergaard. You'll be here to enjoy afternoon tea with us then?"

"It would be my pleasure."

After rinsing my cup and plate in the sink, I wandered out to the garage. There I found Terry's legs sticking out from underneath Elizabeth's Chevy.

"Need a hand?" I asked. "I make a fair tool passer. Or at least I used to."

"Just changing the oil," answered Terry. "But if you could hand me a filter wrench, it'd be good."

I dug a filter wrench out of a toolbox sitting nearby and passed it under the chassis to an oily, waiting hand.

"Thanks. You know how it goes. These filters are supposed to be hand tightened, but sometimes they just don't want to come off when their time's up."

"You using a synthetic motor oil now?" I asked.

"Yep! Costs a little more, but the cars get better gas mileage with it. Easier starts in cold weather."

"Yeah, that's what I found, too," I said.

"Okay, that oughta do it," said Terry. "Can you slide the oil tub out from under the car?"

I did so gently, managing to avoid slopping any of the old, dirty sludge onto the concrete floor. Terry crawled out from under his wife's car and began pouring fresh new oil into the engine.

"That ought to do it for a while longer," he announced. "Climb in there and fire up the engine, will you Amos? Let her idle for mebbe a minute, then shut her down."

I turned the key as requested. The engine caught, clattering a bit until the fresh oil made the rounds, and then smoothed out. We both listened. Neither of us noticed anything amiss. I shut it down and got out.

"Thanks, Amos," said Terry as he drained the old oil out of the tub into a waiting storage bucket.

"Sometimes a third hand is useful, huh?" I said, chuckling.

"You know it! Listen, today's my day for tramping out along the creek. Wanna go along?"

"Uh, you figure you could bag us a couple more of Elizabeth's bear claw rolls before we go?" I asked anxiously.

"Have to be stealthy about it," answered Terry with a grin. "But it's possible."

I followed Terry back into the main house where he

cleaned up and swiped us a couple of warm pastries from a cooling rack on top of the stove. From there we returned to the garage where Terry emerged with a smallish nylon backpack slung over his shoulder.

"Lead on," I said.

It was a nice morning for a walk. We trudged past the Alpaca pens where most of the gentle creatures seemed to be catching a morning nap. There was a gentle breeze, and the sun felt good on my face. About a half mile later we came upon a meandering creek with its crystal clean mountain waters running freely.

"You own this too?" I asked.

"Nah. This is BLM land," said Terry. "Anyone can come back here, but very few ever do."

We walked along a while longer, neither saying much. Just two friends enjoying the sound of the running waters and the occasional cry of a bird overhead. Once we stopped for a moment and watched a red fox drink from the opposite bank. He gave us a wary look, then quickly dashed away into the brush.

You ever get the fever?" asked Terry, pulling a couple of well-worn pans out of his backpack.

"Gold fever?" I said, laughing. "No, can't say as I have. Been a long time since I did any panning. There anything in this creek?"

"Sometimes yes, sometimes no," answered Terry. "You know how it is."

"Yeah, gold's a hard find," I said. "But it can be fun, huh?"

"I've taken a few thousand dollars in small nuggets out of this creek in the years since Elizabeth and I moved here. There's a vein somewhere, but I've never found it. Probably just as well. Word gets out about something like that and pretty soon you've got people tramping all over."

"Seems to me you've got a pretty good life here," I said philosophically.

"I'm happy. So's Elizabeth. The boy's grown and seems to

be doing fine. The B & B brings in enough to keep the bills paid. The Alpacas are just icing on the cake."

"So, like, no need to be a gold magnate, eh?" I asked.

"Nope. No desire for that at all. Still, I like coming here to pan every now and then. Either that or fly fish. There'll be good trout fishing here in the spring. Elizabeth's got a thing she does with trout meat, almonds, and spices inside a thin crust. The guests love 'em."

"She's a good woman," I said, nodding.

"That she is. Can't imagine my life without her."

We continued panning, with Terry occasionally finding a little color in the bottom of his pan. I wasn't even finding color. But then my luck changed.

"Well, what do you know about that?" I said, smiling as I looked at the bottom of my pan.

"Waaa hooo! Look at that! You hit the jackpot, boy!" exclaimed Terry excitedly.

Down in the bottom of my old pan among the other rock and debris were two plump gold nuggets smiling up at me. I picked them out and examined them critically.

"Think they're worth much?" I asked.

"They'll bring a little more than spot because they're big enough to be mounted. You're looking a six, maybe seven hundred dollars there, Amos."

"Beginner's luck," I said. "Well, nearly beginner, anyway."

I stuck the two nuggets in my shirt pocket, and the two of us continued panning for a while. Terry found some more tiny flecks of gold which he expertly plucked out of his pan with a pair of tweezers. I didn't find anything else.

After a while, Terry looked up. "You about ready to head back?" he asked.

"Yeah, I think so," I said. "Might be a message for me at the house. I left your phone number with the airframe mechanic. Asked him to leave word when he was finished."

"You staying here tonight though, right?"

"Yeah. I already promised your wife. Can you drop me off

at the airport in the morning?"

"No problem. Just say the word."

I took the two gold nuggets out of my pocket and looked them over again.

"Terry," I said, "I tell you what. You take these into the assayer's and get cash for them, okay? Tuck the money in your wallet and forget about it for a while. But when your boy Jake comes to visit and brings his lady friend, you scoot off and pick up a few bottles of Dom Perignon to celebrate with. Tell him Uncle Amos sends his regards."

"Amos, that's uncommonly generous," said Terry. "And Elizabeth will love it."

"Being uncommon is one of my guilty pleasures," I said with a grin.

Chapter 33

Terry dropped Zoom and I off at the Ely airport early the next morning. First stop was the FBO office to pay my fuel and repair bill. I found a rather stocky, slightly balding fellow sitting at the dispatch desk.

"Good morning," I said. "I'm Amos Westergaard."

"Will. Will Cameron," said the man, sticking out his hand. "We spoke on the phone yesterday. I'm the one who fixed your Cessna."

"Excellent!" I said, shaking his hand. "Are we good to go?"

"All set. It was just a minor repair. I also performed a general safety check of the other control surfaces and fuselage. Your ship appears to be in very good condition for her age."

"That's always good to hear," I said, handing over my Amex card.

Will Cameron slid my card thru the reader. A few seconds later the terminal began to hum and produced the usual invoice for my signature. Then another printer began to cycle and spit out a repair record for my maintenance log.

"Thank you, sir," said Will Cameron, handing me the paperwork. "Um, if you wouldn't mind, there's one more thing," he said, pulling out a well-worn copy of A Wanderer's Wisdom from a desk drawer. "My mother's a fan. I'd consider it a kindness if you'd autograph your book for her."

"Certainly," I said, by now used to this occurrence. "Lend me your pen."

We shook hands again, then Zoom and I headed out to reclaim our winged chariot. Cessna One Sierra Tango was standing there confidently, ready to take us wherever we needed to go.

Zoom hopped into his customary back seat digs to settle in while I performed the walk-around and pre-flight routines. Finding nothing amiss, I lit the fire in the engine and we were underway once again.

I circled around to gain a little altitude and then pointed the nose east towards the Schell Creek Range. A little while later we cruised through the gap in the Toyabe National Forest and crossed over into Utah. The sun was shining high overhead and it felt good to be at the controls again. I monitored the Flight Watch circuit and was advised of a good tailwind aloft. Ascending another couple of thousand feet, we were rewarded with an additional twenty knots of airspeed, gratis. The winds remained steady, and I was able to steer us safely into Colorado without having to refuel.

A little after one in the afternoon we received clearance into Walker Field, the fine little airport outside of Grand Junction. I landed, taxied over to the fuel pumps, and shut down the engine.

"Fill 'er up, please, with one hundred low-lead," I said to the lineman. "Is there a restaurant in the terminal?"

"Yessir. A really good one. Just inside the door and take the stairs to your right. If you want, just leave your plane here. I'll keep an eye on her while you eat."

"Thanks, that'll be fine," I said. "Be advised, my cat's asleep on the back seat."

The lineman nodded, and I walked across the ramp in search of a late lunch.

I like eateries in the smaller airports. They're almost always top drawer and feature home made specialties unlike the processed fast food one normally finds at the big international jet ports.

The Pegasus Café at Grand Junction proved to be no exception. I enjoyed a generous bowl of turkey-vegetable soup, followed by a delightful wedge of fresh blueberry pie.

"Anything else you'd like," asked my attentive waitress.

"Just a small amount of water - in a paper cup if you please. My cat's out in the plane and he'll want to wet his whistle before we take off," I explained.

"Aw, your kitty flies with you? That's sweet," said the young woman. "I'll be right back."

She quickly returned with my bill and a small cup of water with a lid over it. And yet another cup containing a few morsels of shredded chicken.

"Never knew a kitty yet that didn't like chicken," said my waitress, smiling.

"You've been very kind," I said. "My little pal will enjoy this."

I returned to my waiting aircraft, left the food and water for Zoom, then went in search of the lineman in order to pay for my fuel. A few minutes later we were waiting our turn for takeoff, being number three in line behind a Piper Seneca and an ancient Stearman.

So far we'd enjoyed good flying weather that day. But things were about to change. There was a report of moderate to severe turbulence over much of the Rocky Mountain area. The further east I flew, the worse it got. I listened in as other pilots in the area continue to file reports of turbulent air at various altitudes. There didn't seem to be any flight levels that were better than others. It was proving rough all over out there.

After about an hour of being bounced around, Zoom started to complain.

"Maaa-ow! Maaaa-ow!" he shrieked over the engine noise.

"Hang in there, little buddy!" I yelled back over my shoulder. "It'll be okay."

"Maaa-ow! Maaa-ow–ow-ow!"

I grabbed my navigation chart, beginning to consider Plan B. Most often, Plan B involved running for the barn when the weather turned unpleasant. Besides, we'd already made good progress for the day. No reason to push our luck.

Deciding on Eagle County airport near Vail, I called the Flight Service guys for a weather update.

"Cessna One Sierra Tango, Eagle County reporting partly cloudy with visibility ten to twelve. Winds are out of the north, with gusts to twenty knots."

"Denver Flight Service, roger gusts to twenty knots. I think that's where we're heading, then. Cessna One Sierra Tango thanks you. Out."

"Maaa-ow! Maaa-ow!"

"Okay, okay. I hear you. We'll be landing soon. Chill out," I yelled over my shoulder.

"Mrrrrrrrr-ow!"

The winds didn't seem die down any as I began my slow descent toward the airport. We continued getting buffeted and smacked around pretty good. I did the best I could to control the airplane, but it wasn't a pleasant ride at all.

Mercifully, there was little activity at the Eagle airport. With a generous amount of left rudder and a little extra airspeed, I touched down just past the runway numbers and rolled out safely.

"Cessna One Sierra Tango, welcome. Turn left at the next intersection. Contact ground on one three three point two," said the tower controller.

"We made it, little buddy! It's over!" I yelled over my shoulder at Zoom, who gave me a sour look.

It wasn't until after we'd taxied to the tiedown area and shut down that I discovered Zoom had tossed his lunch.

"Well, that's a first," I said to Zoom, who was looking embarrassed.

"Mrrrrr-eeew."

Chapter 34

Zoom and I had visited the Vail Grand Lodge a year or so previously and had enjoyed a pleasant stay. Rightly figuring I'd have no trouble getting a room during the early fall season, I called there first. The reservations clerk mentioned that my usual suite was available. I said that would be fine and asked to be picked up at the airport as soon as possible. She said the hotel limo would be around in about fifteen minutes.

I finished tying down the Cessna for the night and went inside the terminal to check in with the dispatcher and await our ride. Zoom was tired, cranky, and kept squirming on my arm as though he couldn't get comfortable.

"Just a little longer," I pleaded. "A nap, then a little food, and you'll be your old self again."

Vail is a spectacular sight in the fall. I marveled at the kaleidoscope of color on the trees as we rode into town. It was quite cool and there was a promise of winter in the late afternoon air.

The front desk clerk, a young Latina, welcomed the two of

us with a gracious smile and proceeded to register me in an efficient, practiced manner. By the time I got us upstairs to our suite, the drapes were already drawn open and my bag had been delivered.

I filled a small glass with Colorado Rocky Mountain water and set it down for Zoom. My little pal enjoyed a long drink, then immediately trotted into the bedroom where he settled atop the bed for some well-deserved slumber. I broke open a fresh bag of kibble and left it where Zoom would find it, knowing he'd want a snack upon awakening.

Admittedly, that pure, cold mountain water expertly quenches dehydration. I enjoyed a couple of glasses of it myself while gazing appreciatively at the mountain view from my balcony. After that I headed off to the bathroom to hit the shower and wash away the day's tension.

Toweling myself dry, I listened to the daily news on the television. It seemed a rather slow news day from the sound of it. Ah well. Who was it that opined "no news is good news?" I finished dressing and went downstairs.

The lounge at the Vail Grand Lodge is everything it should be. Open and airy with high vaulted ceilings, lots of intricate wood paneling, and sporting an exquisite stone fireplace complete with blazing logs. I took an empty table near the fire that also afforded a view of the approaching sunset through the patio glass.

A tall, leggy brunette approached.

"Good evening, sir," she said with an English accent that I couldn't quite place. "My name is Janet and I'll be serving you. What would your pleasure be?"

"Janet," I said, "I think I just want to relax and enjoy the fire for a while. I've been flying hard all day and, for the moment, I'd like a Perrier water with lime, if you please."

"Coming right up, sir," said Janet, who then scurried away.

The sun was fast dropping down behind the mountain, leaving a brilliant orange glow in its wake. Janet arrived with my drink.

"Here you are sir," she said, favoring me with a smile.

"I'm a guest in the hotel," I said. "Probably better if you run a tab for me," I said.

"Certainly, sir. I'll just need to see your room card."

I produced the card, which she ran through a portable scanner on her tray. Technology.

"Janet," I said, "I can't quite place your accent. It's not Brit, but neither is it Aussie."

"I'm from New Zealand," she said with a giggle.

"Ah! That explains it. From Auckland, perhaps?" I asked.

"Devonport," she said. "Most people have never heard of it."

"Ah, Devonport," I said with a grin. "Know it well. Fell in love there once, years ago. Took many a long walk, arm in arm, in the big park that overlooks the harbor. I remember a fish and chips venue there in the park. Best fish I ever ate. Not far from the fleet landing."

I looked up from my musing to see a tiny tear trickle down Janet's face as she struggled to maintain her composure.

"Forgive me, Mr Westergaard," she said. "My daddy used to take me for walks in that same park when I was just a little girl. He's gone now. I haven't thought of those happy days for a very long time."

"Forgive ME, Janet," I said. "I didn't mean to make you tear up. I'm no good at all when women cry," I added, feeling embarrassed.

"It's not your fault. I haven't been home in a long time. Just nature's way of reminding me of some things I'd stuffed into my mind's closet," said Janet, regaining her composure.

"How'd you come to be in Vail?" I asked.

"Came for the skiing, loved it, and stayed," she said. "I was thinking only a few days ago that I'd work through one more ski season, and then if nothing happened to change my mind, I'd fly home to New Zealand come next spring."

"Home is where your heart is," I said.

"Quite so," said Janet. "Excuse me, but I must get back to work...."

I was pondering that when a four piece combo arrived and took to the small stage adjacent to the bar. They were really quite good, playing a medley of smooth jazz designed to put weary travelers at ease. It seemed to work -at least on me.

Enjoying the fire and the music, I motioned to my server Janet.

"Janet, I don't really want to dine in the restaurant. Do they serve appetizers here in the lounge?" I asked hopefully. "I'm enjoying the lounge too much to leave for the restaurant."

"Certainly," she said. "Tonight's special features Thai spring rolls. They're stuffed with duck, and come with some light summer vegetables and a nice dipping sauce."

"Spring rolls are a favorite of mine," I said approvingly. "Um, is there any champagne? I'm not sure I want a whole bottle, though..."

"We have splits of chilled Perrier Jouet," said Janet.

"Excellent! That'll do nicely," I said.

Janet smiled at me again and then turned away. I continued listening to the music. There was now a fifth person on the stage, a pretty, animated blonde who began gently cooing the words to "Feverish Delights." The band backed her up skillfully and the people in the lounge applauded with a genuine enthusiasm.

The food arrived, expertly prepared and with a creative presentation. The Thai spring rolls were heaven on a plate. Delicate crust, beckoning aroma, and made with rare spices I could only guess at.

I sat there a while, just nibbling at the fine food and enjoying the music. A young woman carrying a martini with an olive in it sat down at the table next to mine. Designer dress, high heels, expert make up. An MBA on the prowl. She attempted to engage me in small talk. I smiled and was polite, but did not encourage her. She moved on.

Janet came back over to my table and asked how I was doing.

"Excellent!" I said. "The spring rolls are the best I've ever eaten."

"The chef will be pleased to hear that," she said.

"I need you to do a couple of things for me," I said. "Bring me a full sized, unopened bottle of this Perrier Jouet. Ask the chef to visit me. And then tally up my bill so's I can sign it."

"Done and done," said Janet.

A couple of minutes later she returned with the fresh bottle. I signed the bill, adding a generous tip.

"Thank you, Mr Westergaard. Hope to see you again," she said, obviously pleased.

I continued enjoying the band's repertoire and finished the remainder of my champagne.

A young Chinese fellow dressed in kitchen whites approached my table.

"Sir, I am Marcus Chin. You asked to see me?"

"Mr Chin, I am Amos Westergaard. Just wanted to thank you for a splendid effort. Your spring rolls are the best I've ever had anywhere in the world. You're a credit to chefs everywhere and a blessing to weary travelers," I said.

"Thank you VERY much, sir! Actually, the recipe is an ancient family tradition. I learned it from my venerable grandmother."

"Then my thanks to her, also."

"She'll be pleased to hear that, sir. She's very old, but still works in the family restaurant in San Francisco from time to time."

"Mr Chin, is cooking your calling, or are you just here as a ways to a means?" I asked.

"I truly enjoy working in the kitchen, sir. But all the same, I'd like to eventually try my hand at running my own place. You see, I'm the youngest of eight children. And while the family restaurant is always there, I'll be too old to care by the time management falls to me."

"I understand completely," I said. "One more question. Do you have a woman here?"

"Yes sir. Married five months ago. In fact my wife will be picking me up to take me home soon. She's in the process of completing a hospital internship here in Vail."

"Ah! Very good," I said. "It is my wish, then, for you to take this bottle of champagne home with you, along with my thanks," I said.

"My wife will like that very much," answered Chin, bowing slightly.

"A very good evening to you then," I said.

Chin smiled, bowed a little deeper, took the bottle, and returned to his duties in the kitchen. I dissected the last spring roll, extracted a few morsels of duck for Zoom, and returned upstairs to my suite.

Back in my room, I cracked the patio door an inch or so to let in the cool, sweet mountain air and then hand fed my little pal the delicate bits of duck I'd saved for him. Zoom was looking much better. I was feeling pretty good too, having dined exquisitely and with a half bottle of fine champagne sloshing around my insides.

I placed a call to the beautiful and wondrous Cyndi Cheyenne. She answered in person. We proceeded to talk as lovers do, well into the night.

Chapter 35

Zoom woke me early the next morning for no good reason that I could understand. I was sound asleep when he decided it was appropriate to hop upon my chest, hunker down, and stare at me until I began to stir.

"Okay, okay," I said. "I'm up. NOW what?"

I got no answer, but then I didn't really expect one. Sometimes there's a reason for this early morning reveille (like an empty kibble bowl) but other times it's just his way of getting the day started.

The room service operator recommended the day's morning special of freshly squeezed orange juice, a bacon-egg quiche, and coffee. I said that would do nicely and then went off to shower and shave. By the time I finished dressing, breakfast had been delivered. I turned on the television and listened to early news while I ate. Zoom went back to sleep on the bed.

The weather report didn't sound promising. A low pressure front was moving over the Rockies from up north. Rain, freezing rain, and snow were among the possible outcomes later in the day. I went downstair to the hotel business center to get an aviation weather forecast from the FAA over the internet.

I was surprised to find Janet, my waitress in the lounge the previous night on duty there in the business center.

"Good morning, Janet," I said.

"Well good morning, Mr Westergaard! Nice to see you again!" she exclaimed, giving me a genuinely warm smile.

"Working double shifts?" I asked.

"Regular attendant called in saying she couldn't make it. So the hotel asked me to fill in at the last minute. The job's not that strenuous compared to serving drinks in the lounge. And a girl can always use the extra money."

"I need to use one of the terminals," I said.

"Well, you can take your pick. They're all up and running except the one nearest the door."

"But first I'd like to wire some flowers," I said. "You can arrange that for me, right?"

"Certainly," answered Janet. "Piece of cake."

"Okay, I would like two dozen long stemmed red roses delivered to Miss Cyndi Cheyenne at the Half Moon Inn, Sausalito, California. Preferably late this afternoon or early evening."

"What would you like the card to say?" asked Janet.

"With love from Amos," I answered.

Janet nodded knowingly and picked up a telephone. I wandered over to the internet terminals and began my inquiries.

The weather picture appeared threatening. I didn't want to get stuck in Vail, and my beloved Cessna isn't designed or equipped for operating in extreme conditions. Zoom and I would be making a run for it, hoping to clear the Rockies before the storm hit later in the day.

I filed a flight plan online, knowing I'd probably have to

amend it from the air later. But it'd save time, and that's what I needed at the moment.

"Excuse me, Mr Westergaard?" asked a tall, patrician looking fellow in a hotel jacket.

"Guilty," I said.

"Sir, I'm Reginald Caruthers, the resort's general manager."

"Pleased to meet you, Reggie," I said, sticking out my hand.

Reggie looked pained at being addressed that way, but shook my hand anyway.

"Sir, I'd like to thank you for visiting us here once again, and ask if, in my official capacity there's anything I can do to improve our service on your behalf."

"Actually, there is," I replied. "Join me upstairs in my suite while I'm packing, and we'll talk. I'm pressed for time this morning. And, if you could notify the transportation desk I'll need a ride to the airport in about twenty minutes, that would help."

"I'll see to it right away, Sir," said Reggie, hustling off.

I went upstairs and began packing.

"Get ready, little buddy," I said to Zoom. "We're out of here shortly."

Zoom, rightly figuring that getting us underway was my job, simply rolled over and went back to sleep.

There was a knock at the door, and I admitted Reggie the manager.

"Mr Westergaard, the hotel limo will be waiting downstairs for you," he said.

"Thank you, Reggie. Always a pleasure doing business with people who know their jobs," I said.

Despite being addressed in such a familiar fashion, Reggie forced a smile.

"But there's two people here I want to single out," I said. "These are people of the sort every good organization looks for. They are superb at what they do, have a great attitude, and should be promoted to the extent you're able. If you're smart, you'll move them up in both pay and responsibility."

"Who are these people?" asked Reggie.

"The first one is a chef in your restaurant named Marcus Chin. He comes from a restaurant family in San Francisco. He's talented, creative, and quite articulate for such a young man."

"I know Chin," replied Reggie with a nod. "Has a good work ethic and understands the value of team playing."

"Take care of him," I said. "It'll be worth the investment."

"Who is the other person? You said there were two."

"The other is the young lady on duty in the business center this morning." Her name is Janet and she was my cocktail waitress in the lounge last night. She's smart, attractive, and very efficient. She's capable of a lot more. She'll stay through the upcoming ski season, but she's homesick. Give her a couple of weeks off when the snow melts along with a plane ticket home as a special thanks for a job superbly done. And then offer her a better position. She'd be dynamite as manager of conventions, special affairs, or something along those lines."

"Mr Westergaard, I thank you very much for these recommendations. I assure you I'll take a special interest in these people. It's not often that a hotel guest will take the time to discuss such matters."

"Reggie, I learned a long time ago the value of surrounding myself with the right people. And I make it a point to nudge exceptional individuals along any chance I get. Frankly, it pleases me to do so," I said solemnly.

"May I help you downstairs?" asked Reggie, seeing I had finished packing my belongings.

"That's very kind of you, sir," I said with a nod.

I roused Zoom for the trip to the airport, and then Reggie escorted us downstairs to the waiting limo.

Chapter 36

It was already slightly overcast when we departed the Eagle County airport near Vail. Cessna One Sierra Tango, being full of fuel (and therefore heavy) struggled mightily to gain altitude in the thin Colorado mountain air. It was going to be slow going, and I fervently hoped we'd make good enough time to evade the approaching weather.

Eventually though, we chugged past the little airport near Golden and then the big new Denver airport to the south. I breathed a sigh of relief, knowing that if nothing else we'd avoided being grounded in Vail and perhaps having to deal with early season snow or ice.

But the weather system charging down from the north wasn't going to be denied; that much was clear. I kept pressing eastward, having to change altitude every now and again to satisfy minimum requirements. But it was becoming obvious that at some point soon we'd have to set down and wait it out. By now the airports behind me at Denver and Colorado Springs were both reporting rain and marginal visibility at best.

And the weather reports that the Denver Flight Service people were occasionally feeding me weren't encouraging. It was time to start looking for a safe harbor.

"Denver Flight Service, Cessna One Sierra Tango requests current weather at Burlington, over...."

"Cessna One Sierra Tango, Burlington currently reporting overcast with visibility 3-4 miles...."

We landed safely at the Burlington Municipal Airport in eastern Colorado about a half hour later just as it started to rain. I tied us down, registered at the FBO, and rented us the only car available.

Burlington is a small farming community and the hotel pickings were predictably modest. As we drove through town with the windshield wipers fully engaged, it became clear that there weren't any of the larger national hotels, only smaller motel/coffee shop accommodations. The trick was going to be finding one that would accept Zoom without my getting drowned during the hunt. Zoom positively HATES being rained on. And I had no rain gear either, although my leather flight jacket would keep me at least partially dry.

I stopped at a place calling itself the Red Brick Inn and walked inside, leaving the car running. A fat fellow wearing overalls was sitting behind the counter watching television. He didn't look up when I came in. I stood there for a minute, and then finally rang the tiny bell for service.

"Yeah?" the man said, not even looking up.

"Would you have a room for the night?" I asked.

"Fifty five dollars, plus tax," was all he said.

"Do you allow cats to stay in the room?"

He finally looked up, annoyed. "Ninety eight dollars if you have a pet," he said.

I was feeling a little irritated myself by now.

"No thanks," I said, walking out. He continued staring at the tv screen while I drove away.

Okay, it wasn't the money. It was the attitude. I just can't abide shabby treatment.

I had just about run out of town. The last place that presented itself on the far eastern side of Burlington was the Silverside Motel. It appeared to be fairly well maintained and there was a small restaurant next to it.

"Yessir," said the woman at the front desk. "Can I help you?"

"Save me from drowning," I pleaded. "Would you have a room available for tonight?"

"Certainly," she replied, giggling. "How many people?"

"Just myself and my cat," I said. "Is that acceptable?"

"Yes," she replied. "But we require an extra twenty dollar deposit if you have pets. It's refunded when you check out as long as there's no damage to the room."

"A sensible policy," I said. "My furry pal's a seasoned traveler though, so you'll not have any problems."

"I have a nice room just down the main corridor with a king sized bed."

"I'm sure that'll be just fine," I said as I handed her my credit card.

"So, just tonight then?" she asked.

"Far as I know," I said. "Sort of depends on the weather, though. We're flying, and our plane's over at the airport until the rain lifts. I'll have a better idea of how things will be in the morning."

The room turned out to be surprisingly comfortable and thoughtfully furnished without that plastic composite motif that seems to have swept into so many of the nation's inns. I went back out to the car to retrieve Zoom and my overnight bag. He seemed relieved we were stopping and cowered a bit when thunder boomed out overhead.

"Relax pal, we got it made," I said.

Zoom wasn't convinced and buried his head in my shoulder, shivering slightly. All was forgiven once we were inside the warm, safe building and he was being cooed over by the desk clerk.

"Boy, aren't you the handsome fellow?" she asked.

"Mrrrr-wow!"

Some things never change.

Chapter 37

It continued raining throughout the rest of the day. I got up early the next morning, peered out through the drapes, and noted it was still coming down in buckets. Didn't look like we were going anywhere today. At least not by plane.

I called the Flight Service Station and asked for the morning aviation weather. The good news was, while it was still raining throughout most of Colorado, the forecast was for partial clearing sometime during the evening. If that prognostication held up, we could make good our departure early the next day.

The lady on duty at the hotel's front desk seemed pleased when I called to say we'd be staying over another night. With nothing better to do, I went back to bed and dozed off for a while.

Eventually, hunger conspired to get me up and moving in search of calories. By now there was a lull in the rain and I managed to get next door to the coffee shop without getting drenched. I asked for a couple of french dip beef sandwiches and cole slaw to go. And quaffed down a large orange juice while I waited.

Safely back in the hotel room, I turned on the local jazz station and read USA Today while I ate. Zoom came in, pleaded for a couple of bites of the roast beef, then returned to his pursuit of the ultimate nap.

I checked my voice mailbox and retrieved two messages. One was from Dolly Barton reporting that she and her baby had made it safely to Portland. The other was a promising, very personal communique from the fair Cyndi Cheyenne.

Finished with the newspaper, I turned on the television. I watched two movies, one of which I'd seen at least twice already. The rain came and went throughout the day. I was bored out of my skull, but there was nothing to be done about it.

Finally about five thirty I wandered back over to the next door coffee shop and took a seat. The daily dinner special was baked cod, which turned out to be most excellent. A little salad combined with a couple of crusty rolls and I was good to go.

"Yeah, but go where?" I thought to myself. The weather appeared to be clearing, but Burlington wasn't exactly a hotbed of night activity. With a sigh, I picked up my dinner check and headed towards the cashier.

Walking out of the front door, I noticed a large poster fixed to the glass that I hadn't seen earlier.

Two Nights Only! Brother Stowe's Traveling Salvation Show! Featuring the Shiloh Sisters Choir! Under the Big Tent! County Fairgrounds, etc, etc...

I began to get an idea.

The lady tending the hotel desk was helpful.

"You know how to get back to the airport, right?" she asked.

I nodded.

"Just keep heading south on airport drive past the terminal about a mile. You'll see a sign - turn right and the county fairgrounds are maybe a mile further. You won't have any trouble finding it."

"Thanks," I said.

"You going to the big revival meeting there tonight?" she asked. "It's a big deal. We'll be full here in the hotel afterwards."

"One of the benefits of being something of a nomad is experiencing new sights and sounds," I said. "Besides, I'm naturally curious."

I went back to the room and roused Zoom.

"Hey little buddy! Get yourself together. We're going out tonight."

Zoom somehow got the message, and began the laborious process of washing himself as cats do.

Picking up my cell phone, I made some more calls to those in the west coast pacific time zone.

"Amos my boy!" cried Bernie the Attorney. "Where on the planet are you?"

"Beautiful downtown Burlington, Colorado, pal. Stuck here while the rain passes through," I said.

"Well, the good news is, the insurance company settled on your, ah, former pad down in Arizona. Courtney deposited the check in your trust account yesterday. The bad news is, you and Zoom still aren't welcome at CID Studios."

"Win some, lose others," I said.

"Listen, I have a client waiting," said Bernie.

"Catch up with you later," I said, terminating the call.

Cyndi Cheyenne didn't answer the phone in her hotel room. I dialed her cell phone and left a cheery message for her to retrieve later.

Then I dialed up Caesars in Tahoe, hoping to catch Curly Mike on duty. I was curious to know how his niece was recovering after that gruesome auto accident. The transportation captain told me Curly Mike was off on assignment, but that Shannon continued to progress well according to what he'd been told.

"That's excellent news," I said. "Please tell Curly Mike I called."

"I'll be sure to do that, sir."

I terminated the call, and looked over a Zoom.

"Saddle up, pal," I told him. "We're movin' out!"

My little pal was so excited that he managed a slow yawn.

Chapter 38

The rain had eased up and there were a few patches of blue to be seen in the late afternoon skies. Looked like we'd be getting out of there in the morning for sure.

On the way to the county fairground I stopped at the airport to check the tie downs on the Cessna and advise the dispatcher of our planned departure in the morning.

"She's fueled and ready," said the woman behind the desk. "Ready when you are."

I nodded, returned to the rental car, and headed off towards the fairgrounds.

The lady at our hotel had given me good directions and I found the place without getting lost in the process.

Honestly, I can't say I was prepared for what I found. The tent that had been erected for the revival meeting was simply ENORMOUS. I hadn't seen anything this big since I was a kid at the Ringling Brothers Circus. The tent would seat several hundred, easily. There were acres of cars, busses, and vans already parked. I found a spot out on the perimeter, grabbed

Zoom, and locked the car doors. It looked like we were a little late; there were few people about and I could hear music coming from inside the tent. With Zoom riding on my arm, I walked to the main entrance and peeked in.

It looked like it might be standing room only. I saw a great sea of humanity already in place, most of whom were busy cheering and clapping to the music. I stood there for a moment taking it all in, allowing my eyes to adjust to the dim light and listening to the music.

There were six women on stage, all blonde and dressed in pale turquoise. I presumed these were the Shiloh Sisters. They were augmented by a four piece band that clearly had done this gig a time or two before. Their numbers might've been small, but they'd managed to get the crowd seriously worked up.

The music began to tone down, and the Shiloh Sisters did one of the sweetest renditions of 'Amazing Grace' that I'm ever likely to hear. The crowd applauded politely and Brother Stowe walked on stage.

Stowe is a big man (picture the late John Wayne) with a commanding voice to match. He wore a simple black suit, white shirt, and a plum colored tie. A craggy face, medium length jet black hair and expertly trimmed mustache completed the look . I stood there listening for a while as he taught from the bible, exhorting the people to eschew the things of this world and seek after the Lord. It was an old theme, but then things of quality have little fear of time. Despite all the people (and LOTS of children) in attendance, the tent was quiet except for Stowe's great voice ringing out from the stage. Brother Stowe knew how to work an audience.

I continued to listen while walking slowly down the main aisle and watching for an empty seat. Every now and then a child or two would spot Zoom riding on my arm.

They'd poke a parent, point at us, and I'd smile. Soon I was near the bottom end of the aisle, close to the stage, and still no place to sit. I was about to turn around and trek back up towards the entrance when Brother Stowe stopped me dead in my tracks.

"Brother," he said, pointing a long finger directly at me, "I sense the Spirit is strong in you. Would you join me here and perhaps share a word with us?"

I froze like a deer in the headlights. I could hear my heart throb and felt the blood rushing. But then Zoom began to purr, easing my tension. A cranial lightbulb switched on and an idea formed.

The drummer in the band beat some soft licks as I mounted the stage. The crowd began to murmur. More kids saw Zoom, and I could hear their tiny, delighted voices.

"Look at the kitty, mama! He's PRETTY!"

I shook hands with Brother Stowe who handed me his microphone. The drummer took his cue and the music began to fade.

Chapter 39

"Brother Stowe," I said, "I am honored. Ladies and gentlemen, how about a round of applause for Brother Stowe, the beautiful Shiloh Sisters, and all these talented musicians here with us tonight!"

The crowd stood, clapping and whistling enthusiastically. The Shiloh sisters beamed and the band members beat out a few licks. Brother Stowe's head was bowed and his eyes were closed, as if in silent prayer.

"I have a few words for everyone here tonight," I said. First, I'd like all the married men here to raise their hands for me."

About two out of three men in attendance raised their hands.

"Okay, keep 'em up for a minute, please," I said.

There were a few smiles, and a low murmur as everyone looked around.

"Husbands," I said, "you are to love your wives. Not the honeys you see on television. Not the fashion models in magazines or those in the movies. Not the cocktail waitress at the local bar. Love your wives even as Christ loves you.."

There were a few hoots from the crowd, but I continued unabated.

"Now I'd like all the married women here to raise their hands for just a moment," I said.

"Ladies, respect and honor your husband, for he is the head of the household. When you open your mouths, let wisdom and kindness fall out of it. Not the shrieks and complaints of old wet hens."

At that there was great laughter and some good natured rib-poking.

"Fathers," I said, "it's up to you to set a good example to your sons. They need you to teach them HOW to BE men. If they don't learn it from you, they'll get it wrong from television, movies, and such. Too many boys today grow up and have no real concept of what it means to BE a man. And that's the great tragedy."

There was murmuring and general assent.

"Mothers," I continued, "it's up to you to teach your daughters well. You may not realize it, but they watch your every move, every single day. The things girls see in their mothers, the good and the bad, will stay with them all their lives. Set good examples and worthy goals for your girls, and watch them become valued women."

I looked over at Brother Stowe, who was actually smiling.

"For the children and all the young people here, I have a special message. You are to love your parents, and help them all their days. They're not perfect, none of us are. But you're far better off as part of a family than not. There's a world out there waiting to devour you, alone and on your own. Families protect each other. So avoid rebellion and remain safe among your own clan."

One of the Shiloh Sisters appeared at my side, taking Zoom off my arm and giving me a break from his weight. It appeared she was a cat lover, knowing exactly how to rub my little pal's folded ears. I put the microphone in Zoom's face, knowing he'd purr loudly as if on cue. He did, and the crowd loved it. For the umpteenth time in our years together, he'd made me proud.

"And now," I said, "I'd like all the single men to raise their hands for just a moment. That's it - all you single dudes, raise your hands and keep 'em up for me."

They did, and everybody looked around.

"Now I'd like all the single, unmarried women here to raise their hands."

There was some giggling and a few heads shook, but they did it for me.

"Guys," I said, "these single ladies you see with hands raised are your mates. Godly women who'll be virtuous wives and help create a fine home for you. They'll be a treasure worth far more than gold to you. When you leave here, watch for 'em."

More murmurs, a few guffaws and laughter followed.

"Single ladies," I said, "these single dudes with their hands still in the air are your husbands. You'll note these guys are HERE tonight, most of them carrying bibles, and seeking after the Lord. When they could just as easily be sucking down suds at the local beer bars and shooting pool with their pals instead. These are loyal men. The kind you want to ride the river with. Watch for 'em. "

There were more polite murmurs. I gave the band their cue. The Shiloh Sisters began to sing a lively tune based on the Song of Soloman. I turned and gave the microphone back to Brother Stowe, who seemed quite pleased. Zoom was returned to my arm. After shaking hands with Brother Stow, I turned to walk off the stage.

"Beloved, we've been especially blessed tonight," I heard Brother Stowe say as I walked off. "I recognized our special guest Mr Amos Westergaard almost from the moment he walked in to celebrate with us. I feel certain many of you have read his best selling work 'A Wanderer's Wisdom,' or perhaps you've seen him on television. And his little companion is Zoom, a wondrous cat indeed."

The crowd erupted in applause and I immediately felt a strange satisfaction and kinship with all those people. I can't really explain it. I've never felt quite that way before, despite all the interviews and tv appearances in my recent past. And I have to say I liked it.

Still having no place to sit, I walked slowly back up the main aisle. The focus was still on me, and I was obliged to stop every few paces to shake an outstretched hand or allow a small child to stroke Zoom's fur. The thought came to me that I was stealing Brother Stowe's thunder. So I picked up my pace and hurried on towards the main entrance.

Stopping just outside to allow my eyes to adjust to the dark, I stroked Zoom's fur and briefly contemplated what we'd just experienced.

Zoom just continued doing what he does best – purring gently while riding comfortably on my forearm.

Chapter 40

By now there were stars high in the nigh sky, the air was clear, and tomorrow seemed to hold the promise of good flying weather. The trick was to find our rental car among the acres of parked vehicles. I felt a little panicky, having only a vague recollection of where I'd left it. Couldn't even recall what the make and model was. Only that it was white.

Coiled and hidden behind the mammoth tires of a yellow school bus was an anxious, angry serpent with oversize florescent red eyes. His forked tongue flickered every now and then, testing the night air. Zoom and I walked by as I searched for our car. The snake hissed, but not so loudly as to allow me to hear. Zoom heard it though, his ear cocked back.

"Maaaa-ow! Maaa-ow!" he yowled. I could feel him tense on my arm.

"Steady there, little pal," I said. "We'll be at the car soon."

"Maaa-ow!"

Well, something had set him off, although I didn't know what. I held him a little tighter so as to reassure him, and continued the looking for our rental car.

I was just at the end of the longest row and turning up the next when two very pale, scraggly- looking men wearing torn blue jeans stepped out in front of me.

"Evening, mister," said the taller of the two.

I just nodded.

"Nice cat you got there."

"Thank you," I said, my face revealing nothing.

"Would ya sell him?"

The other man thought this was funny and cackled loudly. I noticed he was missing several teeth.

"I don't believe so," I said.

"Come on mister; give us the cat and maybe we won't cut you."

Both men simultaneously pulled switchblades out of their pockets. I could hear the audible CLICK as their blades popped open.

"What d'ya suppose fried cat tastes like?" the toothless one asked his partner.

"Probably better'n spotted owl," hooted his pal.

Swell. Just swell. I took a step back and looked around. Nobody else in sight. I could hear gospel music coming from the big tent.

"Boys," I said, "you're not going to get my cat. Think about what you're trying to do here. You know it ain't right."

The two men just laughed and gave each other the high five. I took a couple of more steps back, my nose wrinkling. These idiots were obviously strangers to soap and water.

There was no way I'd give them Zoom, even if it meant watering the ground with my own blood. I couldn't outrun them and still carry my little pal. There had to be another way.

Just when I thought things couldn't get any worse, two more guys appeared, stepping out from the side of monstrous motor home. These were big fellows. Long hair, bearded, and each carrying what looked like a hickory axe handle. Both smacked the wood on their palms and made it clear they were open for business .

"You in a heap of trouble," one of them announced calmly in a deep baritone voice.

Lord help me, I thought to myself. This wasn't going to end well.

The two newcomers stepped past me; they were remarkably quick on their feet for big men. These guys were bikers, I realized. Each wore a leather jacket adorned with patchwork on the backside that I couldn't quite make out in the darkness.

I don't know who was more surprised, me or the knife wielding bad boys when the two bikers walked past me and confronted them.

"Drop the knives, gents," ordered the taller biker.

The two dummies just looked at each other, hesitating a moment too long.

"Thwack! Crack!" came the sound of hickory against bone.

"Owwwwww! You son of a .... You BROKE my wrist!" howled the one with the missing teeth.

"Shoulda listened to me, boy," said the biker with the droopy handle bar mustache.

The other fellow, seeing his pal in anguish, wisely dropped his blade and took a step back from the action.

"Now you two clowns get out of here. And don't let us see you in town either," snarled the other biker.

The two would-be assailants slunk away, walking towards the main highway.

I turned to the two bikers who'd saved my bacon.

"Evening, " said the tall one.

"Glad you came along when you did," I said. "Things were lookin' grim there for a while."

"Meth monkeys," said the other biker, shaking his head. "They'll do anything for a few bucks or another fix. Their brains are fried by that dope."

"We're sort of volunteer security here tonight for Brother

Stowe's show. Mostly we just help people park and direct traffic afterwards. Almost never have to play cop. Still, every now and then....well....things happen."

"My little pal and I owe you," I said, gratitude in my voice.

"No you don't," both said in near-unison.

"It's what we DO," said the tall one.

"And besides, we know about you, Amos. What goes around comes around."

I just shook my head, not knowing what to make of this.

"Seems you have me at a disadvantage, gentlemen. You know my name but I don't know yours."

"Gabe" said the tall one, sticking out his hand.

"Mike," said his friend.

Chapter 41

I was just about finished with the morning pre-flight routine on the Cessna when I heard the dispatch lady calling my name.

"Mr Westergaard? Mr Westergaard?"

I closed the engine cowling, wiped my hand with a rag, and looked towards the FBO building. The dispatcher was walking my way and had a curious looking fellow in tow behind her. A short, trim fellow wearing a red bow tie and carrying a briefcase.

"Mr Westergaard, this is Doctor Gladstone," she said, pointing to the man beside her.

"Nice to meet you, Doc," I said. "What can I do for you?"

"Mr Westergaard, I'm scheduled to give a lecture in Kansas City this afternoon. My son was flying me up there, but we've been grounded here with a blown turbo. This lady says you're going that direction. Any chance I can beg a ride?"

Now, I don't normally like to pick up hitchhikers. But the man seemed in real need of help.

"Really," I answered. "Tell me Doc, what are you lecturing on?

"Ethics," was all he said.

"Hop in Doc. I can think of few things the world needs more of than a good dose of ethics. Be a shame for you to miss your meeting."

"I'm grateful, sir. Means a lot."

"Here, let me put your gear in the back," I offered.

Walking aft to the small storage hold, I stuffed his modest valise in there with the other cargo and locked the hatch.

"Tell the Doc's son I'll get him there in one piece," I said to the dispatch lady. She nodded and walked back to her office.

Doctor Gladstone was adjusting the co-pilot's seat when Zoom woke up from his back seat digs and sensed we had a visitor.

"Maaar-ew?"

"You're not allergic to cats, are you Doc?" I asked.

"Not so far," he answered. "Never have seen one flying in a light plane before, though."

"This is Zoom the Wonder Cat," I said. "Zoom, meet the doc. He's going with us today."

I lit the fire in our engine and listened closely as it settled into its customary smooth hum. Then I plugged the spare headset into the com panel and handed it to our passenger.

"Can you hear me?" I asked through the intercom.

"Just fine," said Gladstone.

"How's your shoulder harness and safety belt?"

"Nice and snug," he said. "I've done this before a few times."

Releasing the breaks, we began rolling slowly down the taxi way towards the run up area. I performed the customary safety checks and listened on the radio for any other aircraft who might be coming or going. But it seemed we were alone that morning with no other traffic about.

"Cessna One Sierra Tango, taxiing into position for takeoff, runway three-zero, Burlington...." I broadcast in the clear.

"Ready to go, Doc?" I asked.

"Let's do it," he answered.

"Cessna One Sierra Tango departing runway three-zero, Burlington..."

We were airborne a few seconds later, climbing into the cool morning air, the runway disappearing behind us. I trimmed up the nose slightly, made a right turn out, and set us on course for Kansas City.

"So, are you like a college professor, Doc?" I asked over the intercom.

Gladstone just laughed. "No, Mr Westergaard. Actually, I'm a retired computer software engineer. Had my own company for years. Then a consortium of my competitors decided it was better to buy me out than continue losing business to us. Made me an offer I couldn't refuse."

"Let me guess - you got bored being rich and retired, right?"

"Exactly! I found out I could travel around the country as a guest lecturer and share the value of what I'd learned in thirty years as an entrepreneur. So that's what I do a few months out of the year. Colleges, corporations, sometimes even government entities."

"Where do you call home?" I asked.

"Denver," he answered. "Most of my family's there, including my wife. Sometimes she accompanies me on these trips, but not this time."

"Well, I'm happy to have you aboard this morning, Doc. Glad I could help. My little Cessna's not turbo'd, so it'll take us a while longer. Looks like we're getting a bit of tailwind though; we'll be in K.C. in good time."

We hummed along during the rest of the clear morning. It's always great flying after a storm's moved through an area. Visibility is mostly unrestricted and you can see for miles and miles. I let my mind wander back to the previous night's close encounter and thought once again that Zoom and I had been extremely fortunate to walk away unharmed. Our right-seat passenger seemed alone with his own thoughts, mostly watching out the side window.

We made it to Kansas City without the need to refuel. The weather continued to be excellent. I landed, shook Doc Gladstone's hand, and sent him safely on his way. That afternoon Zoom and I were the guests of honor at the grand opening (and fund raiser) for a no-kill animal sanctuary. The organizers auctioned off signed copies of 'A Wanderer's Wisdom' for surprisingly big money. That evening we were treated to fine KC barbeque and the smoothest of smooth jazz. Livin' large is good....

Chapter 42

Zoom and I slept in late the next morning, being in no great hurry. The hotel staff in Kansas City was predictably excellent, and the mid-morning brunch the room service waiter delivered was superb.

I read the morning paper, enjoying a bit of smoked ham and cornbread with honey along with the hot Kona coffee.

The flight service station report indicated that the flying weather would be good all along our route. I glanced at my watch and decided it was time we headed back over to the airport.

I gave Zoom the last morsel of smoked ham, scratched his ears, and marched off to the bathroom to wash my hands. Honestly, I would like to have stayed over another day.

That didn't seem to be in the cards, however. An old shipmate of mine was marrying off his daughter the next day. I'd missed the weddings of his two elder sons for one reason or another in times past. This was my last shot, the girl being his only remaining unmarried offspring. Besides, she'd always been a favorite of mine. Didn't seem right not to be there on her special day.

I called the desk and asked for a shuttle over to the Wheeler Downtown Airport. The lady at the desk said she'd have one out in front waiting for us in ten minutes or so. That gave me just enough time to scour my teeth, brush Zoom, and finish packing.

Traffic was congested, both on the ground and in the air around Kansas City. By the time we were finally clear it was almost two in the afternoon.

Fortunately, it wasn't all that far to our destination. Cessna One Sierra Tango kissed the runway sweetly at the Joplin Regional Airport and was welcomed by the resident FBO with a tie-down spot close to the terminal. I rented a new Chevy Impala, drove into town, and checked Zoom and I into a very pleasant Ramada Inn just before supper time. After a light meal, I returned to our room and spent a delightful couple of hours on the phone with my beloved Cyndi Cheyenne who seemed very pleased that I'd called.

"Amos, I'm missin' you and Zoom constantly," she admitted. "I've got at least another week's work here, but I'm already counting the days until we're in Montana together."

"Me too, baby. Me too......" I said.

"Promise me you'll stay safe."

"We pilots don't take unnecessary chances," I assured her. "G'nite!"

"Nite, my love...."

I turned in for the night and enjoyed the sleep of one who knows he's loved by a beautiful woman.

Chapter 43

Morning in Joplin meant fog, drizzle, and slick roads. Zoom got me up early for a hearty breakfast in the hotel coffee shop and check-out immediately thereafter. I soon found myself trying to navigate on unfamiliar back country roads with directions that proved faulty. Twice I had to double back and get clarification from the locals. The map I'd taken from the rental car agent proved woefully inadequate for my needs.

Fortunately, we weren't in any great hurry. The wedding wasn't scheduled until later that afternoon. But I wanted to show up early and be able to spend a little time visiting with my old friends before the ceremony.

I drove cautiously in the fog, passing a series of farm operations and rundown hamlets. The longer I drove, the worse the roads seemed to be. Even in the almost new rental car we were getting bounced pretty hard. Zoom didn't like it and complained regularly.

There didn't seem to be any radio stations out there either;

the signals kept fading out despite my best efforts at re-tuning.

But, nothing lasts forever and as the morning wore on, the fog began to lift a little. At least to the point where driving wasn't such a hazzard.

Of course, it was then I unexpectedly hit something VERY slick and lost control of the car. I wasn't traveling fast enough for it to really scare me. But I did manage to slide off the road, onto the unpaved shoulder, and halfway down the adjacent ditch.

"Great! Just great!" I muttered to myself, feeling exasperated.

We weren't injured, and neither was the car. But we were stuck in the oozing mud; the tires could do nothing but spin and gain no traction.

I got out to see if I could push the car, or rock it back enough to get us out of the worst of the mud. No chance. We were stuck good, and it'd take either a tow truck or at least a couple of strong men to shove us out. I flipped open my cell phone only to find out there was no signal.

"Little buddy," I announced to Zoom, "it looks like we're going for a walk."

It had quit drizzling, but it was still a foggy, gloomy day.

Zoom gave me a sour look as I tucked him inside my jacket to keep him warm.

"Mrrr-eeew!"

"Yeah, I know, I know," I said.

I crossed the road, facing any oncoming traffic (hadn't seen any so far, but you never knew) and began walking. Unknown to me was a medium sized snaked with large florescent eyes that was stalking us from behind.

About a half a mile down the road I came to another cluster of small, rundown houses much like the ones I'd passed before. I knocked on a couple of doors, but nobody answered. It was an odd feeling. There were no barking dogs, no birds, just an eerie quiet. I could sense eyes watching me, but despite by now having knocked on at least eight doors, no one answered.

Not knowing what else to do, I continued walking down the highway figuring that sooner or later I'd find some help.

Another half-mile down the road a large building began to emerge out of the morning gloom. And there seemed to be a lot of cars parked around it.

"Aha!" I thought. "Signs of civilization!"

The sign out front read Boaz Baptist Church. There didn't seem to be anyone outside. I walked through an open gate towards the main entrance, finally remembering that after all it WAS Sunday. Surely I could borrow a phone in the church office or plead for help in getting my car out of the ditch. I glanced at my watch, knowing time wouldn't be on my side much longer.

I decided that the best approach was the most direct one. I opened the right side of the huge double doors that led inside and walked in. Zoom and I immediately found ourselves at Sunday morning worship services and in the midst of a sea of black faces. Boaz Baptist Church was obviously what the media would label an American "black church." Seldom have I been so conscious of being a white man.

But, in for a penny, in for a pound. I took a seat on the aisle of the rear-most pew. Quite a number of the brothers and sisters turned around and stared at me. I smiled and focused my attention on the immaculately attired choir and the curious make-up of the band. There was a drummer, a bass guitarist, a lady on the keyboard, and a really old dude with gray hair sitting behind a washboard.

The reverend continued his sermon from the Book of Timothy, eliciting shouts of "amen!" and "hallelujah!" on a regular basis. He had a deep, commanding voice and a presence that resonated with the conviction of the gospel. I found myself liking him almost immediately.

A few minutes later he began winding up his Sunday lesson and the choir skillfully began to hum gentle and low. The band kicked in smoothly, rendering a beat that bespoke African origins. The members of the church began to sway with the music; there were a series of praises to the Lord, along with lots more amens and hallelujahs. The Boaz Baptist Church was clearly a traditional black church at its finest.

From up near the front came an angry shout that I absolutely didn't expect.

"Throw out da white devil!"

More murmuring, this time louder. And just about EVERYONE turned and looked back at me, some glaring menacingly.

I looked down at Zoom, who looked up at me from where he sat on my lap..

Get back, honky cat?

Chapter 44

The murmurs and glares directed towards me from various church goers seemed to be picking up momentum. I didn't like where this was heading. And apparently neither did the reverend, who remounted the stage and took his customary place behind the pulpit. The choir began to chant and hum.

"Oh my lord, lord, lord, lord.........mmmmmm hmmmmm.......mmmmm hmmmm...."

The reverend looked over at me, and I made eye contact with him. He seemed unsure of what to do next. I motioned to him that I wanted to approach. I got a quizzical look in reply, a nod, and then he beckoned me to come forward.

Gathering up Zoom, I walked slowly towards the stage. The choir continued to chant, backed up by the musicians. The old gent playing the washboard scratched out a compelling ditty. Every eye in the place seemed to be on me.

"Oh my lord, lord, lord, lord.......mmmm hmmmm......mmmmm hmmmm....."

Okay, I admit I was probably emboldened by my

performance a couple of nights back at the tent revival meeting. I mean, I just don't see myself doing what I was about to attempt. But it really did happen this way.

I took a cordless microphone from the outstretched hand of the reverend, turned slowly towards the assembled people, and walked boldly to the center of the stage. Zoom was riding on my arm as he customarily does, unconcerned by all the goings on. The choir's chant became a whisper, and the band faded out as I began to speak.

"Ain't no white devil," I proclaimed with authority. "Ain't no brown devil. No black devil, either. There's only the devil. Ole Satan himself. The great deceiver."

"Oh my lord, lord, lord, lord......."

"And I tell you the truth," I said, continuing, "that the man who hates his brother will never reach the Promised Land."

This got a couple of nods and a "hallelujah!" from a woman down in front.

"This is a house of worship; our Lord's house," I said. "And the devil won't prevail here among God's people. The presence of the Holy Spirit is too strong for him...."

"Oh my lord, lord, lord, lord......."

"Uh huh! Unh huh! Um hmmmmmm...."

The wash board player skipped up tempo and the bass player kept time with him.

"For even as you find yourself wandering through the valley of the shadow of death, facing all kinds of hardship and temptation, demons snappin' at your heels, be strong and of a good courage, my friends. For the Living God is always with you; always your protector. Always your friend."

"Oh my lord, lord, lord, lord........mmmm hmmmm....."

By now the crowd was beginning to come over to my side. There was a lot of swaying and occasional clapping interspersed with praise.

"These are the rivers that for the Christian run very deep," I said.

More 'hallelujahs.'

I looked over at the reverend, who had a look of pure astonishment on his face.

I was on a roll.

"As for me," I continued, "My name is Amos. I'm just a travelin' man. Had some car trouble down the road a little ways. Stopped in here knowing I'd find help among God's people."

The lead singer in the choir, a very attractive woman in a snow-white robe, broke into song and was backed up by the others in her group.

"Well, Amos was God's prophet man!"

"Oh my lord, lord, lord !"

"Best y'all listen whenever you can!"

"Oh my lord, lord, lord....."

"Mmmmm....hmmmm......mmmmm ....hmmmm."

I cued the band, and they toned it down once again for me.

"My little pal here is Zoom. He's my faithful companion kitty. Goes everywhere I go," I said. "He's my constant reminder of God's blessings upon me."

Lowering the microphone for Zoom, he once again purred on cue. The crowd loved it and went wild with applause.

"Well, God marched in the animals two by two...." sang the choir.

"Oh my lord, lord, lord, lord....." chimed in the worshippers.

"He saved all the critters and he'll save YOU!"

"Oh my lord, lord, lord, lord....."

"Mmmm....hmmmm......mmmm....hmmmm....."

Chapter 45

The morning service wound down about twenty minutes later. Zoom and I found ourselves honored guests at the social hour that followed. The ladies auxiliary provided some of the yummiest coffee cake I'd ever eaten. And the coffee wasn't bad either.

"Mister Amos, Sir, I'm the reverend Alan Isaac," said a deep baritone voice beside me.

"Pleased to meet you, Reverend Al," I said, shaking his hand. "And thank you for allowing me to speak."

"Mister Amos, you can't know how much you inspired me this morning. You have a way of getting to the heart of the matter. You said more in a few minutes than I sometimes manage to get across in a whole sermon."

"Don't sell yourself short," I replied with a smile. "I heard part of your sermon this morning. You've got what it takes and the people here know it."

"Mister Amos, I am sister Eloise Dumas."

"Ah, the charming gospel singer that lent my little

performance credibility," I said, taking her hand and kissing it gently.

That seemed to score me some points with the other onlookers.

"Ms Dumas, you should sing professionally," I added. "And the musicians in the band do some of the best back-up I've ever heard."

"Why, thank you, Mister Amos. But we just make a joyful noise as the Spirit moves us," she said, clearly pleased just the same.

"Reverend Al," I said, "please pass along my thanks to all the ladies who've so generously provided the cake and coffee. Looks like my cat has something to be thankful for too," I added. Zoom was busy lapping up a saucer of milk.

"Sister Sarah's watchin' over him with her Sunday School class, looks like," replied the Reverend Al, with a deep chuckle. "He's in good hands."

"Mister Amos," I'd like you to meet my son D'artagnon," said Eloise.

I reached over to shake hands with a very handsome fellow. Young Mr Dumas looked to be maybe seventeen or so. Give him a little more time and he'd be a real heart breaker, I thought.

"D'artagnon Dumas," I said, smiling, "I like it."

"Aw, mama! I told you to call me Dart," he said, looking over at his mother, somewhat embarrassed.

"Hmmm.... Looks like you're at something of a crossroads, my man," I said.

"Why....what you mean?" asked D'artagnon.

"Seems to me you have a choice to make," I answered. "Now, the D'artagnon of old was not only a bold, courageous hero. He was also a leader of men. People looked up to him. And the ladies.....aw man.....the ladies couldn't get enough of that handsome young fellow. And the men of his day respected him. Wanted to be like him. Because they knew D'artagnon was loyal and could be trusted to keep his word."

"Yeah, man, I read the book," said D'artagnon. "Been teased about it all my life."

"I don't doubt that," I said. "Children can be cruel. But you're almost a man now. Time for you to stop payin' attention to people with small minds. Show 'em what you've got. They'll quit teasing you and rally to you instead."

"You think I can do that?" asked D'artagnon, incredulous.

"This is the United States of America," I said. "You can do anything you set your mind to."

Young D'artagnon pondered that for a moment.

"Now let's consider Dart for a minute," I said, continuing. "Dart is just a street name. Like a million other losers out there. No pride or respect to it whatsoever. Dudes like Dart roam the inner cities all over the country. I know because I've seen them many, many times. One step ahead of the po-lice if they're lucky. Always workin' on their next scam. No future. Dart's friends aren't really friends, they're just parasites feeding off him. And what kind of woman wants to be with a street runner like that?"

"D'artagnon, I think Mister Amos has a real point there," said the Reverend Al in a gentle voice. "It's a decision you're going to have to make for yourself. And soon."

"Reverend Al," I said, "let's put my little thesis to the test."

"What do you have in mind?"

"Here in my hand are the keys to a new Chevy Impala. It's down the road a little ways, stuck off the highway. Now, I'd trust my friend D'artagnon and a couple of his loyal companions to shove it back onto the road and bring it back here. To help their friend Amos get on his way. But I'd NEVER trust a street dude named Dart with something that important."

D'artagnon looked at his mother, who looked at the Reverend Al.

"Decision time, D'artagnon," said Reverend Al. "What's it going to be?"

D'artagnon snatched the keys from my hand and went over

to corral three of his friends who were busy trying to make time with a trio of cute girls.

"C'mon, man, we got a little job to do," I heard him say.

"Aw, Dart, I was talkin' to Missy Malone," said a complaining voice.

"Now listen, fool! From now on it's D'artagnon, you get it?" hissed Eloise's handsome son. "Let's go..."

The Reverend Al, Eloise, and I watched the young men troop out the door with D'artagnon in the lead.

"Mister Amos, you are a real piece of work, you know that?" said Eloise, flashing me a radiant smile.

"Comes of desperation," I answered. " I have a wedding to attend. Needed to get be on the road about a half an hour ago. The father of the bride's an old shipmate of mine. His youngest child. Lord help me if I don't make it on time."

"We'll pray for you, Mister Amos," said Eloise Dumas.
"Can't ask for anything more," I said.

Chapter 46

After driving like a maniac for another half hour, I pulled up alongside the farm home of James and Jennifer Mack. The wedding ceremony was being held outside and I could see that the multitude of guests were already seated. I heard the wedding march begin to play and watched from the side yard as the bride and groom stepped off down the aisle. As soon as they reached the altar and stopped in front of the waiting minister, I raced quickly across the lawn and settled into one of the few empty chairs near the rear.

"Dearly beloved, we are gathered here......."

Alone with my thoughts while the wedding ceremony played out, my mind drifted back through the years. I remembered bouncing Jilly Mack on my knee when she was about two. I sported a reddish brown mustache in those days, and she'd always loved playing with it. Such a happy child. And here she was now, grown and marrying.

"And do you, Jillian Mack take this man....."

It looked like Jilly Mack had snared herself a young sailor.

The groom was a Navy petty officer wearing an immaculate dress blue uniform. My, my.....how the world does turn!

"I now pronounce you husband and wife. You may kiss the bride...."

With that, the crowd cheered and applauded. Even Zoom got in the spirit of the occasion and let out a happy yowl. The newest bride and groom marched back down the aisle looking like they'd won life's lottery. I have to admit that the smallest of tears escaped and trickled down my cheek. Guess even we crusty old dinosaurs aren't entirely immune to such things.

My old shipmate Jimmy Mack spotted me and came hustling over and grabbed me in a great bear hug.

"You old son of a ..... I thought you weren't going to make it," he said.

"It was close," I admitted. "Had some problems on the road. But a few new friends saved my bacon and got me underway again."

"C'mon! I want you to meet my new son in law!"

"With pleasure," I answered. "And here's the lovely Jenny Mack!"

"Amos Westergaard, you oughta be hung! We thought you weren't going to make it!" said Jimmy's wife Jenny.

"Forgive me, dear lady," I said. "Was delayed on the road, but all's well now."

"Well, just so you know....you're staying here tonight," she said. "It's already arranged."

"Orders received and understood," I said, laughing.

"We'll go fishin' on the lake in the morning," said Jimmy.

"You MEN are all alike!" said Jenny, laughing. "Fishing indeed!"

The three of us went over to where the groom was surrounded by well wishers.

"Eric Stone, I want to introduce you one of my oldest friends in the world," said Jimmy Mack. "This is Amos Westergaard. He's known Jilly since she was a little girl."

"A pleasure, Petty Officer Stone," I said, taking his hand. "Congratulations. It pleases me to see Jilly carrying on tradition. A Navy family indeed!"

"Thank you sir, " said young Mr Stone. "Am I correct in thinking you're a former sailor yourself?"

"Roger that," I replied. "Your father in law and I both served aboard the same destroyer back in the dark ages."

"And somehow lived to tell about it," chimed in Jimmy Mack, laughing.

"So where are you and Jilly off to?" I asked.

"I've got a month long leave ahead of me, sir. Then off to a service school in San Diego for two months. After that, change of station orders to the USS GOLIC, home ported in San Diego."

"A destroyer?" I asked.

"Yes sir. Arleigh Burke class."

"They're fine ships," I replied. "I managed to get invited to the christening of a brand new Arleigh Burke class guided missile destroyer a while back. Had a long talk with the CIC officer."

"It'll be a first for me," said Stone. "I've only served on a carrier before this."

"It'll be a challenge, then," I said. "On destroyers, it's not enough to just do your job and keep your gear operating. Destroyer duty will make a more traditional sailor out of you."

"I think I'll like that," said Stone. "I like being at sea. Yessir, being at sea and having a gorgeous wife back home waiting anxiously for my return to port appeals to me...."

"Do you think you'll make a career of it?" I asked.

"I'm not entirely sure. But I've just re-enlisted, and have at least another six years ahead of me. For me and a lot of my friends, it's about being part of something important. Oh, I know most of us could make more money on the outside. But it seems like this is a critical time in our nation's history, and we're needed right where we are. I don't know how else to

explain it, really."

"You did just fine, and you're doing us all proud, Petty Officer," I said. "May God watch over the GOLIC and all who sail in her."

Turning to Jenny, I asked, "Now, where's Jilly? I need to see her?"

"In the house, upstairs in her room being tended to, I imagine. You know the way, Amos."

I excused myself and made my way across the lawn towards the big two story farm house. I knew a few of the other guests and was obliged to stop here and there to shake hands and allow Zoom to be petted. A platoon of young men were busy setting up tables and chairs for the wedding feast. There were a dozen or so barbeques in use, and a handful of young women with trays were passing out chilled flutes of champagne. Still balancing Zoom on my arm, I managed to grab one without spilling it and greedily sucked it down.

"Thanks," I said to the serving girl. "Must be a little dehydrated."

"Well then, best you take another one, sir," she suggested, smiling.

I did so and made my way inside the house and up the stairs.

The door to Jilly's room was closed, and I had both hands full. So I gently kicked the door with my foot. A moment later a large woman I did not recognize opened up.

"Jilly's busy right now. She'll be down later," she said.

"I understand," I said. "But time is short and I need to see her."

I pushed my way past the astonished woman and made my way into the room Jilly had grown up in. It still looked like a teenager's digs, but I knew that would soon change.

Jilly was sitting in front of a large make up mirror being fussed over by three other young women. She looked beautiful and radiant, just as a bride should on her special day. And I was forced into the realization that she was indeed every bit a woman. She looked over and saw me. I watched her eyes grow large, and I smiled.

"Uncle Amos! And Zoomers! You both MADE IT!" she yelped.

The other women didn't know quite what to make of this outburst and gave way to me. Jilly jumped up from behind the vanity table and hugged me fiercely.

"Mrrrr-ow–ow-wow!"

"And you too, Zoomers!" laughed Jilly, rubbing his ears and stroking his fur just the way he likes it.

"Ladies, I don't mean any disrespect," I said to the others in the room. "But time is short and I need a few minutes alone with Jilly."

Jilly nodded and sort of swept the other girls out the door with all the authority of a new bride. I placed Zoom on her bed. He sat down and watched both of us expectantly.

"Jilly," I'm sorry I couldn't be here earlier. I tried, but had some trouble on the road," I explained. "I wanted to talk to you before the ceremony but it just didn't work out that way."

"It's OKAY," she said. "I'm just so happy you're here. And I know Dad is, too!"

"I've already talked with your husband," I said. "He's a fine young man. Makes me proud I once served. I know our Navy's in good hands."

"Eric and I have known each other since junior high school," said Jilly. "We were always friends back then. And somehow along the way we sort of fell in love. And I DO love him, Uncle Amos."

"I know you do, Jilly. I can see it in your eyes. His too. You're both going to do just fine together."

"We'll be moving to San Diego, long as Eric's orders to the GOLIC hold up. Can we come up and visit you sometimes? I looked at the map, and it appears like it's only a couple of hours from San Diego to your house."

"You'll always be welcome, Jilly. Never doubt that."

"That means a lot to me."

"Now listen, Jilly. Being a new wife is one thing, but being a Navy wife is a challenge all by itself. It'll be hard on you when Eric deploys overseas with his ship."

"I think I understand that, Uncle Amos. Dad talked to me a LOT about how hard it is on the women who wait at home. I won't know how I'll hold up until I actually go through it. But I can be pretty strong when I need to be. You know that."

"Indeed I do. You might also find yourself having to help other Navy wives who don't have that same character."

"I'll get along okay. When Eric's away, I'll go back to school. I've already checked into completing my B.A. in computer science at Cal State San Diego."

I handed Jilly one of my business cards. "You need anything, and I mean ANYTHING, you call me, you hear? I'm still traveling a lot, but you can always leave a message at this number and I'll get back to you."

She tucked the card into her wallet and then leaned over to hug me again.

"I'm so lucky to have you in my life," she sighed.

"One more thing," I said. "Running a house on Navy pay isn't the easiest thing in the world. And the cost of living in San Diego is notoriously high."

"Just another challenge for the new Mrs Eric Stone, right?"

I nodded, and handed her a sealed envelope with her name on it. She looked at it curiously, unsure of what to do.

"Go ahead; open it," I commanded. "It's got your name on it, girl!"

Jilly slit the envelope open with a long finger nail and dug out the contents.

"Oh, Uncle Amos! This is too much! Much too much!" she wailed, continuing to stare down at the bank check made out to her.

"This is between you and me," I said. "Tuck it away for

now and forget about it."

Jilly leaned over and kissed me on the cheek. "I don't know what to say."

"Get yourself together, girl. You've got guests downstairs to greet and a honeymoon to get to. Now, I'd better let your friends back in before they start telling tales."

Jilly giggled. I picked Zoom back up and headed towards the door.

"See you later, Mrs Stone," I said.

Chapter 47

The big old Missouri farm house was quiet that next morning. I rousted myself from the depths of the warm comfortable featherbed and made my way to the bath for a quick shower and shave. After that, Zoom and I crept quietly down the stairs to the kitchen. There wasn't anyone stirring yet, but I knew that'd change quickly. These were farm folk, and even the big wedding the day before wouldn't alter their routines by much.

I put the coffee on and then began foraging among the leftovers in the refrigerator. I was rewarded with blueberry muffins, Canadian-style bacon, and a few clusters of red seedless grapes. I warmed the muffins and bacon in the microwave oven, being careful not to overdo them.

"Mrrr-ow!"

Ah yes. And some leftover grilled chicken breast for Zoom.

I assembled my little feast on a large paper plate, poured fresh steaming coffee into a black ceramic mug, and settled in the front porch swing to eat. I was admiring the fine morning when I heard the door behind me open.

"Mornin' Jimmy Mack," I said.

"Smelled the coffee," he said. "You ain't lost your touch, Amos. You still make the best coffee...."

"Don't let Jenny hear you say that," I chuckled.

"Too late; she already knows."

"She still asleep?" I asked.

"Yeah - late night for her."

"Hope you'll forgive me for begging off early last night. I needed to sleep," I said.

"Yeah, you ain't as young as you used to be, huh?" said Jimmy Mack, yanking my chain. "No matter. That cat of yours kept everyone entertained and in stitches until something like three this morning."

"I'm not surprised," I said. "Zoom's happiest when he's got an audience to perform for."

"Well, he done good last night, that's for sure," declared Jimmy Mack. "Couple of the women tried to sneak out the door with him."

"Not the first time THAT'S happened either," I said with a smile. "Zoom loves the ladies, and they love him...."

I went inside to refill my coffee mug and grab another blueberry muffin.

"We still going fishing?" I asked Jimmy Mack when I returned.

"Need to," came the reply. "Helps clear my head."

Zoom was busy engaging in that time-honored game of capture the cricket when Jimmy Mack and I tramped off towards the small lake that adjoined their property. There were lots of crickets hopping around on the porch and down in the grass. I figured my little pal would enjoy that for a while. Jenny could let him back in the house later.

Kitties, of course, have their own mind. About fifteen minutes after Jimmy and I had shuffled off through the woods towards the lake, Zoom dispatched the last cricket of the morning and decided to follow us. I, of course, was unaware of this.

It wasn't far to the lake and there's an easy, well-worn footpath through the brush. Like most furry animals, Zoom can smell water and knew instinctively where I'd be. Walking purposely along the path, stopping here to sniff a wildflower, there to swat at a white moth on the wing, my little buddy was having a fine time. He dashed off the trail for a moment to relieve himself discreetly behind a suitable shrub. And was nearly bush whacked in the process.

"Hisssssssssssssssssssss!"

Zoom leaped away a nanosecond before the evil viper struck, causing a near miss.

"Hisssssssssssssssssss! Hisssssssssssssssssss!"

"Mrrrow! MRRRROWWOWOW!"

Zoom arched his back and for a moment thought to stand his ground. The snake slithered up closer, his pointed tongue flickering out. But when its eyes flashed red, Zoom thought better of the idea. Glancing around, he quickly scrambled up an old oak tree and ran out on the limb nearest the ground. The snake didn't like this much. It raised its head as high as it dared, and hissed some more. It appeared they'd achieved something of a stand off. But Zoom knew eventually I'd have to come back that way, so all he had to do was stay put.

"Hisssssssssss!" The snake was really angry. His eyes continued to flash their blood red glow.

"Mrrrow! Mrrrow!"

Ah, but it was an ancient oak tree Zoom had climbed to safety. It had witnessed many decades of heat and cold in the Missouri wilderness. And its lowest limbs were weak from abuse by insects and the ravages of time.

"Crrrrrrack!"

It took only Zoom's added ten pounds to bring the limb down, snapping it off clean from the old oak's trunk.

"Mrrrrooooowwww!" howled Zoom, falling with the

branch eight feet or so to the ground. Right above the hissing snake.

The snake wasn't near quick enough. And Zoom, like all cats, instinctively righted himself and leaped away just as the wood hit the dirt, pinning the snake beneath the heavy oak limb.

"Hzzzzzz...." A weak protest. More like the air coming out of a beach ball than the bold threats the snake had uttered only moments before.

Zoom, being nobody's fool, saw his chance and ran away fast as he could. Down the dirt path and directly towards the lake.

By now, Jimmy Mack and I were about eighty yards offshore and busily paddling the creaky old boat out to the middle of the lake.

"Maaaa-ow! Maaaa-ow!"

I looked over and saw Zoom running frantically back and forth on the shore.

"MAAA-OWOWOW!" His cries were louder and seemed more determined.

Jimmy Mack looked over at me, and I just shrugged.

"Let's paddle back over and pick him up," I said. It'll only take a few minutes. Dunno what he's so upset about."

Jimmy just nodded, and we began the process of turning the boat around.

"Mrrrrow! Mrrr-ow!"

"Hey! We're coming! Hold on!" I yelled across the water.

"Mrrrrow!"

Zoom continued running frantically on the shore, exhorting us to hurry. Finally he could stand it no more, and he did something that astonished even me. Jimmy and I had maneuvered the boat to within about forty yards of the shore. Both of us were paddling determinedly when I looked up to see Zoom step gingerly into the water and began SWIMMING out towards our little boat.

"Well I'll be dipped!" exclaimed Jimmy. "Never, EVER saw a cat do that."

I didn't know what to say, so I just shook my head.

Zoom continued paddling out towards the boat as if he did this sort of thing every day. "Come on, Zoom! C'mon little buddy!" I yelled, beginning to cheer him on.

When he got close enough, Jimmy stuck out his paddle as far as he could and Zoom scrambled up onto it. I reached out and got a hold of my little wet friend and yanked him into our boat.

"Towel in the tackle bag," said Jimmy.

I reached in, found an old blue towel, and began drying Zoom's fur as best I could. The good news was, by now the sun was shining and I knew he'd dry pretty quickly.

"Think we might get in some fishing now?" asked Jimmy.

"Maaaa-ow!"

Chapter 48

I pulled in a fat bluegill and examined it critically as it wiggled on the line.

"Catch and release?" I asked.

Jimmy nodded. "Got enough wedding leftovers at the house to feed the First Division of the Fifth Corps for a month."

Zoom, by now almost dry, swatted lazily at the still dangling fish.

"Mrrooow!"

"Guess that makes it unanimous," I said, pulling the hook out of the fish's mouth and tossing it unceremoniously back into the water.

"Jimmy, I gotta tell you, I'm flat amazed that your little girl ended up marrying a sailor."

"Tell me about it. After everything you and I went through back in the old days, huh?"

"He's a good man, though," I said. "Got his head together better than we ever did at that stage."

"And that's the gospel truth. We thought we were such suave, sophisticated Joes back then. But we were really dumber than a fence post, I think."

I nodded. "It's a different world, Jimmy. In our day all we worried about was our next port call, booze, and willing women."

"Amos," said Jimmy philosophically, "I'm just a simple country farmer. A redneck country bumpkin to a lot of folks. I read and listen to the news, and wonder what it's all about. Tell me, since you've traveled in rarified social circles in recent times, what's it all about? What's really going on?"

"The world's changed a lot since you and I were sailors," I said. "Our navy no longer exists. It's been replaced by one far smaller, much smarter, better led, and with vastly superior technologies."

"Tell me about it," said Jimmy Mack. "You and I rode that old destroyer to 'Nam. Did all those dirty, dangerous jobs they ordered us to. Didn't make any difference, though, did it? Saigon still went down the tube and we all watched it. The fruits of failure."

"Those were bad times for a lot of us," I said, agreeing.

"Yeah, I remember. Came home to a bad economy, terrible inflation, no jobs. Couldn't even wear your uniform in public without invitin' trouble."

"The pendulum swings both ways," I said. "And it seems to me like the smart people are beginning to understand just how essential our modern, volunteer military is to the free people of the world. The Persian Gulf war helped some. And the September 11th murders in New York woke up a lot more people. Oh, there'll always be the anti-war factions. Those who think it's easier to appease and bow down, rather than living free like God intends. But those people aren't representative of our national character. And I believe the days of folks spitting on our uniformed service people are behind us."

"I hope so," said Jimmy Mack. "I know I don't want my son-in-law Eric to have to go through the same stuff we did."

"I don't believe that's going to happen, at least not this time around," I said gently. "I've noticed in recent years a grudging acceptance by the public that what they did to us after 'Nam was really shameful. I don't know that our generation of the military will ever get that long-over due tickertape parade, but maybe it's no longer important."

"I think I understand that," said Jimmy Mack. "Just so long as the kids returning from war today don't end up getting the same shaft we did, it'll be okay. I can live with that."

"Listen, give it a little time, and if Eric's orders to that DDG hold up, you and Jenny fly down and tour his ship. Talk to the XO. Wear your Tin Can Sailor hat. You'll be surprised how much the youngsters today look up to those of us who went before them. And afterwards, drive up the coast to visit me. We'll do the town."

"That sounds like a good idea," mused Jimmy. "I'd like a better sense of what our Navy's like today."

"Looks like you got one," I said, pointing to Jimmy's straining line.

This time it was a fat brown trout.

"You're lucky, fish," I said as Jimmy pulled the hook from its mouth. "Any other time, you'd end up pan-fried with herbs and sliced almonds."

"Well, we'll put him back for next time," said Jimmy, tossing the scaley critter back into the lake.

"What I want to know is, can we WIN this time, Amos? Is the resolve there?"

"I believe so," I answered. "This is a determined enemy we face in the Age of the Terrorist. It requires thinking ahead, rather than simply reacting. An ability to peer over the horizon is essential. Some of these guys are smart, but they're not brilliant. And their insane hatreds will eventually betray them."

"Time to head back?" asked Jimmy, looking at his watch.

"Yeah, I think so.

"You stayin' for lunch though, right?"

"Told Jenny I would. Then Zoom and I have to drive back to the airport."

"Beats me how you can fly that little plane all over the country," said Jimmy. "I'd be petrified. I don't even like flying the big commercial jets all that much."

"Flying for me is like fishing is to you," I said. "Helps me clear my mind. Gives me a sense of freedom I don't get any other way. Besides, I'm not the only one. I know of at least three of our former shipmates that also fly."

"Is that so? Well, I guess I shouldn't be all THAT surprised. We destroyer sailors have that long-standing reputation for boldly steppin' out....."

Chapter 49

Zoom and I made our good by's to Jimmy and Jenny Mack. Ever the thoughtful hostess, Jenny packed us a bag of goodies to munch on during the day.

"Just you don't stay away so long next time, Amos Westergaard," admonished Jenny.

I hugged her, and shook Jimmy's hand.

"You fly safely, you hear?" ordered my old shipmate.

"Oh, absolutely!" I answered. "That's the only kind of flying I know how to do..."

Putting the rented Chevy Impala in gear, I pulled away thinking how lucky I was to have friends such as these. A man just can't have too many friends.

I managed to get us back to the airport without getting lost this time. After checking in the rental car, I pre-flighted the Cessna for takeoff. Finding nothing amiss, I lit the fires and spent the rest of the afternoon and the next day humming along under clear blue autumn skies.

Mostly we stopped for food and fuel at small county or

municipal airstrips. The people that run these small operations are almost universally helpful and friendly. Belonging to the general aviation fraternity makes me feel special. May it always be so.

The daylight hours were getting shorter, and it was nearly sunset when we touched down at Standiford Field in Louisville, Kentucky. Standiford was busy, and the ground controllers had their hands full keeping tabs on everything from heavy transports to relatively little guys like me piloting the Cessna. I ended up having to taxi all the way across the airport, being mindful of giant C-130's from the Kentucky Air National Guard that were moving skillfully along the same stretches of asphalt that we were. As we pulled up in front of the FBO, a gasoline truck approached. Kentucky hospitality.

"Top her off, sir?" asked the fuel service man.

"All the way to the top," I said, tying down the Cessna for the night.

Finding a hotel proved more difficult than I would've thought. Seemed there were competing conventions in Louisville that night. Not a room to be had at any of the major inns. After several phone calls, I gave up in exasperation. I rented us a car and drove out toward the edge of town. Finally on the fifth try, Zoom and I managed a room in a small drive-in motel. I was tired, needed food, and felt cranky after the long day. I tossed our gear on the bed, put out food and water for Zoom, and walked across the street to a Subway store that was still open. A few minutes later (with a very large sub in hand) I went next door to a mini-mart and bought a quart of cold Budweiser. Things were looking up.

The motel was modest, but the room was clean and looked to have been recently refurbished. Zoom was already asleep on the bed. I turned on the tv and found nothing of interest except for a music channel that played a continuos string of jazz.

I settled into the chair and began unpacking my sandwich on the small table in front of me. The chilled Budweiser tasted especially good, and before long I could feel the tension disappearing. I looked at my watch. Too early for Cyndi Cheyenne to be back at her Marin hotel. Maybe later. As I sat there in the near-dark listening to the sweet jazz on the tv and munching my sub, I contemplated our good fortune at having found this modest little motel. Zoom and I had fared far worse in times past. Naturally, we'd grown accustomed to more upscale inns. But small motels like this one, mostly mom and pop affairs, had often provided us sanctuary when we needed it most.

While I continued gnawing on my sandwich, I noticed through a small crack in the drawn drapes that the parking lot was mostly full. A few people came and went. Most returned later carrying bags of fast food. Burgers, fries, tacos, burritos, pizza, hot dogs, chicken, Chinese take-out. The staple of travelers across the nation. America on the go.

Noting sadly that my giant sub was mostly devoured, I concentrated on the remaining beer. A large white sedan pulled into the empty parking slot next to my rental car. Looked like we were going to have overnight occupants in the room next to ours. I watched through the small opening in the drapes as the car disgorged five tall, painfully skinny young men. With me sitting in the near-darkness, I doubted they were aware of being watched.

The tallest of the five was the driver and presumed leader. He hurriedly opened the door to the motel room next door and returned to direct the offloading of their vehicle.

They spoke in hushed tones, and I could not make out what they said. Whatever language they used, it wasn't English. Which made sense, because these men all had the look of being from the middle east.

It took them longer than one would expect to unload the trunk. I watched closely as many medium sized soft bags, along with a dozen or so zipped long rifle cases were removed and carried into their rented room. I began to have an uneasy feeling.

The guy I'd dubbed their leader finally closed the trunk lid and after a quick furtive glance around returned to their room, slamming the door behind him. I could hear their muffled tones as they spoke among themselves, but I understood none of it.

Things were about to get worse; they turned on their tv with the volume much higher than it needed to be. It was a foreign language channel, probably Farsi or Arabic but I couldn't say for sure. Shortly thereafter it became apparent all these guys were chain smokers. It didn't take long for the second hand smoke to start drifting into my space from under the locked door that adjoined our two rooms. Zoom didn't like it either. He woke from his nap, sniffed the foul air, and immediately voiced a whiney protest.

"Yeah, I know," I said. "Just our luck, huh?"

I got up and opened the window up in front and then did the same to the small one in the bathroom. With any luck, it wouldn't be that cold overnight. Zoom, seeing I'd done the best I could, hunkered down beside me on the bed and both of us dropped off to sleep.

Sadly, there wasn't enough alcohol in the beer I'd sucked down to keep me in securely in the arms of Morpheus. The idiots next door kept their tv on all night. Between twangy, sing-song music, occasional overheated voices, tobacco smoke, and Zoom being restless, I found myself mostly napping off and on. About dawn, I gave up in disgust.

After checking the aviation weather, I filed a flight plan and headed off to the shower. Zoom and I would bid adieu to this place, grab some breakfast, dump the rental car, and be on our way before the morning crush at the Louisville airport.

With Zoom already occupying the front passenger seat, I tossed my bag in back and prepared to drive away. Something was still nagging at me. I took notice of the license plates on the white sedan. Out of state. Might well be a rental car, I thought.

Driving off, I still felt unsettled. I stopped for a red light and then pulled into a parking lot a half mile or so from the motel. With the engine still idling, I dug around for my cell phone and placed a call.

"Federal Bureau of Investigation; how may I direct your call?" came a voice over the airwaves.

"I'm calling from Louisville, Kentucky," I explained. "I need to know if there's a counter-terrorism unit operating nearby."

"Sir, that would be in Lexington."

"Can you transfer my call?" I asked.

"Yessir. Please stand by..."

There was a pause, a couple of whirrs and clicks. I thought for a moment I'd lost the connection.

"This is agent Robert Nighthawk. With whom am I speaking, please?"

I gave him my name and told him where I was calling from.

"Westergaard? I know that name. You wouldn't happen to be a writer would you?" asked Nighthawk.

"Guilty as charged," I replied.

"What can I do for you sir?" asked the G-man, quickly getting down to business.

"Agent Nighthawk, what I'm going to tell you might be just the product of an over active imagination. But just the same, I'm inclined to report it."

I told him what I'd witnessed the night before, with the five skinny guys unloading a huge cache of suspected weapons. Their chain smoking, the Farsi (or Arabic) tv station all night. All of it. Nighthawk listened carefully and only interrupted me twice for clarification.

"That's an interesting story, Mr Westergaard," said Nighthawk.

"Well, listen," I said. "I feel a little foolish about calling you. With any luck at all, it'll be a dead end."

"Are those men still at the motel?"

"Far as I know. I just pulled out of the parking lot a couple of minutes ago, and their car was in the lot as I left."

"The FBI appreciates your call, Mr Westergaard."

"Listen, one more thing," I said. "Just in case this amounts to something, I'd appreciate you keeping my name out of any press releases. I'm not looking for face time with the cameras. Far as I'm concerned, you and your people deserve any accolades that might result."

"I can't promise anything except that I'll try to respect your wishes. How can I reach you if I need to later?" asked Nighthawk.

"I travel a lot. Sometimes the cell phone works and sometimes not. Here's the number," I said, rattling it off. "And I'll also give you my lawyer's number in California as a back-up contact."

"Where will you be the rest of the day?"

"Can't say for sure; I'm off to the airport right now," I answered.

"Flight number?"

"I fly my own aircraft," I answered.

"Okay, I understand then," said the FBI agent. "Thank you again for calling this in, Mr Westergaard. I have to get to work now. Good by."

FBI agent Robert Nighthawk stared at his phone in disbelief for a moment, stifled a yawn, and then poured himself more coffee. He'd been on duty all night. Stirring in an ample amount of sweetener, Nighthawk speed dialed another number.

"Kang? Yeah, it's Bobby Nighthawk. You were right; by all that's holy! They deviated and went west to Louisville. They're there now. Just got a tip from a citizen. White sedan and the plates confirm it. Blue Lake motel just off the interstate. Roll your team, and take 'em down, quickly and as quietly as you can. And listen, our citizen tipster says they unloaded a large number of soft tote bags. Might be detonators and explosives besides their personal weapons, so watch yourselves. Yeah, yeah.... the tip feels right. Solid citizen. Sometimes we just get lucky. I'll be waiting to hear.

Call me. Good luck."

Agent Nighthawk hung up the phone and stared at the clock on the wall. Nothing to do now but wait. That was always the hardest part.

As for me, I drove off towards the Louisville airport, watching along the way for a promising eatery. And in supreme ignorance of everything I'd just put in motion.

Chapter 50

A day and a half later found us humming through the old Virginia countryside. The weather was splendid, the glorious fall colors were everywhere, and my Cessna was running as smoothly as ever.

Zoom and I had fared somewhat better the previous night, being welcomed at an elegant Sheraton Inn. My night's lodging included a delightful massage and steam bath afterwards. The food service was superb and the staff even whipped up some special kitty canapes for Zoom. Both of us slept well that night and were well-rested for our morning departure.

Pretty soon the lush green horse farms below started giving way to signs of civilization. I began paying close attention to my navigation. We were getting nearer Washington, D.C., some of the most closely guarded airspace in the world. I got a hard fix on the little town of Springfield, Virginia, and could see the Potomac River a few miles beyond that. There was a small general aviation airport on the opposite bank where I planned to set us down.

Despite all my travels, I'd never been to our nation's capitol. This visit would fulfill a promise I'd made many years earlier.

Closing on the west bank of the Potomac, I strained my eyes trying to make out some of the historical buildings in D.C., but I was a little too far out. There was also some haze over the city, giving testimony to the exhaust of many, many cars below.

Okay, get your head back inside the cockpit, pay attention to the gauges and dials, I told myself. I was just resuming my normal scan when I realized I had company nearby. Sliding into position just beyond my port wingtip was a Navy attack helicopter.

Now folks, I want to tell you this scared the willies out of me. This sort of thing just doesn't happen. It's not done. I tried to keep my mind on the business of flying my airplane and at the same time watch the helicopter. I mean, there was no possibility he didn't know I was there. So what was going on?

I watched and a moment later, the pilot began hand signaling me. Fingers. Okay. One finger. Then two fingers. Then one. Then all five fingers. Aha! I tweaked my radio frequency to 121.5 and gave the Navy pilot a thumbs up.

"Cessna One Sierra Tango, this is Navy Leg Iron Three Zero One transmitting on guard, over...."

"Good afternoon, Navy Leg Iron. This is Cessna One Sierra Tango. What's on your mind?" I asked, trying to sound casual.

"Cessna One Sierra Tango, Leg Iron Three Zero One, sir, I need to know if Mr Westergaard is aboard, over..."

"Navy Leg Iron, that's affirmative," I said. "You're speaking to him."

"Cessna One Sierra Tango, roger that, stand by...."

A moment later he got back to me.

"Cessna One Sierra Tango, be advised, your flight plan has been cancelled. You are directed to follow me. Steer course zero-seven-zero and maintain altitude."

I was shocked. I knew I'd violated nobody's airspace.

"Uh, Navy Leg Iron, what's this about?" I demanded.

"Sir, I can't tell you anything else. I have my orders. You are directed to follow me. Anticipate landing at Andrews Air Force Base."

I mulled that one over for a few seconds. Civilian aircraft never EVER land at active air force bases except for dire emergencies, or unless they're already in deep trouble with the authorities.

"Cessna One Sierra Tango, Navy Leg Iron three zero one, change frequency to Andrews approach, one two four point seven five, over...."

"Navy Leg Iron, roger that, changing frequency," I answered.

A moment later I heard, "Navy Leg Iron three zero one, roger that, return to station, break, Cessna One Sierra Tango are you up on this frequency, over?"

"Andrews approach, this is One Sierra Tango, over...."

"One Sierra Tango, good afternoon sir. Squawk zero two three seven and ident, please."

I dialed the numbers into my transponder.

"Cessna One Sierra Tango, radar contact. Steer zero six five, descend to two thousand."

"Andrews approach, roger that," I said. "Can you tell me what's going on?"

"Sir, I'm not able to tell you anything at this time. Anticipate a left downwind approach to runway zero three."

"Cessna One Sierra Tango, roger left downwind for zero three."

My mind was racing ahead and I had to fight to control my thoughts. I needed to focus on this unplanned landing and getting us down safely. I glanced over at Zoom, asleep on a pillow in the co-pilot's seat. He didn't seem worried.

"Cessna One Sierra Tango, looking good sir. Switch to Andrews tower, one two seven point niner, over...."

"One Sierra Tango, switching."

I checked in with the tower controller, who was obviously waiting for me. She expertly called my base and final legs. The immense runway loomed ahead of me. It seemed to extend all the way to the horizon, but of course that was necessary in order to accommodate some really heavy lifters.

"Andrews, One Sierra Tango's on a half mile final to runway zero three," I radioed.

"Roger that, sir. Winds are light and variable out of the north at five knots...."

I touched down smoothly, rolled out, and exited at the first high-speed taxiway that presented itself..

"Cessna One Sierra Tango, welcome to Andrews. Stay right where you are; we're sending the truck out to guide you. Switch to ground control, one three two point five...."

I changed the radio frequency again and waited for the truck. I still had no idea why I was at Andrews. I decided that since we'd landed safely, there wasn't much to do now except enjoy the sights and keep my wits about me.

A small air force utility truck showed up a couple of minutes later with a big "FOLLOW ME" sign mounted in the bed.

"Cessna One Sierra Tango, please follow the truck...." came the voice of the ground controller.

"One Sierra Tango, roger the welcome wagon," I said.

The little truck began moving slowly down the taxiway with me following behind at a safe distance. Andrews is an immense facility, especially for a Cessna pilot like me. It seemed like we taxied for miles, and not knowing where we were going made it seem longer than it probably was. We passed all kinds of aircraft. Fighters, helicopters, giant C-17 cargo haulers. We even cruised past an immense hanger that housed Air Force One. There seemed to be dozens of technicians swarming all over her.

"We in the tall cotton now, Zoom," I said to my little pal, who'd awakened and was staring outside the window.

"Mrrr-ow!"

"Cessna One Sierra Tango, we'd like you to turn in just beyond this hangar. Nose out toward the runway, sir, and prepare to cut power," came voice from the truck ahead of me.

"Roger that," I said.

Just past the giant hangar I could see a young airman ready to direct my parking efforts. I swung in like I'd been doing it all my life and began my post-flight routines before I killed the power. The welcome wagon sped away, and was quickly replaced by a battery powered golf cart containing a female air force captain.

In for a penny, in for a pound, I thought to myself.

"C'mon little buddy. Let's go see what this is all about."

By the time I got exited my trusty air chariot, the air force captain was standing at attention waiting for me.

"Good afternoon, sir, and welcome to Andrews," she said, saluting.

I was dumbfounded, but managed to keep my head together.

"Thank you, captain. Now, suppose you tell me why I'm HERE?" I asked.

"Sir, I'm under orders. I can't tell you anything. Please accompany me inside."

Now, I knew better than to argue with this woman. So I just shrugged and mounted the golf cart. Zoom continued riding his customary spot on my forearm.

"Nice cat, sir," said the lady captain.

"He likes women," I said.

I have to admit to being overwhelmed. Here I was in a golf cart being driven by a really sweet looking lady air force officer. And rolling along inside a giant hangar containing the regal Air Force One. There was also no shortage of security people. Several men in black gave me the once-over as we drove by.

Toward the back of the immense hangar I could see a series

of smallish executive offices. My escort pulled up at one of the doors and stopped.

"This way please, sir...."

I got out and followed. The young captain stopped at a closed door, knocked loudly twice, and went inside. Inside was a very plush office with all manner of electronic communications and computer equipment. Behind a polished mahogany desk sat a blonde, thirty something fellow wearing a power suit. The captain stopped in front of his desk, came to attention, and saluted.

"Mr Westergaard, sir," was all she said to the man.

"Thank you, captain. That will be all for now," said the suit behind the desk.

The lady captain turned and briskly walked out, closing the door behind her.

"Mr Westergaard, I am Nicholas Stanton. Deputy to the White House Chief of Staff," he announced somewhat grandly.

I just nodded.

"Yes, well....I'm sure you're wondering how it is you come to be here."

"Don't patronize me, Nick," I said.

"Yes, ah, very well....." answered the young deputy. "Well, first off, we apologize for cancelling your flight plan and diverting you here."

"Who exactly is WE?" I demanded.

"Sir, your flight plan was cancelled at the express order of the President. I have been asked to invite you to dine at the White House with the President and First Lady tomorrow evening. The First Lady has asked that you also bring your, ah, cat...."

"And you couldn't just call and ask me this?" I said, incredulous.

"Mr Westergaard, let me again express our regrets at upsetting any travel plans you have for today. There's more that I haven't been told, I'm sure. But the President wouldn't order your diversion to Andrews like this on just a whim. It's not his way."

I nodded, not quite ready to let this young man off the hook.

"And, I'm also to inform you that if you're unable for any reason to accept this White House invitation, we stand ready to refuel your aircraft and send you on your way immediately."

I nodded, scratched Zooms ears, and listened to him purr for a moment while the deputy White House staffer sat fidgeting.

"You may tell the President that I'm at his service," I finally announced.

"Splendid! He'll be most pleased!"

"Is this to be a formal state dinner?" I asked.

"No sir, it's more of an informal gathering. You might expect to meet at most a couple of dozen other individuals. A business suit and tie will suffice."

An idea began to form.

"Now see here, Nick," I said. "It just won't do for me to show up at the White House by myself."

A pained expression. "What do you have in mind, sir?"

"I have a special lady friend that lives nearby. You'll have to send someone to pick her up, though."

"And, just who would she be?" asked Stanton.

I told him the name, and he smiled.

"I'm sure I can get that approved," he said.

"Please endeavor to do so, I urged him. "It's important."

"Can my people arrange hotel accommodations for you while you're here, Mr Westergaard?"

"Four Seasons," I replied.

"Consider it done."

Our business concluded, we shook hands and I walked out the door. An unmarked black SUV driven by an air force sergeant whisked Zoom and I to the Four Seasons Hotel.

The truth was, I knew little more about the actual reason for our being there than I did when we first landed. And I found it rather unsettling.

Chapter 51

Lady Melanie Sherwood was far too old to be surprised by much of anything. All the same, she allowed herself a tiny, crooked smile as she hung up her telephone.

Well, well, well......she mused. A White House dinner invitation, compliments of that rather amazing Amos Westergaard. The boy DOES get around, doesn't he?

Lady Sherwood had become acquainted with Westergaard the year before in the course of her ongoing fund raising activities. He'd been very generous with his wallet, and had even managed to shame a few of the more well-heeled tightwads on the social scene into upping their contributions (all tax deductible, of course). She'd even seen him interviewed on television a couple of times. But she'd not read anything about him or his amazing cat in the last couple of months. Odd that he'd drop out of sight like that. She was sure that it wasn't for lack of social invitations. She'd have to look into that.

Lady Sherwood herself had an interesting past. The widow

of a career British intelligence officer, she'd traveled the world with her dashing husband and dodged more than a few bullets (metaphorically speaking) during the Cold War era. Strikingly attractive in her day, she'd been also been blessed with a keen analytical mind and natural social grace. When her late husband Sir Guy Sherwood had been knighted by Her Majesty for exceptional service to the Crown, it was generally accepted that the honor was as much Melanie's as her husband's.

Sir Guy had been assigned liaison duties in Washington, D.C. as part of his pre-retirement sunset tour. While working in the American capitol he and Lady Melanie had fallen in love with the Chesapeake Bay area and purchased an elegantly restored stone cottage on the bluffs overlooking the water. With so many friends in the American government and industry, the two would feel very much at home.

Sadly, it wasn't to last. Sir Guy succumbed to a massive stroke and died less than two years after his well-earned retirement. Lady Melanie was heartbroken, but managed to carry on in the finest of British traditions. It was unthinkable to her that she remarry. She needed no one to take care of her. And in her mind, the adventures she and Sir Guy had shared over their lifetime together could never be supplanted by another man, no matter how good he might be. Better she treasure those memories in her heart, she thought, and leave well enough alone.

After a suitable mourning period, Lady Sherwood pulled herself together and embarked upon a new calling. She began rekindling all her old social contacts, managing to get her name and picture in the society pages a few times. She then established Cavalry Rescue, an international humanitarian and disaster relief organization. In the beginning there were the usual scoffers at the slogan she'd adopted, "Hang on; the Cavalry's coming!" But after nearly a decade of hard work, Lady Melanie had built Calvary Rescue into a well respected international entity. Earthquakes, firestorms, floods, avalanches, hurricanes, tornados; it didn't matter. Wherever people were hurt and dying, the Cavalry would go charging in to provide emergency medicine, technicians, food, and water.

Despite now being in her late seventies, Lady Melanie continued working tirelessly to secure donations. She was always in need of medical supplies, volunteer doctors, nurses, and above all the cold cash needed to send people and cargo racing across the globe on a moment's notice. By day she worked her contacts in the U.S., Canada, and Latin America. At night she lobbied and cajoled those on the other side of the globe. Her Rolodex files bulged with the names and numbers of hundreds of her late husband's contacts in foreign governments and private industry throughout the world. It was a schedule that would crush the ordinary person. But Melanie had long ago discovered she was one of those rare birds that thrive on action. It simply wasn't in her to sit on the front porch and wait for death to come calling.

Yes, she would certainly attend this White House dinner courtesy of young Mister Westergaard. That she'd been the recent guest of the President and First Lady would eventually be noted in various society pages, she knew. And THAT would help her immensely when it came to drumming up contributions for Cavalry Rescue. Besides, she'd never met the current president and was curious about him and his lovely wife.

But before that would all happen, Lady Melanie decided there was enough time for a little snooping. Picking up a well-worn telephone, her first call would be to London.

Chapter 52

President Ian Zane Conroy pushed aside the mound of papers on his desk, deciding he'd earned a break. Lighting up a thin cigar and savoring its unique aroma, his mind wandered back to the Colorado Rockies. There would be snow covering their majestic peaks very soon, he knew. He missed the high country. Missed his Colorado ranch.

"How in the world did I ever end up here?" he asked himself for the thousandth time in the past year.

Conroy was at heart a cattle rancher, his Scottish ancestors having migrated to North America in the years after the American civil war. When his father died, Ian had gladly taken over the job he was born to. With a quick mind and a natural business sense, he'd built the family ranch into one of the biggest in the state. It was in the year just following his father's death that Ian had discovered silver on his land -one of the largest veins ever found. So in addition to being a cattle baron, Ian found himself a mining magnate. Married to an Arapaho Indian princess, he was the father of two boys and a girl, now grown.

No one was more surprised than Ian when years earlier the Colorado party bosses had come knocking, asking him to run for governor. It was during a time when the state economy was in shambles, and the unpopular incumbent (a lifelong politician) was perceived as highly vulnerable. Conroy had no political experience and had never run for anything. But he was genuinely unhappy that his beloved Colorado with its near-unlimited potential should find itself in such wretched condition. After talking it over with his wife, he made the decision to enter the state's upcoming primary.

And the rest, as they say, is history. Conroy won a narrow victory in a four-way primary contest. And then won going away in the fall general election. The voters liked what they saw. A tall, thin, imposing figure of a man with a square jaw. He spoke softly, but with great conviction and authority. And if the electorate liked Ian Zane Conroy, they positively adored his wife. Nearly as tall as her husband, Lori Conroy's finely chiseled features and piercing black eyes exhibited all the dignity and pride of the Arapaho people. In truth, Ian and Lori Conroy looked like they might've been sent from Hollywood's central casting. They were the stuff of dreams for political campaign managers.

As governor, Conroy proved to be no pushover. He immediately set about slashing state spending and eliminating all together any state agency that had outlived its usefulness or simply didn't perform. There were no sacred cows, and his political opposition howled in protest. The newspapers soon turned against him, railing that he'd 'overstepped' his bounds. Ian didn't care. As he saw it, he'd been elected to turn things around. And that couldn't happen if the business-as-usual mentality prevailed. By the end of his first year in office his poll numbers had sunk so low he couldn't have been elected street sweeper. There were rumblings of a recall election.

A year later, things began to turn around. Business, spurred on by lower tax burdens, began hiring more people. A informal network of trade schools sprang up, encouraged by Conroy. Funded by seed money from ranchers, mine operators, and the tourism industry these schools began turning out hopeful, motivated young job seekers with just enough formal training to fit in to all the new entry level jobs that were being created. Seeing the opportunity, businesses from other states began relocating to Colorado or expanding their presence there. Private enterprise was once again succeeding brilliantly, and at almost no expense to the taxpayers. Conroy's job approval ratings soared. Colorado's economic turnaround became the standard by which other efforts of other states would be judged in future years.

Nearing the end of his first term as Colorado's governor, Ian stunned practically everyone by his announcement that he'd not be seeking re-election. As he saw it, he and his operatives had paved the way to a better future for Coloradans. It would be up to new leadership to build upon the solid foundations he'd worked so hard for.

With that in mind, the Conroys bid adieu to the governor's mansion, happily returning to their life on the ranch. By now the Conroy kids were nearly grown. The eldest son would eventually become the chief engineer aboard a nuclear submarine. His brother moved to Silicon Valley and established a computer software design firm. The youngest, a girl, and the apple of Ian's eye, was in medical school training to become a pediatrician. The nest was empty, and both Ian and Lori Conroy deeply felt that void in their lives.

Four years after they'd returned to life as ordinary citizens, party officials once again came calling on Ian Zane Conroy. This time they wanted him to run for president of the United States. At first he spurned the idea. In his own mind, Conroy was content to run out the clock right there on his ranch. Spending each day just a little more in love with his wife and overseeing the cattle and mining operation was about as much as a man might hope for. But the truth was, with the children gone, things just weren't the same anymore. The more he wrestled with the idea of running for president, the more he began to seriously consider the notion. Ian and Lori Conroy discussed the possibilities for weeks. They sought counsel from close friends and political operatives. Their grown children all thought it was a 'cool idea' -provided that's what their mom and dad really wanted.

And so it came to pass that Ian Zane Conroy was sworn in by the Chief Justice of the Supreme Court as president of the United States on a cold gray day in January. He'd now been in office a little less than a year. And like so many of his predecessors at that point in their administrations, Ian wondered if he'd done the right thing.

Conroy's thoughts were interrupted by a discrete knock at the door to the Oval Office. The door swung open, admitting a familiar face.

"Good afternoon, mister president," said Cyrus Brown, the White House Chief of Staff. "The ambassador to Cuba is cooling her jets outside. Her body language tells me she's anxious about something."

The president sighed. In post-Fidel Cuba, its people had experienced a world they never knew existed along with all the problems of a fledgling democracy. The Cubans were being helped along by the discovery of vast natural gas resources and a booming tourist industry. But when it came to playing in the international arenas, they had a long way to go.

"Escort her in," ordered the president. "And ask Humberto to send up more cigars, will you?"

"Yessir," replied the chief of staff. "Oh, and by the by, here's the list of confirmed attendees for the First Lady's dinner party."

The president quickly scanned the list, and nodded approvingly.

"Very good. I see we were able to nail down Westergaard. Excellent. I want to see him privately sometime in the course of the evening, Cy. As discretely as we can manage it."

"I'll work it out, sir," promised the Chief of Staff.

Chapter 53

The phone in our Four Seasons suite rang early, rousing me from a deep slumber.

"Amos my boy, you DO get around, don't you?" said the booming female voice at the other end, sounding for all the world like Margaret Thatcher.

"And a gracious good morning to you too, Lady Mel," I said. "Up a bit early aren't we?"

"Perhaps so, but then it's not every day a girl has to get herself together for a White House dinner, you cheeky bugger!" she replied merrily.

"Seemed like the right thing to do at the time," I said.

"I'm grateful, Amos. I really am. Now listen, I've arranged for the president's people to pick me up a little early and take me to your hotel. I want a bit of time alone with you before we're overwhelmed by White House events later in the evening."

"That'll be great, Lady Mel. Plan to meet me in the hotel lounge, just off the main lobby. I'm sure your minders will be familiar with it."

"I'm told we should arrive at your hotel about six o'clock."

"I'll be ready," I promised.

"Until then, Amos! Ta!"

Hanging up the phone, I was sorely tempted to go back to sleep. But Zoom was already prowling around, giving me that "where's breakfast?" look. So I reluctantly rolled out of bed and got things moving. After paying a visit to the bathroom, I picked up the phone again and arranged a breakfast delivery to include lots of hot coffee.

"Right away, sir," promised the room service attendant.

Next I placed a call to the concierge.

"I need a few things," I explained hastily. "White House dinner this evening. My hair needs trimming, my suit needs to be cleaned and pressed, and I need for my cat to be picked up for grooming and returned to my suite not later than early this afternoon."

"No problem, sir," said the lady concierge. "We have a staff here that's been specially trained to deal with White House protocols."

"Excellent! Send them up to my room in about an hour, will you?"

"Certainly, Mr Westergaard. Is there anything else we can help you with?"

"I'm going to need a car and driver for about three hours. Some local matters to attend to."

"Will you require a limo and tourist guide?" asked the concierge. "We can easily arrange that."

"No, nothing so formal," I replied. "An ordinary car with a driver who knows the city and speaks passable English is all I'll need."

"One will be ready and standing by. Call down when you're ready to leave the hotel."

I thanked the concierge lady and sped off to shower and shave. By the time I emerged from the suite's elegant bathroom, breakfast was waiting along with the morning edition of the Washington Post.

A little later, with coffee having been consumed and newspaper scanned, I admitted a very proper Korean fellow to my room.

"Good morning to you sir," he said in perfect English and bowing slightly. "I am the hotel's protocol advisor for our guests scheduled to visit the White House. May I see the suit, shirt, tie, and shoes you plan to wear this evening?"

I walked over to the mirrored closet, extracted the garments he'd requested, and handed them over.

"The suit and shirt will certainly be acceptable once properly cleaned and pressed," he said. "But the tie has seen better days. I will ask my assistant to join us momentarily and bring an assortment of new ones for you to choose from," said the Korean as he flipped open his cell phone.

I listened to him give some clipped orders (presumably in Korean) to his assistant on the other end of the phone. I understood none of it, but then I didn't need to.

"Now, your shoes please, sir?"

I pulled them out from underneath the bed and watched as he eyed them critically.

"Your shoes are not in the best of condition, but I have an expert among my group that can work miracles," he said. "He'll replace the rundown heels and polish them to a mirror shine."

"I would like that," I said. "I dislike breaking in new shoes."

Another knock at the door. This time I admitted two more people, a shorter man carrying a rack of silk neckties and a pretty young woman.

"Mr Westergaard, I'm Ellen Banes from Cat's Delight. I'll be escorting your cat over to be groomed as you requested."

"Ah! Very good," I said, looking for Zoom. "You'll have my little pal returned this afternoon?"

"Yessir. Sometime between four and five depending on the

usual traffic variables."

Zoom, always liking the ladies, came trotting out from the bathroom and let out a happy meow.

"Looks like he's ready to go, Ellen," I said. "See you later, little buddy."

Ellen picked up Zoom gently and left the room with him on her arm.

I turned to the waiting assistant and picked out a white tie with tiny pale blue stars.

"An excellent choice, sir," said the Korean approvingly.

"Thank you gentlemen," I said. "Your assistance is most prized."

Both men bowed slightly, gathered up my clothes and shoes, and promising they'd be returned later in plenty of time for my White House appointment.

Morning business completed, I called the concierge desk once again and advised them I'd be down immediately.

"Your car and driver are waiting for you at the main hotel entrance, Mr Westergaard. A maroon colored Lincoln. The driver's name is Tony Van Voorden."

I thanked her and headed out the door. The hotel elevator whisked me quickly and silently down to the lobby. As promised, I found a highly polished maroon Lincoln Towncar and driver waiting out in front under the hotel portico.

"Good morning, sir," said the polite twenty-something young man. "Where will I be driving you this fine sunny day?"

"Vietnam Veterans Memorial," I replied.

"Yessir. The Wall over on Constitution Avenue," he said, opening the vehicle's rear door for me.

It wasn't that far a drive, but the morning traffic was, well, typical D.C. stop and go. There wasn't anything to be done about it, and my driver and I both knew it. Tony Van Voorden wisely left me alone with my thoughts. He'd escorted more than a few people to The Wall since he'd started working on call for the Four Seasons.

As for me, this little pilgrimage was in keeping with a promise I'd made to myself long ago. The official American involvement in Vietnam was of course ended. But the impact the war had upon the nation and the world reverberates to this day.

"This is as about as close as I can get us," announced my driver as we reached our destination. "I'll park here and wait for you, sir. Unless you'd like me to accompany you?"

"I appreciate the offer, Tony. But this is one trip I need to make on my own," I replied.

"I understand, sir," said my driver, removing his hat as a signal of respect.

It was a cool, pleasant fall day. The sun felt especially good on my face as I made my way along the wide sidewalk that led to The Wall. Its highly polished black granite slabs stand poised and tall as if to weather the ages, and I felt comforted by that. The bronze Three Soldiers stand their silent eternal sentry duty nearby, along with the Vietnam Womens memorial that fosters healing and hope.

There are some fifty eight thousand names inscribed on The Wall, and more than a few are familiar to me. These men remain forever young to we who knew them. And the names inscribed on this simple yet elegant memorial will continue to serve throughout time, a silent testimony to the world that liberty does not come cheaply.

I stood there for a while and allowed mental images to rush unimpeded through my mind. Visions recalling the danger we'd willingly shared, the daily drudgery, hilarious comic pranks we'd pulled on each other, and the many acts of sacrifice I'd witnessed. Remembrances I'd thought lost to time were still there after all.

I got down on one knee, feeling compelled to pray. But I faltered, realizing I just didn't have the words. It didn't seem to matter. God knew what was in my heart.

Almost immediately I felt my spirit washed and then

calmed by a gentle peace. I could hear a bird singing its sweet song of tranquility. It was enough.

Shifting my weight, I began to rise to my feet and then suddenly felt very weak. I nearly passed out; surprising since I've never fainted in my entire life.

"Steady there, sir," came a voice behind me. A strong arm reached out to help balance me upright.

"Arrrgh! Thank you," I said, being grateful to the stranger.

Standing next to me was a fellow who appeared a little older than I, going to gray at the temples. He wore a camouflage boonie hat, aviator shades, and an old green flak jacket sporting the insignia of several army helo squadrons.

"No problem, sir. Happens a lot around here," he said.

"Army warrant officer?" I asked.

"Yessir. One of the lucky ones," he answered, nodding towards The Wall.

"Navy," I said. "Destroyers."

He just nodded and stuck out his hand. I shook it and as I did so, I could see this man also becoming lost in time for a brief moment.

"Owe you destroyer guys," he finally said. "Your big guns saved me and my crew from becoming sure POW's once upon a time."

We hugged each other, with more passing between us than most people will ever understand.

"Keep the faith, bro," he said, turning and walking away.

"You too," I said, my voice a hoarse whisper. "You too...."

Chapter 54

The rest of the afternoon was a little less intense. I paid a
visit to the Lincoln Memorial, Mr Lincoln having been a
personal hero of mine since childhood. The giant seated marble
likeness of the former president is, I think, an all together
fitting and proper tribute. Lincoln's dogged determination and
perseverance in the face of overwhelming odds has become
part of our national persona. Had he lived, the postwar
reconstruction period would've had an entirely different
character to it, I'm convinced.

Feeling spent, I had young Tony Van Voorden drive me
back to the Four Seasons. I stopped at the hotel café for a late
lunch and afterwards ducked into the hotel salon for a quick
tonsorial trim.

Returning to my room for a nap, I found Zoom waiting.
He looked positively dashing; his fur exhibiting a clean,
almost sparkling look. And around his neck was a cute black
kitty-sized bow tie. Dunno how the groomers do it, but they
do.

At four o'clock a knock at the door roused me from sleep. This time it was the regular hotel valet returning my suit and shoes. I don't think either of them have ever looked so fine, even when brand new.

I trotted off to the bathroom to shower, shave, and ready myself to meet Lady Sherwood. Given the D.C. traffic problems, I wasn't entirely sure when she'd get to the hotel. All the same, I'd be ready regardless of when she arrived.

As it turned out, the hotel lounge was practically deserted when I walked in. A cute honey blonde in a low cut white silk blouse busied herself polishing glasses behind the bar. A medley of classical music was playing softly in the background. I seated myself and watched as a tall, distinguished looking gent with perfect silver hair hurried over to greet me.

"Good evening sir; my name is Basil. What can I bring you?" he asked.

"Bas, it's like this," I explained. "I'm expecting to be joined shortly by Lady Melanie Sherwood. Until she gets here, I'll just nurse a bit of Perrier with lime. When you see my guest has arrived, please immediately bring us some well-chilled champagne."

"THE Lady Sherwood?" asked my waiter. "It'll be a great pleasure sir, " he said, hurrying off.

Lady Melanie and president's people were late. I sat there in the lounge for quite a while, just sipping Perrier and alone with my thoughts. I still had no idea why I was REALLY in D.C. The snobby deputy chief of staff I'd met at Andrews had either been deliberately vague about the matter or else knew nothing. Probably the later, I decided. He didn't seem to have been negotiating from a position of strength. No one would ever consider me a political junkie. Oh, I manage to do my civic duty and visit the polls every couple of years, but that's about it. In any case, I figured to be properly awed. Being entertained at the White House by special invitation of the sitting president and his lady is the stuff of memories. I wondered who else might be there.

Deeply lost in my thoughts, I managed to miss the entrance of my awaited guests.

"Mr Westergaard, I'm Lynn Charleston, of the president's security detail."

Startled, I looked up to see two smiling faces. One of which I recognized as Lady Melanie Sherwood, dressed in a regal blue and gold evening gown. With her thick white hair elegantly coiffed, she appeared every bit the lady she was.

"Good evening, ladies," I said, quickly standing. "Lady Melanie, you're looking charming as ever. Ms Charleston, I'm happy to make your acquaintance."

"And good evening to you, Amos. It is quite wonderful to see you again! And, I must say, you look quite dashing in that gray suit," said Lady Mel.

"Mr Westergaard, I'm sorry we were delayed in our arrival here. Traffic was unusually bad, even for this town," explained Lynn Charleston. "I'm afraid we can only allow you and Lady Sherwood about twenty minutes before we have to leave for the White House."

"I understand," I said. "Twenty minutes will have to be enough, then."

"I'll just leave the two of you and remain on station out in front, she said, turning to leave.

"Listen, in order to save time, why don't you go upstairs to my room and bring down my cat? He can wait in the car. He won't give you any trouble; he loves the ladies," I explained, tossing my room key in her direction.

"An excellent suggestion," replied Ms Charleston, expertly snatching the key in midair.

"She really IS a dear, that Miss Charleston," said Lady Melanie as she watched the White House security agent scurry off.

Basil came scooting over to our table with an ice bucket and a promising bottle at the ready.

"With the compliments of the Four Seasons, sir," he announced.

"Why, thank you very much, Basil," I said, eyeing the chilled bottle of Iron Horse.

"And, if you'll permit me, it's a great pleasure to serve you, Lady Sherwood. I'm a great admirer of your work," said Basil, bowing slightly.

"You're very kind," answered Lady Mel, nodding in his direction.

Basil expertly filled two crystal flutes with the exquisite nectar and then hurried off.

"So, Amos, how is it I haven't heard anything of you or your prized cat in the last couple of months?" asked Lady Sherwood.

"It gets a little complicated, Lady Mel," I replied. "But the hard truth is, I just got tired of life in the fast lane. Sick to death of having to be seen at all the right parties. With the right people. Answering the same moronic questions from reporters who couldn't care less. It began to seem pointless, and I realized that I'm just not hard-wired for that kind of life."

"Still, you needn't have dropped out of sight, Amos. You probably don't realize it, but in doing so you've worried more than a few of your friends, myself included."

"If that's the case, I apologize," I said. "I'm kind of finding my way, and it's not been entirely easy. All the same, I have no plans to become a hermit. I'm just re-evaluating who and what is important, is all"

"And, among those people important to you is a beautiful, fair haired country-western diva with a voice like an angel?"

"How'd you find out about that," I asked, incredulous.

"Amos, you forget with whom you speak," answered Lady Mel, her eyes twinkling and merry.

"Okay, I admit I can be naive about some things," I said, smiling back at her. "Yes, it's true. I'm desperately in love with Cyndi Cheyenne, and we're trying to work it out."

"Don't feel bad, Amos. It's not that you've been indiscrete.

But having been married to Sir Guy all those years, I couldn't help but become a master of quiet inquiries."

"Quite so, Lady Mel. Quite so. All the same, I'd appreciate it if you'd keep this to yourself for now," I implored. "If not for my sake, then for hers."

"It shall be as you ask, Amos. Fear not. Now, perhaps you'll tell me how it is you managed to collect a White House dinner invitation?"

"Ah, now THERE'S a mystery indeed!" I exclaimed. "There I was, minding my own business, flying along outside of Washington when I was intercepted and diverted to Andrews Air Force base by a Navy attack helicopter."

"Goodness! I'll bet that woke you up, eh?"

"Believe it," I said.

"Well Amos, if there's one thing I've learned in the years I've lived here, it's that things in Washington are seldom as they appear."

"Meaning what, exactly?"

"That the president has something in mind, and he obviously feels it's important enough for him to have exercised his command authority over you. I wouldn't worry about it. I'm sure you'll find out all about it in due course."

"That's what I keep telling myself. That, and if I was in any sort of trouble, I'd have found out before now."

I looked up to see Lynn Charleston signaling me from the lounge entryway and pointing at her wristwatch.

"Looks like it's show time, Lady Sherwood," I said, getting to my feet.

Chapter 55

Lynn Charleston escorted Lady Mel and I out of the Four Seasons and into a waiting black Ford Expedition. Zoom was waiting expectantly for us and let out a happy meow at seeing Lady Sherwood again.

"Well, hullo there, handsome fellow," said Lady Mel as she stroked his soft fur. "Love the bow tie!"

"Mrrrfff!"

The driver, a predictably serious fellow in black and wearing an earpiece, mouthed something I couldn't quite understand into a tiny lapel mic. Presumably he was advising the presidential security detail we were underway for the White House. Anyway, he put the huge SUV in gear and we rolled away.

A few minutes later our party arrived at the VIP entrance to the White House and we were handed off to a yet larger squadron of security people. I won't go into any detail about White House security screening protocols, except to say it is quite thorough and a curious blend of the tried-and-true melded with some extremely hi-tech wizardry. And not even Zoom was exempt. My little pal sat there with as much dignity as he could muster while being closely examined by serious minded security specialists.

After passing through the screening process, with Lady Melanie on one arm and Zoom riding the other, I followed another fellow in black into a suitably large and elegant foyer. There we were handed off to another lady, the White House protocol official who introduced us to the President and First Lady.

"Mr President," she said, these are the last of our scheduled guests. May I present to you Lady Melanie Sherwood, Mr Amos Westergaard, and ah, Zoom the cat."

"Charmed and delighted, Lady Sherwood," said the president. "Welcome to the White House."

"Thank you, Mr President," answered Lady Mel. "I must say, I'm delighted to be here once again."

"You have visited here before?" asked the president.

"Yes, Mr President. My late husband and I once spent an evening here in the company of President Reagan and his delightful wife Nancy. Those were good days," she mused.

"In that case, welcome BACK," said the president with a smile.

Looking around so as not to be overheard, Lady Melanie lowered her considerable voice.

"Mr President, I also bring you greetings from Her Majesty's government. I have been asked to pass along a word to you. I've been told you'll know what it means. The word is hopscotch."

At hearing this, the president's eyes lit up and he fought to bring a large smile under control.

"Thank you, Lady Sherwood. And, you may tell the prime minister I am extremely pleased and gratified."

Lady Melanie moved on to greet the First Lady, Lori Conroy. I found myself standing face to face with the President of the United States.

"Good evening, Mr President," I said, shaking his hand. I was pleased to discover the president shook hands like a man, unlike many of today's wimpy politicians.

"Welcome, Mr Westergaard," answered the commander in chief. "Thank you very much for coming this evening."

"I must confess though, sir, that I'm somewhat puzzled by the invitation," I said.

"Later," said the president, passing me expertly along to the First Lady.

"Mr Westergaard, I'm very happy you could join us this evening, " said Lori Conroy. "And it's a double bonus you were able to bring along your cat Zoom."

"Let me assure you, Mrs Conroy, that he'd have pitched a fit at being left behind," I said. "It's what he DOES."

The First Lady laughed appreciatively and asked me to follow her. Picking up a secret service agent along the way, I soon found myself in a small elevator going up. We walked down a narrow hallway and into what I'd describe as a combination music and leisure room. There was a white baby grand piano and a few other instruments stacked and hung along the walls. There were also full bookcases and well-stuffed easy chairs. We were greeted there by a very large man, a small girl, and a dog.

"Good evening, Mrs Conroy," said the large man, who was of course part of the presidential security detail.

"Grandmaaaaaa!" yelped the small girl, who appeared to be about five years old.

"Well hi there, princess," said the First Lady. "Are you having fun?"

"Yesssss! Mister Alvin is teaching me to blow the trumpet!"

Zoom wasn't paying any attention to this. His focus was entirely on the medium sized dog sniffing around at my feet.

"Don't worry about the dog, Mr Westergaard," said the First Lady. "She's expertly trained."

"A blue dingo, isn't she?" I asked.

"You know your hounds, sir," replied the First Lady. "This is our Beth."

"And she's MY best friend!" exclaimed the little girl, pulling the dog over to her and hugging its neck fiercely.

"This is our granddaughter Ellie. Ellie, come say hello to Mr Westergaard," directed the First Lady.

I watched as Ellie slowly approached us. "Pleased to meet you, sir," she said, doing the cutest little curtsey. "Grandma, he has a KITTY!"

I bend down so she could examine Zoom and pet him.

"Miss Ellie, this is my cat Zoom. I think he likes you," I said. "Can you hear him purring for you?"

Beth the blue dingo came over and sniffed. Zoom tensed, and then relaxed. I don't begin to understand what passed between them in that instant, but it was clear there would be no hostility.

"Mr Westergaard, you may feel free to leave Zoom here while you rejoin the other guests," suggested the First Lady. "I'm sure Ellie would like that."

"It'll be fine, sir," said Big Alvin. "I'll be on duty here minding Miss Ellie for the duration of your visit. You can leave your cat on top of the piano if you wish. I'm sure we'll all get along fine."

I looked over at the young Miss Ellie, who was clearly delighted at the prospect.

"Looks like you're going to be entertaining the First Grandchild this evening, little buddy," I said, giving Zoom a courtesy scratch before I left the room. "Be back for you later."

"Mrrrff!"

Chapter 56

Back downstairs and mingling among the other White House guests, I saw with pleasure that Lady Melanie hadn't lost her touch. She was busy holding court, herself being the center of great attention. Crowded around her were quite a few others, mostly women, appearing to hang on her every word.

I found my fellow attendees to be something of a mixed bag. A curious blend of those at the top of their chosen professions, while others were more your ordinary citizens. I chatted briefly with the president of a California aerospace design company, a bourbon distiller, a petite comedian I'd once seen do stand-up on the Laugh Channel, and a dentist. There was also an ecology sciences professor, a retired New York fireman, a golf pro, and a hospice coordinator. Rounding out the lot was an interior design architect, a custom jeweler, a kindergarten teacher from Colorado, and an NFL lineman. Or, at least these are the ones I recall. President Conroy circulated among us expertly, displaying a gift for putting people at ease.

If there was a common thread among us, I don't know what it might have been. I did note a conspicuous absence of any Capitol Hill politicians or any other political operatives. It seemed all the invited guests were accompanied by a spouse or other. Given that, I was particularly glad I'd asked Lady Melanie to come along.

There was no live music (apparently the Navy band had been given the night off) but there was a fine selection of classical music piped in, its volume properly low so as not to impede conversation. The White House is everything you'd expect, opulent and princely but without being garish. It has a unique ability to exude the marrow of our nation's character unlike any other structure.

A collection of white jacketed waiters circulated themselves efficiently among the gathering, ensuring champagne glasses were full and serving a variety of scrumptious finger foods. A White House photographer scurried about taking many memorable pictures and promising copies to everyone later. I wandered around the hall and examined the astonishing array of historical artwork on display. Properly overwhelmed by my surroundings, I followed the others into the dining room at the prompting of the chief steward.

The President and First Lady were the last to enter the room. After having seated his wife near him, the commander in chief motioned for the rest of us to be seated around the elegant setting. Mess stewards began immediately filling wine glasses and serving up a fine green salad.

"My friends," began the President, "Lori and I are delighted to have you here as our guests this evening. One of the perks in being president are these small, informal dinner gatherings. Not to mention having a superb staff available to organize them for us. I know that some of you have traveled great distances to be here with us tonight. Others have been able to attend owing to some rather unusual circumstances. I just want you to know that each of you are important to us in your own way, and that Lori and I really feel blessed by your being here."

There were some murmurs and nods around the table. I picked up my wineglass and got to my feet.

"Mr President, if I may, sir...."

The President nodded at me, and I continued.

"Mr President, a White House dinner invitation is a special occasion. For many of us this evening, this gathering will be the stuff of fond memories the rest of our lives. Your gracious hospitality is much appreciated. And I know I'm not alone in saying so. Ladies and gentlemen, a toast to our hosts, the President and First Lady."

There were several cries of "here! here!" as glasses all around the table were raised in tribute.

Dinner was served; a fine meal of braised beef tips, wild rice, asparagus, and cinnamon glazed carrots. The president was said to enjoy simple food, and the meal exhibited this. We would find out later that the superb beef came from his own Colorado ranch.

The conversation around the table was light. The tiny comedian kept us in stitches with her tales of doing stand-up at country fairs around the nation. Lady Sherwood allowed that, for a bunch of "dashed colonials" we'd all turned out pretty well. The NFL lineman (a HUGE fellow) got a laugh when he asked for a doggie bag.

We were finishing dessert (wild blueberry pie a la mode) when the First Lady began to speak.

"My friends, Ian and I have a special surprise for you this evening. As you know, it's traditional for the First Lady to embark upon her own special endeavor during her husband's presidential term. My predecessors have worked on various literacy projects, anti-drug campaigns, and other programs designed to make things better in these United States. This evening it is my pleasure to unveil to you my vision, Operation Stargazer. At the conclusion of our meal, I invite you all into the White House theater to watch a short video that outlines the worthy goals and aspirations of Operation Stargazer."

"Sounds rather futuristic," said the aerospace design chief.

"Please DO tell us more," pleaded Lady Sherwood.

The First Lady beamed and continued.

"Very well. Operation Stargazer will undertake to get the study of astronomy into our public schools, beginning in the fifth grade and continuing on in a series of progressively more challenging classes through grade twelve. Pilot programs in our home state have shown that children who begin a study of the stars at an early age are much more likely to develop an interest in higher mathematics and the sciences. They're not afraid to take what are perceived as the 'hard classes' and their overall academic records are improved in the process. We're going to need these people. Because they are the ones who will ultimately design and produce our next generation of airplanes and space vehicles."

"A bold initiative, if I may say so," said the eco-science professor in attendance. "How do you propose to attract enough qualified teachers for a nationwide undertaking like this? It's not much of a leap to presume that very few of those in today's classrooms have the slightest understanding of astronomy."

"A good question," replied the First Lady. "But before going any further, I'd like you all to join me in the theater at this time. We'll all view an introductory video that explains more about Operation Stargazer. And after that there should be time for questions."

The dinner guests rose and began to filter out, being led towards the White House viewing theater by a couple of the president's security men. I was bringing up the rear of the procession when I was pulled aside by a Secret Service man.

"Mr Westergaard, the President has asked to meet with you privately. Please follow me."

Chapter 57

The secret service fellow escorted me down another narrow hall, paused to knock gently on an unmarked door, and then entered.

Inside an appropriately appointed drawing room sat the president and another man I did not recognize.

"Mr Westergaard, sir," was all my secret service escort said.

The president nodded and the agent departed, closing the door behind me.

"Come in Amos, and grab a seat. You're among friends," said the President.

I did as requested, settling into a comfortable leather chair opposite the two men.

"Amos, this is my Chief of Staff, Cyrus Brown."

"A pleasure, sir," I said, reaching out to shake hands with the distinguished looking gent. Now that I thought about it, I realized I'd seen the president's man on television a time or two.

"Care for a cigar, Amos?" asked the president, holding out an open humidor. "I get these specially made for me down in Havana. A nice gentle smoke. I think you'll enjoy 'em.

Now, I don't normally smoke, but in honor of the occasion, I decided one wouldn't hurt.

"Thank you, sir," I said, removing one of the thin cigars from the case.

"Amos, I want to thank you for agreeing to visit us here this evening. When you hear what I have to say, I think most of your questions will be answered," said the president. "I apologize for any ruffled feathers at my ordering your plane diverted to Andrews. But when we figured out you were in the D.C. area, we didn't want to take a chance on missing you."

"Well, sir, it WAS something of a shock being intercepted by a Navy attack helicopter," I said. "But I was well treated in the process, so I see it as a no-harm-no-foul kind of thing. And a presidential invitation to the White House isn't the sort of thing one turns down lightly. All the same, sir, why AM I here?" I asked.

"You're here for a combination of reasons, actually," answered the president. "For one, my wife saw you and your cat on television and wanted to meet you. I'm told, by the way, that your cat has done a splendid job of entertaining our little Ellie upstairs. In addition, I've read your book and have successfully incorporated some of what you wrote into my ranch and mining operation in Colorado. I've made A Wanderer's Wisdom required reading for my inner circle here at the White House. The third reason, however, is easily the most important. But I have to ask you a question before I go any further."

"Ask away," I said.

"Can you keep a secret?"

I took a deep breath before answering, knowing intuitively that my response would be weighed heavily.

"Mr President," I said, trying to maintain an even voice, "let me assure you that I can be trusted. I have no political ambitions. And the last thing I want to do at this point in my life is attract any more media attention or television cameras my way. You have my solemn word, Mr President, that whatever passes between us, now or in the future, will STAY between us."

The president seemed to ponder that for a moment, and then nodded his head.

"Amos," he said, "I've learned to read people pretty well over the years. And I'm prone to taking a man at his word. I believe your word means something. Shake on it?" he asked, extending his hand.

I shook the president's hand, both of us looking each other squarely in the eye.

"Cy?" said the president, looking over at his chief of staff.

"Mr Westergaard, a couple of days ago you made a call to the FBI. The president believes you're entitled to know the results of that call to Agent Nighthawk," said the chief of staff.

I tensed, sensing that something of significance was coming.

"Your timely call to the authorities enabled one of our special counter-terrorism units to re-acquire a terrorist cell they'd lost on the highway due to an accident. Your tip couldn't have come at a more critical time. Our agents were able to take these thugs down fairly quietly and without injury or loss of life."

"Whew!" I exclaimed. "So, like, score one for the good guys?"

"Indeed," said the chief of staff. "But there's more to it than that. These skunks were heavily armed, as you suggested to Agent Nighthawk. Plastic explosives, long range rifles, handguns, even a few anti-tank weapons. Some of the stuff we recovered is new for terrorists, and we're having to reevaluate our counter-terrorism doctrine accordingly."

"Do we know what their mission was supposed to have been?" I asked.

"Yes, we do. I should tell you that these men are all very

dangerous, very hard core. Their mission that very morning was to shoot up the big Veteran's Administration hospital in Louisville. And when the authorities began to overwhelm them, they'd planned to blow the entire complex up, committing suicide in the process. And believe me when I tell you they had the firepower to do just that."

I sat stunned, not knowing what to say.

"Amos," said the president gently, "your call saved many lives. I'd pin a medal on you if I could, but that's not possible - at least not at the moment."

"Mr President, I'm horrified beyond belief. What kind of evil devises an operation with the goal of murdering injured soldiers and sailors in hospital beds?" I asked, visibly shaken.

"You're not the first person to ask that," answered the president. "I confess, I don't understand a religion that requires death to appease its god."

"I haven't heard anything about this on the news," I said.

"And you won't, not for a while anyway," said the president's chief of staff. "This is an ongoing event."

"Amos, I presume you heard Lady Sherwood whisper to me when you both came in?

Hopscotch?" asked the president.

"Yes, Mr President, I did. And I admit it surprised me a little. But then, I know her late husband was British intelligence. And there's probably a link there, huh?"

"You're quick on the uptake, Amos. Hopscotch was code to me from Number Ten Downing Street. I've just now finished talking with the British prime minister. He confirmed to me that his people had taken down yet another terror cell. This gang was on its way to blow up the tower of Big Ben with enough explosives to take out a city block. What tipped us to that operation was data from the terrorist laptop computer our people snatched during the Louisville take-down."

"Mr Westergaard, your call to our FBI saved not only American lives but a good many more in London, it seems," said Cyrus Brown.

"I appreciate that," I said. "But it seems to me the real heroes are the FBI guys and their Brit counterparts who risk all in these terrorist encounters. Mr President, I hope these people, or at least those you have authority over in this country, are being properly taken care of?" I asked.

"Already done," said the president. "Strangely enough, FBI Agent Bobby Nighthawk with whom you spoke is my wife's second cousin."

"Is that right?" I asked, incredulous. "What're the odds?"

"Remember, Amos, that you can't tell anyone about this," said the president. "We don't know yet where the ongoing investigation may lead us."

"Sir, you have my solemn word," I answered. "Not a peep."

"Amos, your president is proud to call you friend," said Ian Zane Conroy.

There was a discrete knock at the door, and another secret service agent peered in.

"Mr President, some of the guests are leaving," he announced.

"Very well, Don. I'll be out in a moment," answered the president.

Our time together was obviously over, and I stood up to leave.

"Mr President, I'm very grateful," I said. "Thank you again for your kind consideration. You didn't need to tell me any of this, but just the same, I'm very glad you did."

We shook hands once again, and I left the president and his chief of staff alone.

"A rather amazing fellow," remarked the chief of staff.

"Yes," answered the president. "We don't find many like him in today's world. He's something of a throwback, really. Amos Westergaard obviously doesn't give a damn if anyone else knows he's a hero. It's enough that HE knows. I rather liked the way he inquired about our own people being taken care of. Shows character."

"Sir, we should go now," said the chief of staff, rising to his feet.

"Cy, I want us to keep discrete tabs on Amos Westergaard. The American people owe him. The Brits owe him. And this administration owes him bigtime. Maybe we'll be able to return the favor somewhere down the road."

"It shall be as you say, Mr President."

Chapter 58

As I was walking down the hall with my secret service escort, my knees began to shake.

"Whew!" That was a little intense," I said.

"The president often has that effect on people."

"Um, I'm needing a little fresh air," I said. "Can we go outside agent, uh, Don?"

"Certainly, Mr Westergaard," chuckled my minder. "We'll just go out in back."

I followed obediently, and presently found myself outside a rear entrance to the White House. It took me a moment, but I gradually realized I was looking at the lush lawn that serves as a landing pad for the president's helicopter, Marine One. I sat down on a bench and let out a huge sigh.

"Sir, take all the time you need. I'll just wait over here," said agent Don, reminding me that I wasn't alone.

"Thank you," I replied. "I appreciate your courtesy."

It was then that I realized I'd never lit up the cigar the president had given me. It remained tucked in a pocket where

I'd put it earlier and been conveniently forgotten. I plucked it out and stuck it in my mouth. I never did light it, though.

It was a delightful fall evening in the nation's capitol. I pulled out my cell phone and made a call.

"Hello?"

"Good evening, my love," I said.

"Amos! I was just thinking about you. Where ARE you?" asked Cyndi Cheyenne.

"I'm sitting just outside the White House, having dined elegantly this evening with the President and First Lady," I said casually.

"Oh my GOSH! For real, Amos?"

"For real. I'll tell you more about it when we're together. It HAS been an incredible experience."

"What about Zoom? Where's he?"

"Upstairs in the residence. Spent the evening entertaining the First Grandchild, from what the President just told me."

"I can't believe this!"

"Stick with me girlie; we'll go places," I said smugly.

"Did you get any pictures?"

"The White House photographer took lots. He's promised all the copies we want."

"Who else is there?"

"No one you'd know, except for Lady Melanie Sherwood."

"Lady Mel's there? You give her a hug from me, Amos."

"Will do. She'd been here before. During the Reagan years."

"She's an amazing lady."

"Listen," I said, "I don't have much time. I expect the president's people will be taking me back to my hotel shortly."

"I understand. Where are you off to next?"

"Leaving for Nashville tomorrow. Be down there a day or so. After that, Zoom and I are headed west to Missoula."

"I can't WAIT, Amos! I just can't wait! I've been missing you so much."

"Me too, baby. Me too."

"Give Zoom some ear rubbies from me."

"Roger that. He deserves them."

"I love you, Amos."

"I love you too, Cyndi. Hold those thoughts. I'll see you soon."

"Bye!"

Sitting alone in the near-dark outside the White House, I felt a wave of satisfaction wash over me. Not too many guys ever dine with the president, let alone enjoy a private audience with him. Or experience the warmth and love of a beautiful country western diva. And manage to stick it to a bunch of murdering terrorist skunks along the way. Yessir, Mrs Westergaard's boy had come a long way in the world.

The door behind me opened, and another agent escorted Lady Melanie outside.

"The president's people have decided to fly me back, Amos."

"I believe I can hear a helicopter in the distance," I said, turning my ear into the wind.

"Wait until my nosey neighbors see a black helicopter landing on my lawn late at night!" exclaimed Lady Melanie. "You can bet THAT will start the tongues wagging!"

"Keep 'em guessing, Lady Mel," I said.

"Oh, you can believe that I will," she answered jovially.

With that, Lady Sherwood took my hand in hers and looked at me sternly.

"Now, listen, Amos. We probably haven't much time; I want you to pay attention to me. You've helped me enormously by inviting me to this little soiree. Because of your thoughtfulness there'll be lots of people donating to Cavalry Rescue who wouldn't ordinarily give this old dame the time of day. It's the way the game works. And for that, I thank you."

I nodded and said nothing. I find it often works well.

"And one more thing. When you've finished around here, take Zoom and fly west again. Make it your business to claim that beautiful young songbird as your own. It's not good for you to live alone. And when the two of you decide it's time for a break, you come to my house. Nobody will bother you there. And if you wish, I'll happily put you to work on a couple of my projects. Just remember, you and Cyndi have a standing invitation. Zoom too."

"Lady Sherwood," I said, "you're one in a million. I'll remember what you've told me."

There was a great roar of turbines and we both watched as a Marine helicopter landed gently on the White House lawn. The pilot throttled back the engines, but did not shut them down. A crewman opened the hatch and lowered the steps.

"Lady Sherwood, please take my arm," said the security officer standing beside us.

"Good by, Amos! Be well!" said Lady Mel, turning and walking out towards the huge chopper.

I stood there watching as she entered the helicopter. The same crewman retrieved the steps and then closed the hatch. The Marine pilot poured the coal to the engines and lifted off. A few seconds later all I could see was the helo's blinking strobe against the night sky.

Agent Don rejoined me.

"Mr Westergaard, if you'll join us back inside, please? I believe someone is bringing your cat down from the residence."

"Lead on, good sir," I said, still thinking about what Lady Mel had said.

I found Zoom back inside the main salon, riding comfortably on the arm of the First Lady. Sitting attentively at her feet was Beth the blue dingo. I did not see the president again that night.

"Mr Westergaard, I want to thank you VERY much for joining us this evening," said Lori Conroy. "And Mister Zoom here did a splendid job entertaining little Ellie. We're all very grateful," she said.

"Gracious lady, be assured that the pleasure has been

mine," I replied, bowing slightly. "I'll remember the kindness displayed by you and the president always."

"Farewell, Mr Westergaard. And fly safely," said Lori Conroy, handing Zoom over to me.

"Come along little buddy," I said to Zoom. "Time we were getting to bed."

Waiting outside was Lynn Charleston and the same driver who'd brought us over from the hotel.

"Returning to the Four Seasons, Mr Westergaard?" she asked.

"Yes, thank you," I replied.

Back inside the White House, the staff began a return to their normal nightly routines.

"Would you mind taking Beth out once more tonite, Don?" the First Lady asked the secret service man. "I'm heading upstairs to the residence."

"Will do, Mrs Conroy," said Agent Don. I'll have her sent back up afterwards. C'mon girl, we're going out."

The First Lady headed towards the elevator and picked up her minder along the way. Agent Don stopped at the rear entrance, attached a leash to Beth the blue dingo, and escorted her out to the lawn.

"You're not going to be fussy tonight are you girl?" asked agent Don as the dog began sniffing around, searching for the proper spot.

Beth suddenly quit sniffing and looked up. Sensing great danger, the hair on her neck bristled.

"Grrrrrrr....."

"What is it girl?" asked agent Don, suddenly very alert.

Now, Beth the blue dingo had been superbly trained in her youth. But the danger she sensed out on the lawn was very real. And her instincts told her it represented a threat to her family that she dared not ignore.

Barking loudly at her handler, Beth expertly slipped her leash and went tearing across the White House lawn like she'd been scalded. Agent Don ran after her, talking into a tiny microphone at the same time.

"This is Boxer; the hound's loose out back, break, Center, illuminate sector nine, please. Everyone else continue night ops..."

He could hear Beth having her way with something out in the darkness. A moment later high intensity halogen lights were energized. It was then the secret service man saw the dog about thirty yards away over on the perimeter. She was still growling and thrashing at something.

The security man approached Beth warily, continuing to scan the lawn area as a professional would.

"Hey there! Whatcha got, girl?" he said, approaching Beth carefully. "Wanna show Uncle Don? Sit, girl...."

Danger having been dealt with, Beth's training checked back in. She dutifully sat as instructed, as calm as if nothing had happened.

"Well, I'll be....."

"Hey Don, everything okay?" asked one of the night sentries, trotting over from beyond the tree line, gun drawn.

"Yeah, I think so. Will you LOOK at this Louie?"

"Wow! Never saw anything like that before, have you?"

On the ground in front of them was a well-chewed snake with unusually large bulbous eyes. Beth had clearly done a job on it.

"Nope. Never saw a snake like that. Never. And I grew up in the Bayou - snake country," said Agent Louie.

"Is it dead?"

"If it isn't, it's doing a right fair imitation of it."

"Center, this is Boxer. I've recovered the dog. Leave the lights illuminated for now, please," he ordered. "I'm coming back in."

"Okay, Louie, back to station. I'll take Beth here back

inside and then come back out and bag this snake. We'll send it out for analysis."

"Roger that," said the other security man as he turned to leave.

But when the secret service agent returned a few minutes later with a large plastic bag, he could find no trace of the snake. With no other alternatives open to him, he noted the incident in the night log and returned to his normal evening duties.

Chapter 59

Zoom and I were driven back to Andrews Air Force Base the next morning by a lady staff sergeant with great legs. After passing through multiple security checkpoints, we were deposited outside the great hangar that houses Air Force One. The president's ride was gone, and I wondered where he was off to.

Cessna One Sierra Tango was parked right where I'd left her two days earlier. The difference was, she'd been polished to a high gloss in the interim. I could almost swear she was standing a little taller on her struts.

"Morning, sir!"

I found myself confronted by an Air Force Master Sergeant.

"And good morning to you, Master Sergeant," I said. "To whom do I owe thanks for the top drawer detail job on my bird?"

"I'm Master Sergeant Tony Burns, sir. It's pretty much SOP here for visiting VIPs. I have a squad assigned to me that handles that. I also changed your oil and filter. And our fueling captain topped off your tanks."

"You changed my oil?"

"Yessir. I started working on these Lycoming engines when I was just a kid. It was nice to work on one again."

"Master Sergeant, I'm very grateful. Are any of your people around? I'd like to thank them personally," I said.

"Sorry, sir, they're all at school this morning. When Air Force One's away, we use that time for various training rotations."

"I see. Tell me, Master Sergeant; do your people drink beer?" I asked.

"That's a big roger, sir. Well, most of 'em anyway."

"Then my final request of you before I leave is to make sure they're taken care of at the NCO club this afternoon," I said, peeling off a few c-notes and handing them over.

"Sir, that's not really necessary," protested the Master Sergeant.

"I know, but it's important to me," I answered. "Tell them all I appreciate what they've done for me, and that they make me proud I once served."

"Yes sir! And on behalf of me and my people, I thank you very much."

Master Sergeant Burns drew himself to full attention, gave me a proper Air Force salute, and then withdrew into the expansive hangar.

Chapter 60

The flight down to Nashville was wholly uneventful. The weather was mostly good, although we did encounter some bumpy air a few times. Cessna One Sierra Tango hummed right along, her happy engine never missing a beat. Probably liked that fresh Air Force oil.

Nashville itself is a joy to visit. Rich in musical heritage, fine arts, and exquisite architecture, I've always thought of her as the grand dame of the south. Give me a few days there and I end up speaking southernese with the best of 'em. Or at least it sounds that way to me.

And I like the way business is conducted in Nashville. Mostly it's done in a honest, mannerly fashion that appeals to me. As it happens, I am part owner of Antebellum Antiques and Fine Collectibles in Nashville. Something of a silent partner, actually. The day to day work is done by my friend and co-owner Bo Stewart and his loving wife Lilly Ann.

The store was looking good, I reflected as I walked in the front door with Zoom on my arm. The recent redecorating scheme gave the place a certain gentility it had lacked in earlier times. The sales figures seemed to confirm that, too. Antebellum Antiques and Fine Collectibles was becoming a cash cow.

Lilly Ann was busy with a lady customer, and Bo was just ringing up another sale when he saw me walk in. The speakers were playing a medley of Civil War era music in the background, further adding to the sense of history and refinement.

"Amos! Y'all finally made it!" exclaimed Bo. "Lilly Ann said last night she thought y'all might really get here this time. I admit I wasn't so sho. Good ta see ya, partnah!"

I shook Bo's hand, and Lilly Ann came running over to greet Zoom. She'd adored my furry pal since the first time she'd encountered him. Zoom's folded ears and perpetual grin has a way of getting to the ladies. When he throws in that throaty vibrato purr, they haven't got a chance.

"It's good to be back here in Nashville," I said. "Been too long, hasn't it?"

"Sho' has been. How long can you stay?" asked Bo.

"You have to at least stay for supper," admonished Lilly Ann.

"Deal," I replied, smiling. "But you have to be my guests at the hotel. No cooking for you tonight, Lilly Ann."

"Oh my! And me with nothin' to wear!"

At that, Bo and I both roared with laughter. Lilly Ann has a wardrobe that would put Queen Elizabeth's to shame.

More customers entered the store. Lilly Ann hurried off to greet them while Bo and I talked shop.

"Store looks great, Bo. Y'all done a fine job with the new decor," I said.

"It was worth the money, no doubt about it," replied Bo. "We're seeing more upscale customers; the sales numbers seem to prove that. And another thing, your suggestion about cultivatin' widows, undertakers, and probate lawyers seems to be working."

"Startin' to get unsolicited calls?" I asked.

"Yes sir, I surely am. Been buyin' a surprisin' amount of antique furniture and period jewelry through these contacts.

Word's gettin' out I pay a fair price and don't cheat anyone. I think we're on to something really good here, Amos."

"Excellent!" I said. "We're going to expand on the theme, Bo. Keeping in mind this is Nashville, home of the Grand Ole Opry and country music. We're going to display and market historical clothing. Think about it for a moment. A nice enclosed shadow box featuring a waist jacket worn on stage by Patsy Cline. Or a long black frock coat worn on tour by Johnny Cash. You get the idea?"

I could see the gears turning inside Bo's head.

"You know, it just might work. Sho' would draw people in here, once we got enough inventory. And I know there's a lot of people that live in and around Nashville that're surivin' kin to some of the early legends. Either that, or they had kin of their own who toured with 'em. I'll put the word out, and see how it goes. The trick will be authenticating the goods."

I nodded. "Yeah, we don't want to be accused of any false advertising. So be conservative; pass on anything that doesn't come with a reasonably good pedigree. If this takes off like I think, maybe we'll do a charity auction once a year. You know, auction off a couple of choice items to collectors."

"If this takes off, I might have to hire someone to help in here," said Bo. "I'm stretched pretty thin as it is."

"Do what you need to," I said. "Listen, if things go the way I think, I may be able to offer some world-class third party influence to bolster our efforts."

"What y'all up to, Amos?" asked Bo, grinning. "Do tell."

"Can't. Not yet, anyway. Be patient a little longer, okay?"

"You da man," said Bo. "You sure were right about the other stuff. Speakin' o' which, I want you to take a look at somethin' I bought a couple of days ago."

I watched as Bo opened a drawer and extracted a small, worn box.

"Feast your eyes on this," he said. "It's a little over the top for this place, but I decided to take a chance on it."

Inside the box, resting on black velvet, was a stunning

green emerald surrounded by tiny diamond chips. All were set on a simple gold ring.

I let out a whistle. "Man, that's some piece of work," I said. "The emerald looks to go about what, five carats?"

"A little over that, about five point four," said Bo. "Stunning, ain't it?"

"Sure is," I said, still overtaken by the raw beauty of the big stone.

"There's a story that goes with this. I bought this ring from a descendant of a Civil War colonel. The story is, after the war, the old gent returned to his home to find it all burned to the ground. Lotta that going on back then. Through a series of events, he ends up taking a ship to South America, hoping to strike it big in the mines. He never found gold, but he did find a rich cache of emeralds in Columbia. Made it home with enough to restore his estate and then some. The band is platinum, by the way, not gold."

"Bo," I said, "I'm going to do something I've never done here before. I want that ring. Show it as a sale to me, at whatever price you'd decided was fair. Run it through the books and charge it against my share of the store profits."

"Well, sure, Amos. Whatever you say," said Bo, obviously surprised. "You still ain't gonna tell me what's going on, are ya?"

"Nope. Not for now. It's a matter of honor," I said.

"Well, I can understand that, then," replied Bo. "I just hope she's worth it, whoever she is."

"When you find out, you're going to be blown away," I said. "Now, what else do you need help with?"

"I need more jewelry. Doesn't have to be high end stuff, or even real stones. I get a lot of call for fine costume jewelry. Could probably sell lots, but the quality stuff's in short supply around here."

"I have a contact in Vegas that can probably help with that. He's all the time getting people in his store looking to sell that kind of merchandise. You know, former show girls and other people that work the entertainment side of things," I said. "The thing is, his store only sells really upscale, designer jewelry. So he mostly turns them away."

"Sounds to me like he's a guy I should at least talk to. See if I can cut a deal with him, somehow," replied Bo.

I scribbled out a name and phone number for Bo on a piece of scratch paper and handed it over to him.

"Don't be afraid to use my name," I said. "In this case, it'll probably get the door opened for you."

Bo nodded, then folded the paper up and put it in his wallet.

I looked around the store, and checked my watch.

"Lilly Ann!" I yelled. "Lock the doors and turn down the lights. We're closin' a little early this afternoon. Cocktails in the hotel lounge...."

"What hotel?" asked Lilly Ann, instinctively smoothing her hair.

"The Dixie Belle," I answered.

"Oh good! They make an especially good vodka gimlet there."

I drove the rental car back over to the Dixie Belle, deposited Zoom in my suite for his late afternoon nap, and met Bo and Lilly Ann down in the lounge.

"Did I tell you I had dinner at the White House with the President and First Lady this week?" I asked coyly.

"Oh, do tell, Amos! For real?" asked Lilly Ann, savoring her vodka gimlet.

"For real," I said. "Zoom too. My little pal entertained the First Grandchild while the rest of us were downstairs dining."

"Do you have any pictures?" asked Lilly Ann.

"Not yet," I said. "The White House photographer took lots of 'em though. Promised us all plenty of prints later."

"What's President Conroy really like?" asked Bo. "Seems to me he's cut from a different cloth, bein' from Colorado and all. I admit, though, I surely do like his Arapaho wife."

"I think you'd like both of 'em, Bo," I answered. "Doesn't

seem to be anything phoney about either one of them. The president looks you square in the eye when he speaks. The First Lady has a grace and charm you'd expect. But in addition, she's obviously very bright."

"He's got plenty of political opposition," remarked Bo.

"Oh, no doubt. But he overcame a lot as governor of Colorado. I think you'll see this president cling stubbornly to those things that work, as opposed to maintaining those tired old programs that don't. I see him championing initiatives that elevate the individual, rather than the bloated bureaucracy," I replied candidly.

"I recall reading about him during the campaign," said Lilly Ann. "His ancestors were Scottish. I remember when I first saw a picture of Conroy. He's tall, lean, and rather good looking for his age. If he weren't president, he'd look right at home wearing a traditional Scottish kilt."

"I think you could say something similar about Lori Conroy," I said. "She'd be very believable dressed in traditional deerskin and adorned with silver. She has this incredible black hair."

"Well, they've both got their work cut out for them, seems to me," said Bo.

"That's a fact. I'll be prayin' for both of them," said Lilly Ann.

"I think they'd appreciate that," I said, signaling the barmaid for another round.

Chapter 61

Bo and Lilly Ann drove to the airport the next morning for an early breakfast and to see Zoom and I off. It looked like a fine day to fly, and I was anxious to be heading west again. Cyndi Cheyenne had completed her work on the movie she was part of and had returned to the family ranch in Missoula. I saw no reason to keep her waiting. Although I do admit I was a little nervous at the thought of meeting her mother.

"Amos," said Lilly Ann, "you've simply GOT to come back and spend more than a day or two. Promise us you will?"

"It'll happen, Lilly Ann," I answered. "But I'm in an almighty hurry to get back west right now."

"And besides, Zoom's lookin' a little thin," continued Lilly Ann. "He needs some of my country cooking."

"Aw right! Aw right! I give UP," I said, laughing. "Message received and understood."

I shook hands with Bo, hugged Lilly Ann, and then passed through the security gate that led out to the general aviation tie downs. Cessna One Sierra Tango waited on the back row and thus out of view of my friends.

Bo and Lilly Ann retreated to their car and drove away.

"So, what do you think, Bo?" asked Lilly Ann.

"That boy's in love, baby. Bet the farm on it." answered Bo.

"Yeah, that's what I think, too."

Zoom assumed the take-off position in the back of the plane while I did my customary walk around and pre-flight checks. Safety routines completed, I patted my buttoned shirt pocket where the antique emerald ring was residing. Bo had carefully wrapped it for me with tissue paper and tape. I left the tiny antique ring box with him and told him to use it for displaying something else.

"Little buddy, you ready back there?" I yelled over the engine noise.

I got no reply. Peering over my shoulder, I could see Zoom curled up nose to tail and probably asleep. Although with cats one can never be entirely certain.

Flight plans filed, taxi authorizations acknowledged, and now in a 'hold' configuration on the active runway for takeoff, everything looked good for us to go.

"Cessna One Sierra Tango, clear for takeoff," came the voice of the controller over my headset.

"One Sierra Tango's rolling," I said, pushing the throttle to the stop.

My faithful little red and white Cessna dutifully rolled down the runway gathering speed and launched herself into the bright morning sky. My spirits were soaring, knowing that I was finally headed back to my beloved.

I flew hard that day, trying to get as far as I could before fatigue and sunset had their way, with prudence dictating we rest for the night. Oh, I stopped for fuel and the occasional quick sandwich. But mostly I kept us in the air and paid close attention to my navigation. The pilot reports were helpful too. Since I was now heading west, I'd have some headwinds to contend with all along the way. And it became a constant search to find the altitude with the least objectionable winds so as to make the best possible speed over the ground.

After spending an uneventful and quiet night in Wichita, Zoom and I pressed on across the plains the next day. So far, the weather was mostly cooperating and I was able to continue our established routine of fly-fuel-food-fly throughout the daylight hours.

Just before sunset on the second day, we found ourselves at the very pleasant Jefferson County airport northwest of Denver. I wanted to be well rested before pushing across the Rockies, so I called it quits for the day and engaged a local hotel shuttle to transport us into town. Zoom seemed okay with the idea, especially once he lay eyes on the comfortable king sized bed. Yeah, he's a well-traveled kitty, but he likes his creature comforts just the same.

I showered, changed clothes, and went downstair to enjoy an early dinner in the hotel restaurant. Back in the room afterwards, I found a voice mail message waiting for me from Cyndi Cheyenne asking that I call her forthwith. Which I did.

"Amos! Where are you?" she asked anxiously.

"Just outside of Denver, safely hunkered down for the night," I answered. "Headed straight for you, as fast as I can."

"Oh, I'm SO glad! I can hardly wait!"

"Me too, baby. Me too."

"When do you think you'll be arriving in Missoula?"

"A couple of days, if the weather cooperates. I cross the Rockies tomorrow. Probably late the following day. I'll keep in touch," I promised.

"The guest room's ready and waiting for you. Mama redecorated it; she seems to be all a-twitter about your visit."

"I'm anxious too," I said. "Desperate to see you and enjoy some downtime. I've been on something of a tear these last few days."

"Well, when you get here, plan on being totally SPOILED. Zoom too!"

"I can't tell you how good that sounds to me, baby. I'll be getting up early and pressing on at first light tomorrow."

"Well, I better let you get some rest, then. Sleep well, Amos. See you soon. I love you."

I hung up, moved Zoom over to his side of the bed, and was soon fast asleep.

Chapter 62

U p early and, after a light breakfast, Zoom and I caught the first available shuttle back to the Jefferson County Airport. The aviation weather picture was changing. The FAA briefer told me of an approaching storm coming down from Canada that would probably bring rain and snow to the Rocky Mountain region. The good news was, it was a slow mover. If I got underway quickly enough, we'd be long gone before it became a factor in our travel.

I logged on to a terminal at the airport FBO and got an updated radar picture of the aforementioned storm system. Yep, it was a bad boy all right. But no threat to us at present. I paid my fuel bill and went out to warm up the engine. Zoom protested; there was a hint of cold in the air and he didn't like leaving the nice warm pilot lounge.

"C'mon, little buddy! We have to go! I'll turn on the heater in the plane as soon as I can," I promised.

"Maaa-ow! Maaa-ow!"

I deposited my still-grumbling furry pal on the back seat,

completed the needed pre-flight safety checks, and fired up the engine. She caught quickly and smoothed out into her customary pleasant hum. I activated the cockpit heater. It really WAS a little on the cold side. I dug around in the door panel for my deerskin gloves, released the brakes, and began to taxi out for take off.

With a full bag of fuel, I figured to fly northwest over the Rocky Mountain National Forest and make it well inside Wyoming before having to refuel. This would also take us away from the path of the oncoming bad weather.

The fall colors were in full display as Zoom and I departed the Denver area and climbed high into the early morning sky. I was feeling especially good, knowing that every minute took me closer to my beloved Cyndi Cheyenne. Even the air traffic controllers helped, giving me the direct routing I asked for without the usual traffic delays.

Less than an hour later found us skirting along above endless acres of primeval forest, broken up only by the occasional alpine lake. I checked my watch and noted that things seemed to be going according to plan. Of course, it was right then that things started to go terribly wrong.

For no apparent reason, my engine shuddered and abruptly quit. Folks, I want to tell you here and now that there's nothing any quieter on earth. You sit there briefly dumfounded and slightly in shock until years of training kick in and you begin dealing with the situation.

I trimmed up the nose to give us the best possible glide ratio and went through the emergency restart procedures. Nothing.

By now Zoom knew something was terribly wrong and climbed into the front passenger seat to watch.

I tried the re-start again. Still nothing. I couldn't imagine what the problem was; such catastrophic failures are extremely rare. I changed the transponder frequency, causing it to squawk 7700, the emergency distress code.

Picking up the microphone, I sent out a plea for help. We were losing altitude fast.

"Mayday! Mayday! Mayday! This is Cessna One Sierra Tango! Mayday!"

Chapter 63

"This is DiDi Swann with your midday news from around the nation. The Federal Aviation Administration announced this morning that the search for celebrated writer Amos Westergaard, whose plane was lost over the Rocky Mountains, has been suspended due to bad weather. Westergaard, the internationally known author of A Wanderer's Wisdom was believed to have been alone aboard the single engine Cessna when it disappeared off radar early yesterday morning. For more on the story, we take you now to Stacey Webb at our MBM affiliate in Denver. Stacey, what's the latest?"

"Well Didi, as you know, the FAA has necessarily suspended the search for Amos Westergaard. I have with me here Jonathan Rand, commander of the local Civil Air Patrol and its search and rescue team. Mr Rand, what more can you tell our viewers about the search for Amos Westergaard?

"Stacey, it's especially bad out there right now. We had

this early season storm come down from Canada and blanket the whole region with snow and fog. It's a very big area to search, and until the weather picture changes we just cannot risk our planes and pilots."

"Isn't it true, Mr Rand, that sometimes planes go down in our forests and never are found?"

"Well, yes, unfortunately those things do sometimes happen. But it may help your viewers to know that our recovery record is still a very fine one."

"Still, in this weather, what're the odds Westergaard survived at all?"

"Well, that would depend upon a number of factors...."

"Thank you, Mr Rand. This is Stacey Webb reporting from Denver. Back to you in the studio, DiDi."

"Thank you for that, Stacey. In related news, President Ian Zane Conroy released a statement regarding Mr Westergaard, calling him a friend to his administration and urging aviation authorities to continue the search as soon as weather conditions allow."

A raw, bitterly cold wind blew sharply through the trees on the White Star Ranch just outside of Missoula, Montana. The sky overhead was blanketed gray and poised to release its chilling rain. Alone in the room she grew up in as a child, Cyndi Cheyenne watched the flickering television screen and wept bitterly.